Needing Your Love

Pippen Creek 2

Lynn Burke

Needing Your Love

When my ex-wife left me financially ruined a decade ago, I became suspicious of everyone and swore off relationships. But pure temptation in skin-tight jeans, a crop top, and lip gloss has shown up in our small town, making me question that commitment.

Jimmy Riley was always getting into trouble as a teenager, and as Pippen Creek's chief of police, it was my responsibility to step in when his need for attention spiraled out of control.

And now?

Behind his facade, he is still broken, starved for connection, and desperate for praise, calling out to my desire to nurture. But he is also dead set on getting into my bed, raising red flags by using every manipulative tactic in his arsenal.

I can't deny the attraction I feel for him, but he has lied too many times for me to trust him with my jaded heart.

Will my walls hold firm against the tide of his insecurities that threaten to overwhelm me? Or will he find the courage to be honest and give us both the chance for fulfillment we both crave?

Chapter 1

Sutton

17 years ago

"Rich Riley's kid just called in."

Babs's voice broke over the radio, and I took my foot off the gas pedal, slowing my cruiser. It'd already been a long shift from hell, and my guts clenched up in anticipation of her next words.

"He said his dad is dead on the living room floor."

"Goddammit," I muttered, yanking the wheel to pull into the closest driveway, the late afternoon sun blinding me briefly through my windshield. "Is little Jimmy still on the line with you?" I asked, shifting into reverse.

"Yes." Babs's tone usually suggested strength and resilience, but this call had her choked up. She'd been the station's dispatcher long before I'd become chief of police in February and had seen enough shit to last a lifetime.

"Tell him I'm on my way, and I'll let you know if I need an ambulance or the coroner." Figuring the young boy was probably upset enough, I didn't turn on my lights or siren. I gunned the engine, lips in a thin line, forehead furrowed into a deep dent.

Pippen Creek was no more than two main throughways

and half a dozen side roads, but our community was strong and tight-knit. I'd been appointed by our mayor after five years as an officer to keep watch over our town and took great satisfaction in seeing to our residents' needs.

Rich Riley was one of our two town drunks and had spent plenty of nights sleeping off the vodka in our holding cell. Jimmy's mom had died in childbirth, and he only had a single grandparent left who raised him until he was six. He'd been sent back to Rich when they had become too old and sickly to care for him.

And now, the poor kid might not have anyone.

Muscles tightening, I approached the southwestern edge of town. The tires of my cruiser crunched on worn-down gravel as I slowed and pulled in front of the Riley house. I shut off the engine, and heavy silence caused my ears to ring.

Jimmy sat on the stoop, bare legged, a torn T-shirt hanging off his thin frame. Tear streaks lined his filthy face, and he hugged his knobby, skinned knees, arms appearing scratched to hell.

Chest aching over how his lower lip trembled, I climbed from my car and quietly shut the door behind me. "Just arrived," I quietly let Babs know through the two-way.

Wet, blue eyes tracked me as I moved closer, softening my features in the hopes he wouldn't feel threatened by the big guy in uniform with a gun on his hip.

Jimmy sniffed and dropped his gaze, causing more tears to stream over his cheeks.

Phantom pain lanced through my heart as I closed the distance between us, and I tore my focus off his face to glance behind him at the house that had seen better days. A few clapboards hung crooked, ready to fall into the un-mowed grass surrounding the ranch-style home. One shutter clung stubbornly at an angle, and the other three from the windows were long gone. The front door stood open, darkness beyond even though the sun's rays shone on the young boy's pale blond hair.

He peeked up at me as I stopped before him.

"Hey, Jimmy," I stated quietly, laying a hand on his shoulder.

Flinching, he whimpered, and I quickly released my light hold.

First time I'd touched my wife Darla's arm back when we were teens, she'd reacted the same way...

A muscle ticked in my jaw. Did Jimmy have a bruise under that shirt like she had, or was it my bulk looming over him that made him afraid? Sixteen years separated me and the boy, the difference in size substantial. I crouched in an attempt to make myself appear less intimidating, hoping he had a better childhood than Darla.

I doubted it.

Dried crust rimmed Jimmy's nose. He sniffed again, scrubbing at the unrelenting tears. Up close, his arms appeared inflamed from red marks as though he often scratched himself. His legs showed no such signs of scuffed skin or gouges.

Was the scratching an anxious tic?

I ached to hold the kid against my chest and promise him everything would be okay. Wrap him in my arms and ease the emotional pain he was too innocent to be dealing with, same as I often did with my own son, who was a couple of years younger than Jimmy.

"You stay here while I go inside and check on your dad," I murmured, unable to help myself from pushing wavy locks of hair off Jimmy's forehead and smoothing back the matted strands.

He leaned into my touch, and a shuddered sigh made his entire body tremble.

Goddamn, this boy tugged on my need to nurture and protect, same as Darla had all those years ago.

Hugging himself tighter, Jimmy dipped his head in a nod, and I tore my soft touch from his head.

Fucking Riley...if the man was no more than passed out, dead-drunk, I was going to be tempted to smother the life from his worthless lungs. At least Darla's dad had a heart attack a few years after she and I had married so we no longer had to deal with his ass.

My footfalls on the three stairs sounded loud, a dog barking in the distance the only other noise meeting my ears.

The scent of cigarettes clung to the stale air as I paused on the threshold, my nose curling at the offensive, acidic stench. Passing into the interior, I blinked, my eyes slowly adjusting to the dimness. A quick scan of the living room on my left assured me the place hadn't been cleaned in months if not longer. Litter lay in every corner, crushed beer cans, Pedro's Pizza boxes, and Dig-In takeout containers making up most of the mess. Dirty clothes piled on a chair and draped over the back of the couch.

A lump of a man sprawled in between said couch and scarred coffee table, an empty bottle of cheap vodka clutched in his meaty fist.

"Rich," I hissed, not wanting Jimmy to hear in case his dad didn't answer—which it didn't appear like he would.

The man didn't move.

I kicked his bare foot, and he didn't so much as twitch.

Sighing, I bent closer to check his pulse. Maybe the man really was dead—

A snort escaped from his parted lips, and adrenaline

shot through my veins. I straightened, watching his chest rise and fall a few times.

"Asshole," I muttered at his face-down form. "I ought to leave you like this. Maybe you'll get sick and drown in your own vomit. Deadbeat motherfucker." I strode through the hallway toward the bedrooms. "Babs," I said into my two-way, "Riley is passed out, not dead."

"Oh, thank goodness."

I couldn't agree with Babs after seeing Jimmy. Neglect was spelled out in black and white from his filthy appearance to the state of the house. I expected the cupboards and fridge would be empty of anything edible or semi-healthy for a growing child. And I couldn't begin to imagine what discoloring might lay under the T-shirt the child wore.

Lips in a thin line, I grabbed a pillow off the unmade bed in the master and returned to find Rich unmoved. While we were roughly the same six feet and not quite an inch over, the guy had a good thirty to forty pounds on my two hundred.

I moved the coffee table out of the way, rolled him onto his side, and propped his dead weight against the front of the couch. I lifted his head by a nice tight grip on his greasy hair and shoved the pillow beneath before taking the vodka bottle and setting it aside with the other cans and empties on the floor.

Once sure Rich wasn't going to slump forward and possibly end up like his son had suspected, I went back out onto the stoop and settled onto the top step beside the boy— who mindlessly scratched at his left forearm.

"He's just sleeping, kiddo."

My statement caused his filthy fingernails to stop digging into his skin.

I kept my hands to myself when I wanted to ruffle

Jimmy's hair. Maybe sling an arm around his stooped shoulders and give him comfort, which was what the kid appeared to need.

A shuddered exhale made the poor boy tremble beside me, and my body responded in kind, hairs raising on my arms, as though the trauma of the afternoon had somehow connected us.

Although it was late September, warmth still shone down with the sun, but a foreboding lay in the breeze, the scent and promise of a long, cold winter. Harder times with nothing but the spring to look forward to.

I wondered what joys or dreams filled Jimmy's thoughts when he crawled into bed at night.

"Your dad drank too much, but he'll be fine," I reassured him, and his audible swallow had the muscle in my jaw ticking again. "You did the right thing in calling the station, Jimmy. Your dad is lucky to have you. It takes a real man to look after his family."

I'd meant that last bit as a dig at Rich, but Jimmy straightened a bit, swiping his forearm over his wet cheeks.

"You're a good kid."

"I'm a worm," he said, thin shoulders once more rolling inward, and my eyes stung at the confidence in his voice. He glanced over at my cruiser. "*You're* the hero."

How often did he get called names? Having learned all about Darla's childhood, I knew words hurt more than fists in the long run.

Fingers itching to pull my gun and go back inside to take care of Jimmy's problem, I eyed the bones of his clavicles poking through the thin shirt. While committing murder to make his life better wasn't exactly an option, I would do what I could to ease some of his suffering. "You hungry?"

He shrugged. "A little."

"Don't move." I hopped up and retrieved a Snickers bar from my car. Babs had tossed the chocolate to me earlier in the day when I'd been grumpy about one thing or another. She'd informed me I needed a pick-me-up. Thankfully, I'd forgotten about the empty calories until now.

I sat beside Jimmy again and offered the candy to him when I'd rather have taken him home and fed him a proper meal. My son Jamie wouldn't mind having a younger kid to hang with.

Jimmy's hands shook as he accepted the gift, struggling to rip the thin wrapper. With dirt under his fingernails, he tore the candy bar in two and handed half to me.

Rather than argue, I took the chocolate, and we ate in silence, once more seeming to share more than food or space. I couldn't watch as he licked every bit of sweetness from his fingertips.

When was the last time he'd showered?

I expected Rich didn't care for the kid any better than he did the house.

Running a hand over my face, I told myself I would have to call the Department of Health and Human services in the morning and get someone out here to check on Jimmy.

The world-weary look in his eyes suggested he'd lived a lifetime of pain and suffering in his ten years. I knew all too well the path being paved for his future, and it sickened me.

"Are you doing okay?" I asked, keeping my tone calm and kind when I rather would have raved.

He shrugged. "I'll be fine," he answered with words that sounded like a repeated lie if ever I'd heard one.

"I've got a question for you, Jimmy, and I need you to tell me the truth, okay?"

"Mmm," he hummed.

"Your dad—does he ever hurt you when he gets drunk or angry?"

Jimmy swallowed hard and gazed down the dirt road.

"Jimmy," I prompted when he didn't answer.

"No." He whispered what I would have bet money on was another outright lie.

My stomach curdled. "Do you feel safe here?"

He shrugged.

I inhaled deeply, torn over the entire fucked up situation. "I want you to go inside and lock up as soon as I leave."

Jimmy picked at the scrape on his knee. "Is Dad gonna want coffee and pills in the morning?"

"Probably," I agreed. But I expected he'd be after more vodka rather than caffeine.

Jimmy nodded, squaring his thin shoulders, and I wondered how much rested on them. "I'll take care of him," he stated, chin lifting in either stubbornness or resilience. I expected both.

I pulled a small notebook I kept in my front pocket out and wrote my number. "This is my cell phone number," I said, handing it over. "If you ever need a grown-up for *anything*, I want you to call me. Can you do that?"

"Yes, sir." He crumpled the paper in his hand, clutching it tight.

Fathomless blue eyes peered up at me, and the overwhelming urge to wrap him in my arms and promise him that everything would be okay rushed through me again. My fingernails dug into my palms as I stopped myself from reaching for him.

"Head on inside now," I ordered quietly, standing to my feet. "Dad's probably going to sleep in tomorrow morning, so you can make that coffee and set out some pills and water if you want, but you get to school on time. Even if he's still lying there, you take care of your*self* first, you hear me?"

"Yes, sir," he whispered again, pushing upright.

I glanced down, noting how badly the boy needed to bathe. "And make sure you shower tonight. Or sit in the tub and soak for as long as you want—no one is going to tell you to stop wasting water."

Wetness welled in his eyes again, causing his irises to shine like sapphires in the setting sun. He nodded, making me feel a little bit like the hero he'd said I was.

Never had I been more proud of the uniform I wore.

"Go on," I murmured with a smile, nodding toward the house.

Jimmy scurried inside, shut the door behind him, and I didn't turn away until I heard the lock click into place.

Once back in my car, I radioed Babs to update her fully, then sat silent, staring at the Riley house.

Jimmy needed help, and maybe DHHS could give him that since legally my hands were tied.

But I feared, from experience, that this was only the beginning.

Chapter 2

Sutton

9 Years Ago

"Thank fuck," I muttered to myself after sealing the final envelope that would get me out of debt. I tossed the mail atop the pile on my right, eyeing the evidence of hard work and dedication toward rebuilding my bank account and reputation.

Of course, if Darla hadn't seriously fucked me over two years ago, I wouldn't be feeling this satisfaction over getting my life back in order.

Shaking my head, I shoved up from the kitchen table, ready to shower and hit the sack. I'd spent the day at the station, dealing with one headache after another paperwork-wise. At least the officer patrols around town had been quiet.

But having to make apologies to investors, bankers, and contributors for fundraisers and attempting to right all the wrongs Darla had done had been tougher than anything I'd faced in law enforcement.

I'd known Darla was a liar from the day she'd gotten me drunk and suggested I take her virginity out beneath the stars that summer night between our junior and senior years of high school.

We'd been each other's firsts experience with intimacy of any sort, and although Darla had lied to me, manipulated me into getting her out of her dad's clutches through pregnancy, she'd gifted me the best thing in my life—my son Jamie. I'd set aside dreams of playing football in college and had taken care of my family as any good man would have done.

Our marriage hadn't been the greatest, but it was peaceful at least.

Until she'd gotten caught siphoning off town fundraisers she'd headed up as the chief's wife, ruined my credit, and accumulated various accounts of bank fraud. She'd hightailed it out of town like her ass was on fire.

But being the caring bastard I was, I hadn't gone after her for damages. Sure, she could have been sitting in a jail cell, but the hurt she'd endured throughout her childhood, the trauma she'd carried into our marriage, had been enough.

"You're soft." I snorted at myself in the bathroom mirror, eyes tired, beard in need of a trim. Should have pressed charges and let her pay the consequences of her actions.

But I feared fucking up our son in the process and figured letting her simply disappear from our lives would be less painful. He would be sixteen this spring, and I'd decided it was time to sit him down and tell him the truth of why she'd abandoned us.

He'd been livid. Pissed at me for not throwing her in the slammer.

A smirk curled my lips.

My boy intended to play in the NFL someday, but he

would have made one hell of a cop with his preference for truthful communication and doing the right thing. At least he'd gotten that part of me rather than his mother's lack of ethics.

Hot water beat on my shoulders a short while later, and I heaved a sigh, my shoulders sagging.

I was officially debt free.

The shit of my existence that had been Darla was officially gone, and for the first time in I couldn't remember how long, I had the house all to myself since Jamie was spending the night over at his best friend's.

Quietness hovered over the house, and I couldn't wait to crash face-first into my pillow instead of staring in the darkness long into the early morning hours over financial crises.

Rubbing a weary hand over my face, I set my thoughts on scrubbing so I could maybe catch up on the sleep I'd lost over the too-long months since she'd left.

Only two people had managed to thoroughly manipulate me, and I wasn't unhappy the first no longer looked to me for support of any sort. Darla's lying ass could stay gone forever as far as I was concerned.

The other?

A grimace marred my face even though I chuckled while sudsing my underarms.

Jimmy Riley rarely accepted help even though almost every single one of his actions screamed of desperation to be seen, heard, and comforted. He'd done all sorts of scheming over the years, and even though he was still a bit of a runt, his power of persuasion and getting his way when it came to Pippen Creek's Chief of Police was often snickered over by the townsfolk.

I didn't really care what people thought. It was his constant fibbing that irked the hell out of me.

I'd spent years looking out for Jimmy since DHHS had deemed his dad capable of parenting and the house livable. Jimmy had been the first kid to insist on ride alongs, and I'd gotten to know him pretty well—or, at least, what he allowed me to see through the facade of confidence and cockiness he wore as a shield to protect the tender boy beneath.

He'd been deprived of and needy for attention, often crying wolf after that first time I'd gone over to check on him and his dad. Made it hard to trust the kid, that was for damned sure. More often than not, he got in trouble at school, and a *real* wide smile would stretch his lips when he saw me striding in like the hero he'd claimed me to be since his father couldn't be bothered to answer the principal's call.

A soft spot in my chest had remained after we'd split our first chocolate bar, a weakness that didn't allow me to brush him aside as the years passed. I kept a supply of Snickers in my console during the cooler months, because the one person I could count on to be in constant need of me was that boy.

His smile remained in my mind when I finally crawled between the fresh sheets of my bed. He would be eighteen tomorrow, and although he told me once he dreamed of having an emotional connection with a man someday and riding into the sunset toward his happily ever after, I wondered over his plans for the immediate future.

He'd assured me that didn't include college of any sort. Other than working at Mary Wallace's consignment and gift shop, he didn't seem to have any thoughts on pursing anything greater for himself.

The boy could be a con man, take his skinny ass down to Boston, and make a killing schmoozing his way into rich men's lives and their wallets. No doubt he would thrive under a sugar daddy's care, but the idea of him leaving to pursue his desires didn't sit right in my guts.

Wasn't sure why, because I'd have been better off not having to deal with his lies on an almost weekly basis.

Soft.

I snorted at myself and rolled over, burrowing my face in my pillow and allowing sleep to finally claim me.

A loud knock pulled me from a dream of Darla of all fucking people. Guessed paying off her debt hadn't rid me of her memory like I'd hoped for.

Grumbling, I blinked at my alarm clock to find it was only a few minutes after midnight.

The rap reached me through the house again. It couldn't be Jamie—he had his own house key.

"If that's Darla, I swear to fucking God..." I muttered a few more curses, thankful I'd changed the locks. The last thing I needed was her crawling back and begging for forgiveness or a second chance. While I felt bad for the woman's upbringing, I wanted nothing to do with her. Once bitten, twice shy and all that shit. Wouldn't ever trust her again. She hadn't only left my heart jaded, but my thoughts turned suspicious toward just about everyone else too.

A peek out my bedroom window showed a beaten-down vehicle I was well acquainted with parked by the curb and its blond owner below on the stoop.

Frowning, I pulled on a pair of sweats but didn't bother with a shirt before hurrying down the stairs.

The knock came again, more persistent.

I yanked the door open, and a rush of cold air slid over my sleep-warmed skin.

Jimmy huddled in tight jeans and a long-sleeved shirt like he usually wore to hide his scratched arms. His hair was an artful mess of blond waves as though styled even though it was past midnight.

I had expected disingenuous tear-filled eyes, but his blue irises were bright, lacking the haze of alcohol I tended to see more often than not these days. Pink flushed his cheeks, and he shifted on his feet. The boy was up to something...

A knot twisted my stomach as I stepped outside onto the stoop with him. "Everything all right, Jimmy?"

"Fine," he breathed the word with a smirk I'd been receiving a lot over the previous year or so.

My gaze narrowed, lips pressed flat. I should have invited him in from the cold, but my sixth sense and enhanced suspicious nature kept us in the night air. "What trouble are you up to tonight, boy?"

His smile faltered, and a hint of vulnerability flashed in his eyes before disappearing completely. The usual facade of confidence he wore slid into place, and I readied for whatever shit he was about to spew. "I want to give you something."

Darla had said the exact same words on the night she'd manipulated me into sleeping with her.

Surely, I'd heard Jimmy wrong.

"What?" I snipped through my tight jaw.

Jimmy trailed a fingertip from my sternum to my belly button before I realized he'd moved.

I caught his wrist, electrical charges skittering up and down my spine.

He closed the distance between us, and I stood my ground, the cold settling into my bones. His wrist was thin, small in my wide palm, and the look he gave me after tilting his head up to hold my gaze hit me like a boot to the groin.

I'd known Jimmy was gay for years, but this was the first time he'd peered at me with blatant hunger.

"Let me get on my knees for you, Chief," he whispered, already starting to sink.

I yanked hard on his arm, keeping him upright.

"Or you can bend me over." He shrugged, his flirty smirk in place as he pressed fully against me. "I'll spread my cheeks, and you can wreck my virgin hole."

"Jesus—" I choked and released my hold on him, stumbling back a step.

He moved closer, insistent as always, hell-bent on getting his way.

My silence must have led him to believe I toyed with the idea of accepting his gift, because he grabbed hold of my cock, which lay limp inside my sweats—until his hand closed around me.

"Let me have this, Sutton."

Hissing, I jerked away from him as my dick continued to swell. And why wouldn't it? Two-plus years had passed since anyone had touched me below the belt. A simple reaction. Nothing more.

"I don't want you like that," I told Jimmy.

He opened his mouth to argue, but I swung the door shut in his face, cutting off whatever other deviousness he'd planned.

Rock in my gut and ears straining, I stood in the entryway, staring at the oak separating us.

What the fuck had just happened?

And why the hell had I shut him out like that?

The boy hadn't worn a coat.

Or hat.

And it was January for fuck's sake.

Guilt crept in, and I reached for the door handle.

His piece-of-shit car started up, and I listened as he drove away, leaving me in stifling silence.

Had I unknowingly groomed the boy? Led him to believe his hero was interested in pursuing a sexual relationship once he was of legal age?

"Fuck." I ran both hands through my hair before spinning on my heel and stomping up the stairs.

My dick remained wide awake, my first goddamned hard-on in *months*.

I refused to take care of it before trying to sleep again though, because I feared Jimmy's face would be in my mind no matter how I tried to erase the memory of those needy blue eyes.

Hopefully, tomorrow the boy would pretend as though he hadn't propositioned me, grabbed my cock, and felt it begin to thicken with interest before I severed the connection between us.

But the next day, Mary informed me that like the other liar in my life, Jimmy had left Pippen Creek. Unlike Darla's disappearance, however, I secretly mourned the loss of the kid who'd weaseled his way into my heart, woken something new inside me, and taken off without a backward glance.

Chapter 3

Sutton

Now

Unrest burrowed into my bones, and I found myself patrolling the streets of Pippen Creek rather than slaving away behind my desk on paperwork that made my eyes as dry as the Sahara. It hadn't rained for weeks, and the hot August air caused the atmosphere to feel like a desert rather than a valley surrounded by thousands of trees and the mountains beyond that had been home for my entire life.

Change was coming. I could sense it—

My cell rang, and I pulled my cruiser into The Market's parking lot to answer.

"Jamie," I said, a grin stretching my lips.

"I bought him a ring," my son said by way of a greeting.

I barked a laugh, not surprised in the least. "When are you going to propose?" I asked, my heart lighter than it had been in months since he'd moved in with his best friend turned boyfriend.

"After the party," Jamie stated even though his voice hinted at a lack of surety.

Jamie graduated from the police academy tomorrow,

and I looked forward to my son joining the force and working under my command starting next week. We were a small band of brothers, just me, Babs, who was finally contemplating retirement, and two other officers. Jamie would be the perfect addition to the station.

Same as when my son was a young boy, he'd done drive alongs with me when he'd returned home last summer after a knee injury ended his short NFL career. He'd been devastated over the loss of his dreams but had gotten together with Chaz, who he'd always been in love with. A solid win as far as I was concerned. He and Chaz were attached at the hip, and I couldn't have been happier for my son.

I told him as such, and his sigh radiated happiness over the line.

"He's the best thing that ever happened to me, Dad. A couple of years ago, I never could have imagined the life I have now, but I'm so goddamned thankful."

"Same." I smiled and waved at Georgie Ellis, who was loading groceries into the delivery van. "I'm excited to see you at your desk on Monday morning."

"I have to get through tomorrow and the rest of the weekend first." Jamie released another heavy exhale. "I'm scared."

"There's nothing to be afraid of. You've earned that badge, and there's no chance in hell Chaz will say no. I'm proud of you, son." I swallowed hard as tears stung my eyes.

"Thanks for believing in me," Jamie said, his tone low too. "For pushing me to enter the academy—for always having my back."

"Always *will*, too," I promised.

"What are you up to?"

"Patrolling."

Jamie snickered. "Bored, huh?"

I chuckled. My son knew me well. "Tired of paperwork."

After promising to see him at graduation tomorrow, I hung up and turned onto Pippen Street to continue my attempts to make the day pass faster even though I only had the promise of a quiet house waiting for me at the end of my shift. Loneliness had settled in after Jamie had moved out, but I wasn't about to tell him.

That afternoon of patrolling didn't offer me the usual sense of fulfillment in knowing I did a damned good job of keeping my people safe, but at least no need arose that caused me to flick on my siren.

My wanderings led me southwest, and I slowed as I approached the abandoned house I thought of more often than not.

Rich Riley had passed three years earlier, and although Jimmy hadn't returned for the cremation and burial he'd arranged from Boston, the boy had yet to sell the place. According to Town Hall, the taxes were paid every year, and I wondered about his plans for the property. The house and land had been in disrepair over a decade earlier and had only gotten worse with every passing season.

While the one-story home could be rehabbed and inhabited, I doubted Jimmy had any intentions of doing so. I hadn't seen or heard from him since that night I'd turned down the offer of a blow job and shut the door in his face.

I pulled to a stop, eyeing the sagging stoop where Jimmy had huddled all those years ago when we'd first exchanged words. Tall grass had taken over the stone walkway that used to lead to the porch we'd sat atop countless times after that September afternoon. Even more clapboards hung in disarray, and the lone shutter that had hung on for dear life now lay beneath curtained windows hiding whatever filth had piled up inside.

Why didn't he just sell the place and be done with it? Why cling to a building that housed his childhood trauma?

I'd often wondered if telling Jimmy taking care of his dad was a real-man thing to do had pushed him toward defending his abuser when DHHS had come knocking. Guilt lay heavy on my heart since that day, and I expected it would continue to haunt me to the grave.

Exhaling heavily, I drove away, turning my focus on the other houses amidst the trees as sunshine warmed my arm through the cruiser's open window. While this wasn't the best side of Pippen Creek, the residents received the same care and thoughts from their chief.

I didn't allow discrimination. Couldn't see a man's wealth or lack thereof shaping who they were. Our residents had chosen the *Live Free or Die* state, and I'd committed myself to making sure those I was responsible for could do just that.

Twice on my way back downtown, I rolled to a stop and leaned out the window to check in with people enjoying the too-warm day. I scanned every house and business, watched couples and moms with strollers meandering down sidewalks as I cruised past, proud of how our town ran like a well-oiled machine. There hadn't been any major trouble in decades, only skirmishes here and there and a few fender benders to cause a blip in our mundane lives.

But something hovered on the horizon, a similar sense to the one I'd felt all those years ago while sitting beside a filthy kid who had called himself a worm.

Pulling into the station's lot, my mind turned toward the manipulative terror who somehow continued to live rent-free in my head.

Jimmy had always been too thin and gaunt, tiny compared to me and my son who'd passed him in size not long after that first call out to their property. I'd taken to bagging up clothing Jamie had outgrown and secretly leaving them on the Riley porch while on the night shift. Every few weeks, I'd ordered staples from The Market for the Ellis family to deliver anonymously.

Rich might have been an asshole, but he'd never turned the gifts away.

Jimmy had been fourteen the first time I'd let him sleep off drunkenness at the station. While the right choice according to the books would have been for me to call his dad, I'd let the kid sack out on the same small cot Rich sprawled across on a monthly basis.

While Jimmy was tougher than most of the other kids in Pippen Creek's tiny school system, it was the fact he'd tended toward feminine that had gotten him into trouble. But things had changed since those days. No longer did we allow bullying of any sort, and homophobia, while it probably hadn't disappeared entirely, now sat silent in the back of minds of those who refused the "wokeness" that had slowly crept into and rooted deep inside my town's limits.

Jamie and my soon-to-be son-in-law weren't the only queer folk in Pippen Creek. My best friend, Dex, who worked at the fire station on the other side of the intersection was an out and proud gay man. The owner of Scone Haven, Kelly Powell, was as well, along with the lesbian couple who owned Frenchie's, the local bar in town. And while I hadn't announced my own queerness, those closest to me knew I swung both ways.

I hadn't realized the truth about myself until that night Jimmy had wanted me to *wreck his virgin hole.*

I'd become obsessed with Jimmy after he'd left. I'd kept

tabs on him, going so far as to hire a detective to make sure he hadn't ended up in a ditch somewhere. Dex called me a stalker, but I reasoned my infatuation away with years of seeing Jimmy as my responsibility.

I stumbled upon a website's page that showcased him for hire as an escort around the time he'd turned twenty-one. The images of his trim torso and pale, smooth skin no longer marred by scratching shouldn't have made me hard, but the suggestive poses and familiar glint in his blue eyes had fully roused that secret desire inside me.

He was stunning—and all man.

Longing to see the little liar saunter back into town and once more offer that ass many others had paid for swept over me whenever I allowed my thoughts to linger on him. Jimmy Riley had become my obsession, the man I dreamed of at night.

My dick thickened in my uniform pants, and I cleared my throat, denying myself another minute of fantasy. Lips pressed into a thin line, I shoved my cruiser's door open and stepped out into the heat.

"I was starting to think I needed to radio in help," Babs said when I entered the air-conditioned station. Shrewd eyes slid over me as I ran a hand through my hair while passing her desk. "Got a call from Georgie," she continued, and I paused. "He hit the Dixon's lab while out delivering groceries and was pretty upset. He asked for you, but I sent Officer Jones."

"How long ago?"

"Five minutes."

"I'll handle it." I turned toward the door that had just shut behind me.

"You stop right there, Chief Sutton Forrester." My feet paused at Bab's order, same as they always did when she used that tone on me. "You're a magnet to needy people, and they take advantage of your goodness and desire to help—"

She didn't lie. Needy people were my kryptonite.

"—but Jones has this one covered." She set aside a file and leaned onto her desk, arms crossed and gaze probing. "You've got another voicemail from *you know who.*"

"Fuck." I rubbed a weary hand over my beard. Darla had called out of the blue earlier in the year and persisted in begging for a chance to talk to me even though I never rang her back.

Babs was the only person besides Dex who was aware that my ex had skewed my thought processes when it came to believing a person was innocent until proven guilty. At least my suspicion made keeping my town safe easier. "Was she crying?"

"Of course she was," Babs grumbled. "Manipulative little bitch. Are you sure I can't tell her to fuck off next time she calls to wail about her woes?"

Heaving a heavy sigh, I shook my head.

Babs's lips pursed, eyes narrowing. "Don't let her use you again, Sutton—I mean it. She comes sniffing around this town again, and I'm going to have to ask you to look the other way while I pull out the three S's."

Shoot. Shovel. Shut up.

I couldn't stop my lips from twitching. Babs might have twenty-plus years on me, but she was still a feisty force to be reckoned with. "Let's hope it doesn't come to that."

She hmphed, finally settling in her chair. "Have you told Jamie she's been harassing you?"

"No, and I would appreciate if you wouldn't either."

"Fine," she snipped, her annoyance over my shutting down her usual gossip factory spelled out across her face.

"On to better things—how are you feeling about Jamie's graduation and joining our small force?"

The satisfaction I'd felt earlier leaked back in, a hint of excitement over the change I'd been desperate for lately overshadowing the fact a voicemail from my lying ex-wife awaited me. "Can't wait." I stated the honest truth.

"Been missing having him around, have you?"

"More than you could imagine."

Babs nodded, knowing eyes looking over my pristine uniform. "You did a damned fine job raising him on your own after she left. I'm proud of the both of you."

I couldn't keep my mind from turning toward the boy who'd had everything going against him.

"What's the frown for?"

Erasing the furrow between my eyebrows, I tried for a grin. "Just...tired."

Babs raised an eyebrow, calling me out on my bullshit. "Go grab a Snickers," she suggested, and I huffed a non-happy laugh while turning toward my office, my heart aching the slightest bit.

The candy bar had become my favorite after sharing countless ones with Jimmy, and I still had a weakness for the satisfying sweetness.

Kind of like my weakness for the kid himself.

"It was a good thing Jimmy left when he did," I muttered to myself while eyeing the phone on my desk and the blinking light that indicated a waiting voicemail that would doubtless be a woe-is-me story about the latest mess my ex-wife had gotten herself into.

Sure enough, Darla sobbed more than she managed to get words out. Something about her partner? Husband? Taking out his anger on her for their financial troubles in ways I wouldn't usually condone.

No doubt, she'd lied to him.

Manipulated his ass in order to get what she wanted.

And now she was broke and had no place to go.

She probably lied about his abuse in order to draw on my protective instincts too.

I deleted her message, my stomach churning, jaw clenched. Stretching my neck side to side, I attempted to rid my body of tension, needing to think on anything but her.

The Snickers atop my desk called out to me, and I ripped the wrapper open, allowing my mind to fixate on the boy-turned-man who had caused me to question my sexuality.

"The shit out of his mouth was no different than hers," I reminded myself so my walls wouldn't crumble.

Who knew what the hell kind of trouble Jimmy would have dragged me into had he stayed and become a gorgeous man right in front of my eyes and lonely heart.

Chapter 4

Jimmy

Quitting my job at Elite Escorts and driving north on a Friday afternoon might have been the greatest mistake I'd ever made.

Or the most rewarding.

Time would tell if the urge to try to fulfill my pipe dream again held any happiness for me.

I had plenty of money stashed away in the bank thanks to my job as a sex worker and my ability to live somewhat frugally. I'd even gotten my GED since I'd left the back-woods of New Hampshire before graduation.

Boston no longer offered the glitz and distraction I'd enjoyed since arriving as a pimply-faced barely adult who'd had less than a hundred bucks to his name. Working at the consignment and gift shop from when I'd turned fourteen until the day I'd left Pippen Creek had allowed me to save enough for an old piece-of-shit Chevy. The junker had gotten me into Massachusetts and the city in one piece.

Barely.

And I was broken down, literally bleeding and crawling

through gutters for years until landing the job that had changed my life.

Windows open on my brand new red BMW, the one thing I'd splurged on for my twenty-seventh birthday in January, I breathed in the country air while speeding up Route 16 toward a wide-open future that led to who the fuck knew where. I'd ignored responsibilities that should have been seen to three years ago, which was my excuse for the unplanned jaunt northward.

I'd attempted to leave Pippen Creek behind after I'd been denied what I'd wanted more than oxygen, but a piece of my heart—or two, rather—had remained back in that shit-hole town.

Mary Wallace, who I'd called Gram from the afternoon she'd sat me at her kitchen table and placed a plate of chocolate chip cookies in front of me, and Sutton Forrester, the man I'd set on a pedestal. He'd been my hero since the day I'd thought my dad had died, and the chief had walked up to me and got down at eye level, his gaze kind, voice and manner gentle when I'd experienced nothing but harshness from men in authority.

I shifted on my car seat and rested my forearm on the open window, breathing in the air ruffling my hair into a sure mess of blond waves.

Both Gram and Sutton had been the only two people who'd given a damn about me, and I still felt a sense of connection to them all these years later.

While Gram and I had kept in touch the old-fashioned way through monthly letters updating each other on our supposed boring existence—I'd lied about what I did for a living—I hadn't seen or spoken to Sutton since the night he'd rejected my advances and broke my heart.

There wasn't much I wouldn't have done for a taste of

him on my lips, to feel the stretch of my hole around his dick I'd fantasized over from the day I'd learned that sex didn't only have to be between a man and woman. I'd been crushed when he hadn't accepted my offer to suck his dick or bend over for my first fucking.

At that point, his bitch of a wife had been gone for over two years, and I hadn't seen him take any woman out on a date. I figured maybe he ought to switch shit up a bit. Try out a boy's mouth or ass.

I'd stupidly thought maybe I was exactly what he'd unknowingly needed to find happiness again.

Even though he'd said no, I couldn't stop from dreaming about him and how that night *should* have ended. I'd gotten plenty of dick in Boston but never enough to fill up the holes inside me like I somehow inherently knew only he would be able to do.

Sutton wasn't on social media, so the few images I had saved to my phone were from newspaper write-ups over the years. The newest headshot from the town's site promised he'd aged like a fine wine, slight lines in the corners of his smiling hazel eyes and gray peppering his dark hair and trimmed beard.

So. Fucking. Hot.

"God*damn*," I murmured to myself like always when getting caught up in fantasies of the man.

He was still single and not dating, according to Gram, who I'd spoken with over the phone last night, which had led to this unplanned jaunt northward. She was having some struggles, and I had unfinished business left rotting on the edge of town.

I'd expected dread to coil in my guts as familiar landscapes and buildings filled my windshield, but a strange sense of peace radiated through me like warm, summer sunshine caressing my left side. I found myself smiling rather than grimacing considering the details I would need to take care of now that I'd finally returned.

Dad's house sat empty because I hadn't been able to stomach looking at the place. I'd skipped out on his ashes being buried that I'd paid for but had been overseen by Gram. She'd been disappointed by my refusal to see the bastard laid to rest. His rotten-ass soul could burn forever in hell as far as I was concerned.

The thought of laying eyes on the dilapidated building I'd called home for most of my childhood years made my empty stomach churn, erasing the easy smile from minutes before.

Gram had warned me the house was a rat's nest and would need to be cleaned out before I could put it on the market and finally unload the burden like I should have done years ago. The shed out back where Dad used to lock me up some nights, even when snow flew, had caved in and would need to be completely torn down. I wondered if the tarps I used to burrow under lay beneath the rubble.

A chill slid along my spine as though my body still felt the winter winds finding their way through the cracks in the dilapidated shed's walls.

Breathing deeply, I focused on the sinking sun shining through my driver window, soaking in its warm rays as I entered town.

The Moose's Muse Lodge sat at the corner of Route 16 and Main Street and had gotten a serious upgrade since I'd seen it last. Fresh green paint covered the clapboard exterior and made it blend into the pine trees at its rear. Brown shutters bracketed every sparkling window. Groomed flower beds spread along a new front porch that spanned the building. Various wooden rocking chairs sat along the deck's length, quaint and inviting.

I pulled into one of the parking spots out front and climbed from my car, stretching my back while scanning toward my left and downtown.

The Outdoor Shop stood next door to The Moose, Ginny's Salon next, then the police station, where I'd spent quite a few nights during my rebellious teenage years.

Butterflies fluttered in my stomach, causing jitters to affect my hands. I wiped damp palms on my tight jeans while hoping for a glimpse of a blue cruiser and the man of my dreams.

No such luck, but Dig-In Diner behind me and Pedro's Pizza a little farther down the street promised the food my stomach growled for.

But first things first.

I grabbed my two suitcases out of my trunk and climbed the sturdy wooden steps toward the only place in Pippen Creek where travelers and visitors could rent a room.

The screen door squeaked on its hinges as I pushed into an open-concept interior that screamed country chic. Earthy tones on the walls created a warm, inviting atmosphere. Exposed beams spanned the ceiling above simple furniture that cradled blue and yellow gingham throw pillows. The hardwood flooring beneath my feet stretched straight ahead to the antique desk and the fifty-something blonde woman seated behind it.

"Welcome to The Moose!"

I returned the woman's smile and approached, not recognizing her. "I'd like to book a room for the week— possibly longer—if you have one available."

Her eyes brightened even more. "Of course. Kendra Cole." She stuck out her hand.

"Jimmy Riley."

She didn't appear to recognize my name or hesitate in shaking my hand.

"What brings you to Pippen Creek?" she asked while clicking her laptop to life.

"I grew up here and decided it was time for a visit."

Her smile widened. "Welcome home, Jimmy."

Home.

The word echoed through my mind as I gave Kendra my information and bank card, and I didn't hate the peace that continued to fill my chest.

After being denied by Sutton, I'd been desperate to escape this place, never planning to return. But I'd done some growing up while away, learned some hard lessons the chief hadn't been able to impart, and now I wasn't sure what to do with myself moving forward.

I just knew I felt driven to find that golden sunset I'd always dreamed of riding toward, hand-in-hand with the man I loved.

The plethora of dick I'd taken care of as an escort had become a bore. An absolute chore that had caused more yawns than climaxes in the previous couple of months. At first, I'd been thrilled to get my hole stuffed a few times a week while getting a shit ton of cash in return, but now? I wanted more. And that included Chief Sutton loving on my prostate with his fingers or cock.

A shudder ripped through me as blood seeped southward even though I daydreamed of impossible outcomes.

"Do you remember Jamie Forester? You seem about the same age," Kendra said while handing over my room key.

The breath punched from my lungs at the surname, considering the man I'd been fantasizing about not a heartbeat before. "Yeah," I rasped and cleared my throat. "Chief's son."

"The one and only."

I remembered wishing Sutton had stolen me from Dad and made me his other son—until I'd learned what all a dick could be used for and had fallen hard for my hero. I'd been a horny fourteen-year-old with my eyes set on the only man who'd ever given me the time of day.

"Jamie graduated from the police academy this afternoon," Kendra continued, "and there's a party in about a couple of hours over at Frenchie's. It would be the perfect opportunity for you to catch up with the townsfolk since most everyone will be there."

Smiling, I thanked her and made for the stairs, adrenaline causing my knees to shake.

While boredom had me leaving Boston in the rearview mirror, I sensed while climbing to the third floor and room with the window overlooking downtown Pippen Creek that I'd done as Kendra had suggested—come home. For how long, I wasn't sure. Too many variables were involved to set a clear outcome.

But for now, I would shower, clean myself inside and out just in case this boy got lucky tonight, then take a walk down Main Street to reacquaint myself with the little town I'd thought I'd left in the dust.

Two hours later and dressed for attention in tight jeans that hugged my ass and a maroon crop top that showed off my hint of abs and belly button ring, I sauntered outside, ready to face down my future. I strode westward, shoulders back and chin lifted, my pulse thrumming from a combination of excitement and fear.

Pippen Creek—and Chief Sutton—here I come.

If only.

Snickering, I set my sights on Frenchie's, my mouth watering for so much more than food.

Chapter 5

Sutton

Pride swelled in my chest at the sight of Jamie in his uniform. Pink flushed his face as everyone in Frenchie's crowded around him to offer congratulations.

"You did well, Sutton."

"Thanks." I grinned, shifting slightly at Dex's hard elbow to my side. He'd been my friend since childhood, sticking by me at every turn, especially after I'd become a single parent to my son. The reminder of Darla and the sob story from the day before made my lips twist into a grimace. "Guess who left another message yesterday?"

Dex rolled his eyes. "The fuck did she want this time?"

"Same complaint—she got into financial trouble and was hoping I would bail her out like I used to."

"Manipulative little bitch," Dex muttered, and I huffed a laugh.

"That's what Babs said."

Dex eyed me, gaze narrowed. "Tell me you denied her the help she wanted."

"Never returned her call, and I won't no matter how often she cries over the phone."

"Don't answer either."

"Don't plan to," I shot back. "Babs knows to send her straight to voicemail."

"She keeps this shit up, you might want to consider a restraining order."

I sipped my beer, already having decided to do that very thing, considering she'd taken to ringing the station like clockwork every two weeks since the beginning of the year.

"Those boys look good together." Dex thankfully changed the subject and didn't lie.

Jamie and Chaz shared a strong love that seemed to meld them into one entity even when apart. Their latched pinkies sent an ache through my chest, making me wish for the same.

When torn apart for accepting hugs from supportive townsfolk, they always found their way back together, fingers entwining.

Chaz, like Jamie, had gone through the wringer, but both had ended up in a better place than when my son had first returned home. Chaz now had a good relationship with both of his parents, and Henderson Auto, his business, flourished as the only auto shop in town. Jamie didn't know jack shit about car engines, but he spent a lot of his free time at the shop helping out where he could.

"Yeah, they do," I agreed with Dex, well aware my best friend longed for the exact same thing as I did, what those boys shared.

A committed relationship to dispel the loneliness of middle age and an empty house.

But Dex didn't have an ex or the baggage I did, the type that had the power to hold me back no matter how badly I longed for companionship. He also didn't have deeply ingrained suspicion that acted like a fortress around his heart.

My thoughts returned to Jimmy, but another of Dex's elbows to my side helped me remain in the present. "Have you downloaded that dating app I told you about?"

I sipped my beer before answering. "Yeah, but I'm not feeling it." I offered the excuse I'd given him more than once already about other sites he'd suggested. "Everyone just wants to get laid and will promise anything to get at my dick. You know I'm looking for more than that—a real connection. A needy guy I can take care of, someone who will give me a sense of purpose."

"You *have* purpose already," Dex argued. "You keep this town safe. You're every kid's hero." He tapped his empty glass bottle to mine in cheers before moving off.

I huffed at Dex's retreating form. I'd been *one* boy's hero, that was for damned sure. That ache slid through my chest again, and I frowned, scratching through my white button-down shirt while continuing to watch Jamie and his soon-to-be fiancé.

I started their way, getting stopped a few times to accept congratulations for raising a fine son.

Chaz left Jamie to get them drinks, and I studied their interactions even though space lay between them. Salacious, longing looks across the bar stated their desire for each other louder than any bullhorn.

I finally managed to sidle up next to my son. "You're making me jealous."

Jamie tore his focus off Chaz to smirk at me. "Sorry?"

"Don't be. I love seeing you happy."

"Your man will show up one of these days," he promised as though he knew the future, but I didn't hold as much hope.

"Starting to think it's not going to happen," I muttered.

"Welcome to Frenchie's!" Iris and her wife hollered as the door swung open.

"Motherfucking..." I cursed under my breath.

"Jimmy Riley," my son muttered as the boy paused over the threshold, scanning the room.

I drank Jimmy in from head to toe. He was an absolute snack in tight-as-fuck jeans and a short-sleeved crop top that showed off his smooth, pale arms, trim waistline, and a ring through his belly button. I grunted, instinctively bending forward slightly to lessen the sudden rush of blood to my groin.

"*Shit,*" Jamie and I both whispered at the same time Jimmy caught sight of us, blue eyes flaring with a purposeful glint I recognized.

I turned toward my son who glanced my way before jerking his focus toward Chaz who approached us, drinks for him and my son in hand. They shared a few words, but I didn't hear the exchange.

Awareness of Jimmy sauntering closer raised the hairs on my nape. Instincts dueled inside me—wrap the kid up in my arms or flee for my life.

Dex elbowed me with a knowing look.

"Fucking hell," I muttered, tipping back my beer to drain every last drop. "Shut up," I told Dex before he could start in with ribbing over the boy I'd been stalking from afar.

"I'm not saying a word," he said, chuckling and moving off to the bar for refills.

"Dad, what's—"

"Why, Chief Sutton." Jimmy's greeting cut off my son's question, his baby blue-eyed gaze sliding down over me with lust and determination.

Jamie studied me—I could feel his inquisitive stare as

strongly as Jimmy's wish to bend over and grab his ankles. I imagined the offer in his eyes leaving his lips, and temptation warred with my better sense.

I didn't move, didn't allow an ounce of the feelings crashing through me to show on my face. "Jimmy," I said, my tone unmoved unlike the swell taking place in my jeans.

"Miss me?" Jimmy asked with a saucy tilt to his pouty lips, his hip popping out the slightest bit, which drew focus to his trim stomach and the glint of silver in his belly button.

"Nope." The lie sounded obvious to my own ears, and I fought to inhale.

Jimmy allowed me a moment's reprieve by giving my son his attention.

"I hear congratulations are in order."

The two boys shook hands while I attempted to regulate my breathing and talk down my swollen dick trapped inside my boxer briefs and denim.

"Chaz." He next greeted Jamie's soon-to-be fiancé, his brow furrowing a brief moment. "You're a dead ringer for an old co-worker of mine. How did I not realize that before?"

"Yeah?" Chaz didn't sound that interested.

"Any chance you're related to a guy named Zack Briggs?" Jimmy asked.

Jamie stilled, and I wondered how much my son knew about what Jimmy had been up to in Boston. Suspicion pinged my in brain as I scanned all three boys' faces.

"Don't recognize the name," Chaz said, latching his pinkie with Jamie's, his facial expression bland.

Jimmy's gaze narrowed while glancing over Chaz in a slow perusal that held zero hint of lust or flirting. Good thing too. Jamie would have laid the guy out flat. "Hmm.

Could have fooled me," Jimmy mused. "You two could be twins."

Chaz bumped his shoulder into a red-faced Jamie. "You okay?"

"Yeah. Just, uh..." Jamie scratched the back of his neck, eyes flitting everywhere but at Jimmy.

There would be questions...eventually, but right now, the one I'd been thinking about more often than not lately stood inches from me, tension vibrating between us even though he didn't glance my way.

A few more words filled the air around me, but I stared at Jimmy, taking note of his artfully mussed hair, the heightened color along his cheekbones, the button of a nose I wanted to kiss, and the sheen on his plump lips that appeared to be gloss.

I licked my lower lip without thought as the throb in my groin intensified.

He leaned into my forearm a second later, but Dex arrived at my other side, offering me a cold beer and much needed distraction from the heat zapping over my skin and causing goose bumps to pebble where Jimmy's skin rested against mine.

"Thanks," I said, my voice sounding wrecked as fuck. Sidestepping Jimmy didn't rid me of his touch, and I fought off a shiver that would reveal how he affected me.

"So, Jimmy." Dex threw his arm around my shoulders in a possessive hold and maneuvered me away from the boy. He was the sole person on the face of the earth who was aware of my obsession with the young man attempting to get all up in my space. "What brings you back to Pippen Creek?"

"Personal shit." Jimmy studied how Dex squeezed me against his side, his lips turning down in a petulant pout that mirrored the look on his face when I'd refused the offer of his mouth and ass nine years ago. Dex also knew about that night, but again, was the only one privy to that tale.

I forced my focus off Jimmy's glistening lips to supposedly scan the room like I always did when in a crowd, but I was too preoccupied with the gorgeous blond in my periphery to take note of anybody in attendance.

"Anything Chief, here, needs to worry about?" Dex asked.

"Oh no." Jimmy purred the words, shifting a little closer.

"When are you going back to Boston?" Jamie asked, and I kept my focus turned away but strained for Jimmy's answer.

"How'd you know I've been in Boston?" Jimmy asked.

"Uh...Dex!" Jamie claimed, his voice higher than usual. "Dexter told me." My son lied, but my own questions and investigation into why my son who rarely fibbed did so now could wait.

I found my gaze on Jimmy's coy smile without meaning to give him my attention.

"Someone's keeping tabs on me," he murmured. "I like it." With a wink at me, he sauntered away, his plump backside swaying, causing my mouth to dry.

Clearing my throat along with Dex, Jamie, and Chaz, I lifted my cold beer. We seemed on the same page about not speaking a word over all four of us having checked out Pippen Creek's prodigal son's lush ass.

"So!" Chaz said abruptly, breaking the weird, tensed silence that had gone on too damned long. "I have a thing to take care of."

"Yeah," Jamie tacked on. "That."

Dex laughed. "Have fun, boys." He grasped my elbow

and thankfully led me toward the opposite side of Frenchie's from where Jimmy had wandered.

Walking with an ache in my groin wasn't exactly pleasant, but the need for relief eased as long as I kept my back toward the one man who affected me with such potency.

The temptation was real.

But so was the fear of trusting another person with my body and heart.

I might long for a connection, but I couldn't allow myself to go there again. Putting on my chief hat, I focused on eventually getting answers and setting this desire inside me to rest once and for all, because I'd learned the hard way that nothing good came from falling for a liar.

Chapter 6

Jimmy

Shivers had slid down my spine the second I'd walked through Frenchie's door. I could feel Sutton's gaze like a sensual caress, waking every hair follicle on my body yet flooding me with a sense of calm that had filled me in his presence as a kid.

The draw had been as real as it had been nine years ago when I'd knocked on his front door, quaking in my boots and attempting to appear confident.

Same as that night, too, Sutton was one hell of a man.

A white button-down with its sleeves rolled up to reveal veined forearms covered his upper body this time, but I remembered the spattering of hair on his thick pecs and the slight ripple of muscles along his core leading into low-slung sweats.

Now, worn jeans clung to his narrow hips and thick thighs, and I attempted to ignore the temptation to check out the bulge between those tree trunks. He'd always been well-groomed, but his short, square fingernails and strong hands pulled my focus for a few heartbeats, and longing for his touch caused a shiver over my skin.

More age lines betrayed his forty-three years, but he was delicious in my eyes, the slight snaggletooth incisor adding to his appeal and making me want to love on it with my tongue and lips.

His imperfections gave me the courage to flirt, the hope that he could be swayed the dick way and would see beyond my brokenness and accept what he'd once turned down.

The heated stare as conversation flowed among us men suggested I might get lucky if I played my cards right.

Unlike the night he'd rejected the offer of my virginity, Sutton studied me with interest, even though he attempted to squash what the sight of me did to his very *non*-straight ass. Gram could claim what she wanted about Sutton only dating women, but that tall drink of water definitely salivated for a taste of my body.

I could feel his gaze follow after me as I sauntered away from him, my thickened cock trapped in a jockstrap aching to be set free to leak all the fuck over the place. While I'd had sex aplenty while living in Boston, no one affected me in the way the chief of police from this small hick town did. No one had filled me how I'd yearned for, a completion that I expected would only come from a soul connection rather than two men just needing to get off.

Lust for Sutton to hold me down and fuck my hole raw made my slit wet. My balls ached and throbbed for release from either his mouth or hands. I wanted him burrowed into me where we became one flesh, heart, and mind. I could live beneath that man's skin like I'd always longed to do, untouched by danger, free from the emotional turmoil from my childhood I'd been attempting to escape for years.

Swallowing hard, I leaned onto the bar, exchanging pleasantries with someone on my left while waiting to nab the blue-haired, scowling bartender's attention.

"What can I get ya?" she finally barked, and I snickered at her attempts to be a badass, unfeeling woman when she was anything but. Her eyes betrayed that she'd seen too much in this wide world of terror and was nothing but a needy, soft pile of fluff inside. Like called to like, after all.

"You're beautiful, Frenchie," I stated with a grin, and her glacial stare warmed.

"Thanks," she murmured, glancing over my face and my upper body that wasn't hidden by the bar. "Not so bad yourself—for a guy."

"I never came in here before I left for Boston years ago, but the place looks great, and you and your wife make this bar run like a well-oiled machine." I repeated what Kendra had told me before I'd left The Moose for my stroll downtown.

"It's all Iris," Frenchie said about her other half, still smiling.

My grin widened, and I ordered a glass of pinot noir along with a plate of wings Kendra had told me were to die for. Not exactly a great pairing, but the tongue and belly wanted what the tongue and belly wanted.

Frenchie put in my order, and I decided this was my new favorite place to be. There was no sense of judgement, no wary glances at me as I spun around, wine in hand, and leaned against the bar, sipping my drink.

Chatting a little here and there with folks who stopped to say hi and welcome me home suggested I didn't have the bad reputation hanging over me from childhood that I'd expected. I didn't bullshit about where I'd been and what I was doing back in Pippen Creek because of the townsfolk making me feel welcomed. I figured letting everyone know the old Riley house was going to be getting a serious makeover and put on the market could only be a good thing for when the time came.

I watched Jamie and Chaz for a few seconds, finally realizing why my old co-worker Zack had always seemed familiar. While the younger Chaz I remembered from nine years earlier wasn't Zack's doppelgänger, the man Jamie currently draped himself over definitely was. Made me wonder if another lip-gloss-wearing Jimmy walked the earth and if he'd been blessed with a better life than the one I'd been dealt.

Huffing, I turned my focus elsewhere—internally and physically since I refused to dwell on the past. Fuck knew I'd had enough of that since returning.

Sutton stood with his back to me, and I ran my gaze over his broad shoulders that carried the weight of the world for all of the town, same as I remembered him doing when I'd been a kid. He stood tall and strong as an oak, and the way he smiled at people with a confident gaze caused me admire him even more.

His jeans fit him perfectly, from trim waist to thick thighs. Every movement of his muscles flexed his backside and made my mouth water.

"Hot as fuck, isn't he?"

I jerked my focus off Sutton to find Dexter lounging beside me, slightly slouched, elbow on the bar, and crooked smirk aimed across the room. But zero trace of desire lit his eyes as he stared where I'd been focused on seconds before.

"Been stalking me?" I asked since I had no clue how long he'd been close by and watching me salivate over his best friend.

"He's single," Dexter continued rather than answer. "Bisexual and finally on the prowl for dick for the first time ever."

A clutch in my belly stole my breath. "He's...bi?"

"Mmm hmm."

I bit the inside of my lip as tingles raced through my limbs.

"A smart man would pursue the fuck outta the chief. He's a good one and will be gobbled up before you know it."

A suggestion *I* be the smart man or was he laying claim because he had plans to turn his best friend into his lover?

Unsure, I hummed before sipping my drink, trying to rid myself of the cords suddenly tightening in my neck. "Are you going to be the one to do said *gobbling?*"

"He's not my type."

A release of tension eased my insides, and I followed Dex's gaze toward a dirty blond, green-eyed man at the other end of the bar staring back at with him with blatant lust and something...more. Temptation? A dare?

"Who's the hottie?" I asked, expecting I peered at Sutton with those same needy eyes as the blond did to the man beside me.

Dexter finished the long pull on his bottle of beer and tore his focus off the guy who'd held his attention. "No one."

"Sure, Jan."

"So—Sutton Forrester. Chief of Police and my best friend." Dexter's attempt to change the subject was downright laughable, but I went with it because no greater topic on earth could be found.

"You don't have to warn me off him," I stated, angling away to take in the rest of the bar and making note of a few more familiar faces. "He wouldn't want someone like me anyway, so don't concern yourself."

"What's that supposed to mean?"

"You've lived here longer than I have," I said with an

attempted shrug. "Surely you're well aware of who my dad was and all the trouble I got into as a kid."

His gaze flitted over my face as though seeking out the inner self I kept hidden from everyone. "A man can't change and grow? Become a better person?" he asked.

I had done that very thing, but my past had soiled me beyond the worm that used to crawl through the dirt of poverty and abuse. I couldn't begin to imagine what Sutton would think if he knew the truth about what I'd done since leaving here.

As though hearing my thoughts, Sutton finally turned, his gaze going straight for me like he'd been aware of my eyes on him.

The bustle and noise of Frenchie's muffled to white noise as we stared at each other. I swallowed hard, hating how he seemed to see past the facade of confidence I wrapped around myself where the self-conscious, hurting little boy was still hidden from the world.

As though hell-bent on making me see the error of my ways, Sutton excused himself from the crowd around him and moved toward me, gaze locked on my face and unwavering in determination.

Dexter snickered for whatever reason, but Sutton ensnared me so I didn't care where his best friend's mind had gone.

I grew feverish, my insides fluttering.

The chief paused in front of me, eyes searching, his looming presence as intimidating and mouthwatering as when I'd been a teen. I had to tip my head back slightly to hold his gaze.

"What have you been doing with yourself since leaving Pippen Creek, Jimmy?" he inquired in his chief's voice, expectation of my reply being a lie in his tone.

The man was in law enforcement for fuck's sake and probably always asked about people's business like they were under investigation, so I had no right to feel called out —or prematurely judged.

Something inside me longed to be honest and spill the truth of my shit from the previous nine years while gone from his town, but doing so would definitely ruin whatever minuscule chance I might have with him.

Pipe dreams were hard to give up.

"Keeping busy. Making money. Trying to leave my past and Pippen Creek behind," I answered, hoping he wouldn't pick up on the hidden truths I refused to admit to.

A muscle ticked in Sutton's jaw as he glanced away, lips in a thin line of disappointment.

So much for gaining a smidgen of his trust and weaseling my way beneath his clothing.

My shoulders slumped, heart seeming to shrivel up. I couldn't stomach guessing what his thoughts might be. I'd cried wolf one too many times as a kid for Sutton to suddenly believe a word I said simply because I'd grown into a man.

"How long will you be hanging around town?" Dexter asked to fill the sudden tension between his friend and I.

I wish I knew his angle or what he attempted to do but came up empty. "Until my dad's house is sold, Gram makes a decision about retiring from her store, and I feel ready to move on with my life." *That* was the absolute truth, shared as my stare remained on Sutton's strong profile, hoping he believed me.

"And what if that life is best served out here within city limits?" Dexter suggested.

I met his dark eyes, wondering what game he played. "Why do you care?"

He shrugged, shooting Sutton a quick glance before giving me a piercing stare. "Just having my friend's back."

What the hell was going on?

"Here are your wings, good-looking."

I turned to find Frenchie holding a plate of steaming wings slathered in sauce. My mouth watered, but no way could I chow down on those messy things and expect to appear polished enough for Sutton Forrester. He would, without a doubt, be reminded of the filthy kid who'd sucked dirt-crusted fingers free from chocolate, and that would *not* be sexy.

"Can I get them to go?" I asked with an apologetic smile, grabbing another twenty from the front pocket of my too-tight jeans and laying it on the bar top.

"Sure. Give me a sec—and keep the extra tip. I'd rather see you in here another day when you have time to tell me all about your shenanigans down in the big city."

Warmth filled me, not caring the gossip of where I'd been since leaving town had reached her ears. "Deal."

She disappeared into the kitchen, and I glanced in the mirror behind the bar while shoving the cash into my pocket.

Sutton's gaze glued to my backside, pupils large and dark.

Heat rushed through me, causing my heart to race. I arched slightly, swallowing the last of my wine as Frenchie returned with my to-go box.

"Thanks, sugar," I said with a wink. "See you later."

"Promise?"

"Absolutely—and I always keep my promises."

She rapped on the bar. "Good man," she said before moving off to help another patron waving at her.

Sutton still stared, so I wiggled my ass, calling him out.

His gaze slid upward, latching onto mine in the mirror. Breath snagged, I soaked in his lustful eyes before he got a hold of himself and shut that shit down.

Too late, Chief.

I winked, my lips curling into a smirk as I turned to face him, completely ignoring Dexter on my right.

"Chief," I attempted a purr, trailing a fingertip over his starched shirt while clutching my dinner in my other hand. "I'll be underfoot for a while, but I promise to be behave— for now."

I swore he held his breath, a huge rushed exhale sounded in my wake as I sauntered away, every muscle in my body twitchy, my pulse racing.

The tone for our coming interactions had been set, and I could only hope my plans landed me in the chief's bed rather than the jail cell cot.

Chapter 7

Sutton

"That man is either going to be the death of you or your happily ever after."

I scowled over Dex's declaration, my gaze glued to Jimmy's lush ass as he walked toward Frenchie's exit without a backward glance.

I'd hoped to see Jimmy again in this lifetime, but goddamn. He made me salivate as though I hadn't eaten in a week. I thirsted like it was late July and a heat wave smothered our town. Lust tightened my balls when I'd noted his shaped brows and eyelashes were darker than his light, blond hair. And that nose ring, along with the one in his belly and the hint of metal I'd seen through his tongue, made me wonder if there was any below his waistband too.

Thank fuck for tight briefs because the thought of a piercing anywhere near that boy's groin caused blood to head southward again with serious intent. And with how he continuously licked his lips, drawing my attention to their plumpness, how he lowered his voice while sidling up close to me—the boy was pure sex and full of promise of a good time.

He'd had plenty of practice while sowing his wild oats and making some serious cash down in Boston.

Which he hadn't admitted to when I'd asked what he'd been up to since leaving.

Not that I'd expected him to up and spill the truth, but still. Would have gone a long way toward helping me rouse the tiniest bit of trust in the boy.

Jimmy might be all big, innocent eyes and flirtatious smirks, but anyone who'd seen shit and dealt with it on a daily basis would recognize he hid his true self. One that still called to the caretaker and fixer in me even though I knew better to get involved with someone like him.

I couldn't help the desire to tear down his walls, rip off the facade he wore to experience the real man beneath. Every part of my being yearned to take him apart piece by piece until he went quiet and pliant, a sated, blissed-out beauty snuggling against my chest where he would finally find the acceptance and peace he'd been desperate for as a kid.

Goddamned kryptonite.

Needing to adjust myself but not about to offer Dex something else to give me shit about, I turned away before Jimmy slipped out the door, flagging down Iris, Frenchie's wife.

"Another round," I said, holding up my empty beer bottle, hoping a third drink would numb my body enough that thoughts of Jimmy wouldn't make my hormones behave like a teenager's.

Dex set his empty atop the bar as well, accepting a cold one from Iris along with me.

We sipped in silence for a few seconds, both of us lost in own heads.

"He's changed."

I glanced over at my best friend who studied the label on his bottle. "What did you pick up on while hanging out beside him unnoticed?"

"You have eyes in the back of your head." Dex huffed. "Swear to God."

I chuckled and took a long pull.

"He's always been a world-weary wise kid—"

I snorted.

"—but there's substance and maturity that he lacked when he'd lit out like his tail was on fire. You can see it in his eyes. How he talked to other people who greeted him. His smile was real on occasion, especially when asking about them and their loved ones, oftentimes by name. Yeah, he's a flirt, but he uses his words to uplift rather than cause trouble." Dex's throat bobbed as he swallowed a few gulps of his beer.

Heaving an exhale, I leaned onto the bar with my elbows. "Yeah. I'd guess his life in Boston hadn't been the rainbows and butterflies he'd probably hoped for."

Jimmy was also even more alluring than online images suggested, the embodiment of everything I hadn't realized how badly I longed for until laying eyes on him. Beneath that facade, Jimmy Riley was still that hurting little boy, desperate for a word of edification and affirming, affectionate touches.

And I longed to give him both in spades.

Every part of me wanted to wrap him up in my arms and erase the flickers of fear that lay in his eyes when he spoke of his dad's house and selling the property. The place would have to be cleaned out and cosmetic upgrades done before an offer was put on the decrepit home in the worst part of town.

Would he do it by himself?

Face down his demons without anyone to offer support if he needed a helping hand both physically and mentally?

The thought of him standing alone in front of that house of horrors I'd driven by yesterday did *not* settle right in my guts. My fingers itched to entwine with his, offering him something solid to hold onto in case the terror of memories got the best of him. I'd heard him whimper and cry out in his drunken sleep while on the jail cell's cot enough times to know he hadn't escaped his childhood trauma unaffected.

"What's up with Christian Cole?" I asked, ready to turn my focus elsewhere and well aware the guy stared our way.

"What about him?" Dex asked, his tone guarded. He glanced up the bar, and I bit back a smirk as sparks flashed between the two men. If they weren't careful, those two would burn the town down to ash.

"I heard from Kendra and Harry this morning that he applied for the same position you did."

A muscle ticked in Dex's jaw, and he gave his beer his full focus, pink staining his high cheekbones. "He did."

"He doesn't have the experience you do. He also didn't grow up in Pippen Creek and commit his life to keeping this town safe like you have."

Dexter had been hired at the fire station not long after graduation, and he'd been a dedicated firefighter for our town for as long as I'd worn a badge.

Christian had moved to Pippen Creek a few years earlier with his parents who'd bought The Moose's Muse, and while Dex and I had close to decade on the guy, he'd had his heart set on fire chief, same as Dex who'd put in the time and effort to deserve the job.

Both men were competitive as hell, their word spats amusing as fuck even though they often left my best friend in a downright shitty mood and in desperate need of getting laid.

"You two ought to just fuck already," I muttered, noting how both stared at each other without hint of caring over who noticed or what people thought of their supposed feud.

Dex sipped his beer, dark eyes intent on the bar's opposite end. "He's not into guys."

My laugh turned into a snort, the type that caused a man to choke.

Dex slapped my back as I caught my breath.

"Are you fucking blind?" I rasped, clearing my throat once more. "Cole would drop to his knees and worship your cock the second you pointed to the ground." I stated the absolute truth I expected all of Pippen Creek was well aware of. "Fuck already and end this tension everyone in this bar can feel."

"You mean like the same sexual draw between you and Jimmy?"

I shifted on my stool, my lip curling into a snarl.

"Don't deny it, Sutton," Dex stated quietly, a hint of teasing in his voice. "Anyone with eyes could see the truth."

"He's too young," I tossed the excuse I'd focused on before.

"Bullshit," Dex replied as he always did. "Try again."

"He's nothing but trouble."

"Maybe," Dex agreed. "But he could be a fun time for you—hell, an eye-opening couple of days or weeks depending on how long he stays in town."

I sipped my drink, not tasting the hops or even paying attention to the liquid sliding down my throat. "And what do I do when he leaves again, hmm?"

"Sutton."

Lips pursed, I shook my head. "I can't afford to lower

my walls and give him the chance to own my heart if he doesn't have plans to stick around, Dex. Even though I'm scared shitless to let someone in, I want forever, not some sexy, warm body in my bed just to ease the ache in my balls."

"But what an easing it would be," he teased with a waggle of his eyebrows.

I elbowed the fucker, as he was fond of doing with me, but didn't disagree. Considering his experience with sampling from all of the local men into dick and the apps he used to locate said guys, I wasn't about to argue.

But I needed more, goddammit, and I'd been hurt enough in the past that I knew without question what I did or didn't want invading my peaceful yet lonely existence.

Putting my heart on the line by falling into bed with a lying younger man who called out to every single part of me was nothing but absolute fucking trouble, exactly as I'd stated.

Jimmy Riley would eventually grow bored with the old chief's body and head back to Elite Escort's gay branch, who'd supplied him with hungry dick and a well-padded bank account for the previous five years.

No way a sex worker would ever settle down with a man sixteen years his senior whose sex drive would pale in comparison to his energetic ass. The boy would wear me out on day one.

The continued thickness in my shaft argued a different story, but I reasoned my unusually strong desire for release was due to lack of action.

Jimmy was not a safe place for me, however, that truth wouldn't stop me from being there for him as a friend if he needed me.

But further interaction required I keep my own walls

sturdy and remember how being vulnerable only ended with broken hearts. I would be smart to remember the devastation left in Darla's wake and how long it'd taken for healing to allow me some sort of joy in life outside of Jamie.

Never again.

Mind set, I finished my beer, said my goodbyes, and went home to a dark and quiet house where I focused on the plans Jamie had to propose that night and the surety of gaining another son. A smile might have curved my lips while I lay in bed alone, but the heaviness in my chest, the unpleasant ache of longing traveled with me into my dreams as it did every night.

Chapter 8

Jimmy

Adrenaline crashed through me the second I opened my eyes.

Today, I would stand before what had haunted me every day since I'd left Pippen Creek. Putting off the inevitable any longer wouldn't gain me anything but further panic over what was to come.

A cold sweat broke out over my body as I climbed into my car, my stomach a rock. Beads of moisture lined my upper lip and forehead as I drove through town then south-west. Gripping the steering wheel until my knuckles turned white to keep from scratching at my arms, I rounded the final turn onto the dirt road I hadn't traversed in nine years.

Breath burst in and out of my squeezing lungs as Dad's house came into view. Muscles twitched, my instincts demanding I swing my BMW around and get the hell away from there. Doing so was certainly an option. I could have hired a contractor to do what needed done in order for the house to sell without having to lay eyes on it. A cleaning company could have righted the mess inside Gram had warned me about.

But for me to move on, to get rid of the nightmares that riddled my dreams and controlled a lot of the processes in my mind, I had to face this shit. A real man wouldn't tremble beneath the weight of nightmares. I would stand tall. Take care of business. Finally find healing through staring down my fears.

My wheels rolled slower on crunching gravel as my shaking leg attempted to press against the brake.

The car stopped.

I shut off the engine.

Suffocating silence flooded the BMW's interior, and I swallowed hard, rubbing damp palms down my jeans. No words to amp me up filled my mind, and no encouragement rose to give me energy to move.

I stared at the peeling front door, the crooked steps I'd spent countless hours sitting on with Sutton by my side while we'd shared chocolate bars loaded with delicious caramel and peanuts.

His warmth had always radiated through the space between us, offering comfort I couldn't derive from anyone or anywhere else.

Clinging to the pleasant memories of my hero, I climbed from the car on weak knees. Every shuffle closer to the house made my guts clench and shoulders roll inward. I bit my tongue to keep from whimpering but could do nothing to stop the tremble in my lower lip.

A dog barked, and I flinched at the intrusive sound, another fresh rush of adrenaline racing through my system.

One step at a time.

One breath, one blink.

Tearing my gaze off the house, I focused on the fake rock beside the stoop and the key that Gram had assured me still rested inside it.

My fingers shook terribly, and it was a solid two minutes before I managed to retrieve the key from its hiding spot. Blowing out a slow exhale, I forced my feet to lift toward each tread until I reached the landing.

I jolted at the loudness of the key sliding into the lock. The click caused another flinch, and my muscles jerked.

The door creaked open beneath my firm shove, and I gripped the metal teeth digging into my palm, the slight pain giving me something to focus on.

Closure, I reminded myself of why I stood on the edge of possible insanity. Pull up those bootstraps, as Gram would say, and face the shit head on.

I stepped inside, the scent of stale cigarette and rancid grease assaulting my nose.

My entire being froze as the blood drained from my face and left me lightheaded. Lungs attempting to instinctively draw breath, I struggled, blinking flashes of memories, loud and vivid, ripping through my mind.

Smacking face-first into the doorjamb.

The stained, filthy couch Dad had bent me over while whipping my ass and back red with his belt.

A single corner of the room without furniture where I'd knelt, nose against the wall, having to hide my ugly face from him when he couldn't bear the sight of me. More often than not, dry rice had been beneath my knees, digging into tender skin.

Worthless worm.

I blinked hard at the voice in my head that had gone to more of a whisper than scream over the years, but I cringed all the same.

On wooden legs, I passed through the mess of trash, piles of newspapers, and clothing. Detouring past the kitchen entrance, I headed back the hallway I'd crawled dozens of times in attempts to escape that damned leather belt he had wielded like a whip.

I stumbled to a halt at the open bathroom door, the stained tub bringing even more flashes of beatings on my bare skin, a constant rain of hurtful words that tore me down until I had no sense of self outside being a waste of sperm, the cause of my mother's death and of Dad's heartache.

Two more steps landed me in front of the door I'd silently shut the night I'd turned eighteen.

Dad had passed out in his bedroom across the hall, his drunken snores assuring me he wouldn't have heard me slam through the house as I left him behind.

I twisted the handle, pushing the flimsy particle board door inward, and scratched absently at my forearm.

The room had been turned inside out. Mattress flipped against the wall riddled with holes that looked like fists had punched through drywall. The few personal belongings I'd left behind scattered over the floor along with the clothing I hadn't taken with me.

My gaze drifted toward the right—a discoloration of the flooring smashed into me like the memory of Dad's fist into my temple, and I staggered on my feet, a whimper slipping past my lips as it'd done the night I'd finally become a man.

I'd lain there, my mind fuzzy and eyesight bleary as he'd stood over me, kicking me where my oversized sweatshirt would cover whatever bruising he inflicted on my body. It was the first time I'd begged whatever supernatural being or possible god might exist to end my life. Not even the plans I had set, the freedom I would soon experience, made the beating bearable. If Dad had hated me as much as he'd claimed to, why not just end me with a bullet to my brain then his? Put us both out of our misery?

I never fooled myself into believing that at some deep level he cared for the only son he'd created with the woman he'd loved more than anything on earth. The man had been a coward through and through, unable to cope with his brokenness over losing my mom. He'd turned to alcohol, and I'd paid the price for being the cause of her death.

"Never should have been born." He'd spat on me that night, eventually leaving me more alone than I'd ever felt in my eighteen years.

Other similar sentiments whispered on the heels of Dad's final words to me like ghosts from the grave, tearing me down as effectively as they had done years earlier when spewed from his hateful lips.

Worthless.

Stupid.

Ugly.

Unwanted.

Would I never be free of the man I'd tried so hard to please?

Fingernails digging into my left forearm, I stared at the bloodstained evidence of what I had endured. I hadn't grown, hadn't escaped the horrors I'd faced every day as a powerless child when all I'd wanted to do was give my dad back some of the happiness I'd stolen from him by being born.

Uncontrollable shaking took over my body, and I curled in on myself to find some sort of stronghold to lean on—the only person I could trust to hold me tight. But I couldn't voice bullshit words to edify myself. Couldn't grasp onto any hope of rising above the trauma I hadn't escaped. The demons from my past still dug their claws into my psyche, owning my focus.

"Jimmy?"

Tears welled in my eyes at the kind voice echoing alongside Dad's in my mind. The room in front of me wavered as wetness gathered enough droplets spilled from my lashes and over my cheeks.

Weak.

Pussy.

Faggot.

I choked on a sob, clinging to myself tighter.

"Jimmy?"

He'd always been the light in my darkness, the hero I'd mentally clung to whenever Dad stripped me down to nothing more than an instinctive creature who froze at the first hint of anger or trouble.

Even now, I couldn't move. My legs refused to lead me outside to safety where every stuttered inhale didn't coat my lungs with stale cigarettes and decay.

"Jimmy."

My eyelids slammed shut at the relieved tone behind me.

Sutton had shown up when I needed him most.

Of course he had—and there would be no hiding the crumbling facade I cowered behind this time.

Chapter 9

Sutton

Saturday morning, I checked in with the Coles at The Moose's Muse to see what type of car Jimmy drove. I definitely kept an eye on my office window overlooking Main Street, taking note every time a cherry red vehicle drove past.

The BMW he owned snagged my attention not long after my breakfast from Scone Haven, and I craned my head, watching the blond beauty hang a left down Pippen Street.

I grabbed my keys and left the station without incident, climbing into my cruiser mere minutes behind the boy. Either he headed for Mary's or he planned to check in on the residence he'd been paying taxes on from afar the previous three years.

A ride by Mary's and empty driveway sent me farther southwest of town. Expecting Jimmy had no interest in visiting the graveyard where Mary had buried the elder Riley's ashes, I headed toward the house that would doubtless bring back a mess of emotions and memories I didn't want Jimmy facing alone.

In my years as the chief of police, I'd found being nurturing, compassionate, and supportive wasn't enough to change a man's path. If a person didn't want to straighten out their life, they wouldn't.

Had Jimmy had gone to therapy in his absence in the hopes of finding healing? Had he come to terms with the childhood trauma inflicted on him by the one man who should have protected him at all costs? Without answers, I couldn't help but feel responsible for his well-being no matter where he'd driven to.

His car sat in front of the ranch where I'd expected, but Jimmy didn't slouch in the driver seat or on the front steps.

I hopped from the cruiser and strode up the uneven cobbled walkway, my footfalls deliberately heavy on the treads leading to the tilting stoop so he would know I approached. A waft of stale air from the opened door passed my nose, and I grimaced as memories assaulted me of the day I'd figured Jimmy's dad might have drowned his liver. No such luck that afternoon, and by the time his body *had* finally given out after years of alcohol abuse, Jimmy had been long gone.

"Jimmy?" I called out while stepping over the threshold into a mess of filth and trash.

The boy didn't answer, nor did I hear anything but deathly stillness, the house more a tomb than shelter from the elements.

I stepped farther into the dim interior, the stench of the air unsurprising considering how long the house had been shut up. "Jimmy?" I called again but not so loud as to startle him.

A choked sob sounded back the hallway, and I hurried forward, rounding the bend to find Jimmy hugging himself in his bedroom doorway. In profile, his face appeared blanched, tears streaming over his cheeks. Red marks lined his left arm as though he'd been scratching.

While I'd wanted to see him broken down so I could help rebuild him, this went far beyond what I had hoped for. Never would I wish to see a man curled in on himself, a mere shell of the usual sass and energy he'd displayed the night before. I closed the distance between us, desiring to reach out to him and offer comfort, but I kept from doing so since he still didn't seem aware I was there.

Heaviness settled over my shoulders as I stopped shy of his personal space, and my throat went thick at the display of hurt and insecurity overwhelming his entire body.

"Jimmy," I whispered, and his eyes closed, letting me know he realized he wasn't alone. "Are you doing okay?" It was obvious as fuck he wasn't, but I needed to check in with him, hear from his own lips what he was dealing with.

"I want to burn it all to the ground," he choked out, his voice ragged as though his insides shredded to unrecognizable pieces. "Every reminder." His voice broke, and he swallowed hard. "Every nightmare." A shudder ripped through him, and he whimpered, hugging himself tighter with arms streaked red from his fingernails.

Unable to help the draw, I gently cupped his elbow, tugging the slightest bit. "Come here," I murmured, shifting him toward me.

Like an innocent lamb, he allowed me to steer him toward my chest as I'd always longed to do.

He pressed against me with a shuddered sigh, his arms encircling my waist to cling to my uniform as I held him. He shivered and shook in silence when I'd expected harsh sobs.

I closed my eyes, his head tucked beneath my chin,

soaking in the warmth of his slight form. While I finally had the chance to give him the comfort he needed, I hated that our first embrace was due to unimaginable pain he must been reliving from having stepped into this damned house.

Long moments passed as my heart thumped heavy against the side of his face, but at least my groin lay relaxed rather than roused at finally having a body—*him* specifically—plastered against my front like a second uniform. He fit like he'd been tailor-made for me.

Jimmy's breathing regulated, and I readied myself for the second he would pull away, leaving me missing the feel of him.

All too soon, he released his hold on my shirt as I'd feared and stepped back, shoving his hands in his pockets. He hadn't even wiped the damp tracks from his cheeks.

He studied the floor. "I'm going to sell this shithole," he said, his tone wrecked as though he'd been sobbing for an hour or longer.

"Glad to hear it." I fisted my hands at my sides to keep from brushing unruly waves of hair off his forehead and tipping his face up with a light touch to his chin so I could drown in his vulnerable baby blues. "If there's anything I can do to help, let me know."

"Thanks." Jimmy exhaled heavily and straightened his shoulders as though throwing off a weighted cloak that had attempted to tug him toward the earth. He tilted his head back and met my gaze straight on, his still-wet eyes as riveting, yet shadowed, blocking me from reading his feelings. A saucy smirk tilted his lips, and my heart fell as his old facade settled into place like he'd flipped a switch.

"So." He hummed, taking a good, long look at how I filled out my uniform. "Following me around town, are you, Chief?"

A muscle ticked in my jaw as I studied the face shuttered from my perusal. This wasn't the real Jimmy from moments before, the vulnerable man who'd needed me as much as I wanted him. A shiver slid over my spine at the realization this boy already held power over my heart, and it wouldn't take much manipulation on his part to play me for the fool I'd always been when it had come to him.

"I'll admit," he stepped closer, his voice lowering, same as the night before whenever he got all up in my space. His fingertips trailed over the buttons atop my chest, and I held my breath, chin lifted, peering down my nose at him as he attempted to disarm my staunch determination to remain unaffected. "Coming here wasn't easy," he continued, tugging on the button right above my belt, gaze fixed farther south, "but I can think of a few ways to get both of our minds off the bad times we shared on this property."

I caught his wrist in a tight grip and gave myself a bit of space with a small backward step that hurt more than helped.

Jimmy lifted his focus, eyes blank of pain when his voice had been coated with it for one brief moment of vulnerability I wished would last long enough for me to connect with him for real.

Nothing sexual or even sensual, simply a freedom to simply *be* in our feelings.

"Don't be this way, Jimmy. Please." I searched his face, hoping the boy would listen to me.

Wetness slid over his gorgeous irises, and I inhaled deeply, drinking in as the veil he hid behind slid from place. His shoulders wilted, and I released his wrist, allowing him to wrap his own arms around himself since I needed to see his face for this brief moment of honesty he would gift me.

"He beat the shit out me the night I left Pippen Creek,"

Jimmy said, his voice as small as it'd been when he'd been ten and I had first suspected abuse. It was his only admission to what I'd always wondered, what DHHS had decided never occurred. "His knuckles tore through my scalp, and I bled while curled up and defenselessly took his kicks." He nodded toward a stain in the wood flooring, and my insides clenched, hands once more fisting at my sides. I remembered no such injury marring his head or discoloring his hair that night. "He eventually stopped and left me lying there. Once he passed out, I showered, packed up a few personal belongings, and planned to head out of town—if you didn't want me."

I could recall with vivid clarity the memory of big eyes begging me to save him in the only way he thought I could.

By claiming him. Making him mine.

Back then, I hadn't considered the possibility.

But now? I wanted to do both—and feared the repercussions.

A sad, crooked smile lifted Jimmy's lips, and he glanced at me before quickly looking away once more as though ashamed of what he'd done before heading south toward Massachusetts.

"I'm sorry," I murmured, not sure if it was for turning him down, for all the shit he'd endured, or a mix of both. But back then, I hadn't seen Jimmy as anything more than a hurting boy, thank fuck, or claiming the kid would have landed me in hot water no matter the fact he'd turned eighteen at the stroke of midnight.

"Do you regret denying my offer even a little bit?" He attempted to flirt but failed miserably, and I hated the pain that lined his face.

How the fuck could I answer that without laying myself

bare? Opening that can of worms would leave me wasted and broken beyond how Darla had ruined me.

I fought for words that would soothe Jimmy and not open me up to a boatload of hurt but came up empty.

His focus dropped to the floor once more, and I hated that in my silence, I'd failed him yet again.

Chapter 10

Jimmy

I lowered my shields, and that tiny bit of vulnerability still didn't get me where I longed to be.

"I always hero-worshiped you," I admitted. "Wanted you to be my dad for the longest time, was jealous of Jamie because he still had your love after his mom abandoned you both."

A gasped exhale escaped Sutton as though my words wounded him, but I was selfish enough in my own pain not to care I'd reminded him of his own heartache. What a pair we were. Surely, we would be a perfect fit.

Right?

But piles of shit metaphorically and physically stood between us.

I glanced up the hallway toward the filthy living room at its end. The trash in there alone would fill a dumpster. I hadn't yet stepped foot into the kitchen—couldn't envision what I might find in there, or even worse, the memories that would assault me.

Inhaling deeply, I imagined settling my emotions into a block of ice and readied myself to face the rest of what should be done to put my past behind me. Sutton might say he was willing to help in whatever way I required, but he stood firm in denying what I needed.

With a physical connection that would ground me and lead me toward the healing I craved.

"Sorry you had to see that part of me," I said, trying to sound like an adult. "Coming back here pulled shit to the surface I'd hoped was long gone."

"Facing demons is never easy," Sutton said, his low tone soothing as always, making me want to melt into his hard chest again where, for a moment of time, every negative thought and feeling had dissolved into a less intense attempt to ruin me. "Don't beat yourself up for getting emotional, Jimmy. It just proves you're real."

I snorted, thinking about how "real" I'd been since leaving. The townsfolk would judge me for sure. "The people of Pippen Creek wouldn't like who I really am," I muttered.

"How about you let them make their own decisions?"

Shrugging, I moved around Sutton so I didn't end up throwing myself into his arms again and fall apart in my weakness. Chief Sutton might be nurturing as fuck, but he would never respect or give me a chance if he found out how needy I was.

Knowing I couldn't sway Sutton toward where I wanted him to be without putting in some serious time and further planning, I drove away from my childhood house in search of comfort that would be offered without hindrance.

Gram met me at her front door, her welcoming arms and soft bosom the perfect coming home I should have sought out first thing after arriving in Pippen Creek last night.

"Welcome back, Jimmy-boy."

Tears stung my eyes at her kind greeting and loving tone of voice. Add in the frailty of her body that used to be robust, and my heart hurt.

"It's good to see you," I murmured.

"It's been too damned long," she chided before letting me go. Using a cane to maneuver through the entryway, Mary headed toward the kitchen at the back of the hallway.

The air smelled of chocolate chip cookies, and my mouth watered. "Did you make my favorite?"

"Of course I did." She pointed to the table once through the kitchen's archway, and I sat my ass down, intent on the plate of deliciousness I hadn't tasted since the last care package she'd sent to me in Boston a few months earlier.

"Mmm," I hummed around chocolate melting on my tongue. "So good."

"Don't talk with your mouth full," she stated, turning on the coffee pot. "Did you go to your dad's?"

My throat spasmed, and I swallowed hard, needing moisture. "Yeah."

"And?"

I shoved another cookie into my mouth to force my body onward, chewing and swallowing through the dryness before answering. "It sucked ass—and not in the good way."

Gram admonished me, gently slapping my shoulder. "Coffee?"

"Please."

She settled across from me a few minutes later, her brown eyes fixated on my face. "How are you doing, Jimmy?"

I shrugged, unable to hold her gaze, allowing mine to

drop to my forearm. At least the unconscious scratching at my arm hadn't broken skin or left marks. "Worse than expected, but I'm surviving."

"You always were a strong boy."

I huffed a snort. "Didn't have much choice, did I?"

"No, but you do now. What's your plan?"

"Sell that shithole and get the hell out of here again." The second part didn't sit well in my mind and caused my stomach to churn. But unless I could change Sutton's stance on avoiding my attempts to get my hands on his dick or even better yet, sneak my way into his heart and make myself as comfortable as he had in mine, I had no other choice.

"I'm thinking about moving to Florida to be with my sister."

I jerked my focus upward to find Gram studying me intently. "What...what about the shop?"

"I'm getting too old to hobble around that place for more than a couple of hours a day."

"Well, what about your son?" I tried again. The thought of the only semi-family I had in my life creating that kind of distance between us churned my stomach.

Gram pursed her lips. "Kurt is an absolute mess. A loser."

"Gram!"

"Well, he is!" she insisted, and from what she'd written in her monthly letters, I had to agree. The man was a drinker, made zero time for his son, and wasn't exactly queer friendly.

"And DJ?" I asked quietly, expecting she would miss her grandson terribly—and that the poor boy would suffer without her being nearby.

Gram heaved a heavy exhale and sat back, toying with her coffee mug, forehead furrowed, wrinkled lips pursed for a few silent minutes. "He's what is making this choice so damned difficult," she finally shared. "He's only eight, and I've already stayed a couple of years longer than I wanted to. My sister is having some health problems and would really benefit from having me as a roommate."

I could understand the tug-of-war in her mind and wished I had wisdom or a solution to offer her.

She glanced at the antique clock ticking on the wall behind me. "He'll be here soon."

"Yeah?" I asked, grinning even though a sense of heaviness lingered. I'd heard all about her only grandchild but had yet to meet him. Gram's son, Kurt, and his ex-wife, Carrie, had married right before I'd left Pippen Creek. DJ had been born a little while later, but at least I'd gotten printed pictures from Gram so I could put a face to her grandson's name.

"He's a troublemaker, like you were, but sweet as pie, same as you."

I chuckle. "You're only saying that because he has you wrapped around his little finger like I did."

Gram smiled, but zero trace of silliness filled her wise gaze. "I've lived enough years that searching out the core of a person, even one as young as DJ, isn't that difficult. He's hurting, and while not nearly as badly as you did with that awful father of yours, his situation is traumatic."

Gram had told me about Kurt and Carrie's difficult divorce and her son's turn to alcohol, so I didn't doubt the conclusion she'd arrived at.

The doorbell rang, and her eyes lit up. She pushed to her feet, grabbing her cane. "Come meet the other boy who makes me smile."

Once more, my eyes stung, and I followed on Gram's heels into the entryway.

The door pushed open before we got there, and a wild, brown-haired terror came flying inside.

"Gram!" he hollered, same as I'd always done when entering into the only peaceful place I'd found inside Pippen Creek. The boy threw his arms around his grandmother's waist, eyes closed, grinning like a dork as he hugged her tight.

She smiled down at him like he hung the moon in the night sky, her frail hands sifting through his thick hair.

My heart ached over memories of her doing the same with me.

"Mom." Kurt greeted Gram as he stepped over the threshold and dropped a backpack to the floor. I could smell the stench of a hangover wafting off him and fought my gag reflex. "I'll grab him tomorrow night," he muttered.

"Okay," Gram said without argument when she'd bitched through letters how often her son unloaded his responsibilities on her doorstep—even though she enjoyed every precious second with her grandson.

"Hey, Kurt." I bypassed his mom to stick my hand out since it was what Gram would have wanted me to do no matter how much of an ass her son could be. "Good to see you," I lied.

He hesitated but gave me a brief shake before wiping his palm on his jeans. No greeting, not even a sound of agreement passed his lips. Considering the guys in construction in these redneck towns tended to curl their noses at people like me who presented more feminine than masculine, I wasn't surprised.

Skin toughened by years of abuse and all that.

I lifted my chin, giving him a haughty look even though he wouldn't meet my eyes.

"See you tomorrow, Mom," Kurt said over his shoulder as he hurried outside, shutting the door behind him.

Good fucking riddance.

I breathed a little easier, shoulders relaxing.

"DJ," Gram said, turning him toward me, "this is my friend Jimmy, the one I've been talking about."

"Gram never shuts up," DJ said, smirking up at me, his dark eyes full of mischief.

I glanced at her then held a hand to my mouth to shield my lips while leaning toward DJ. "But she makes the *best* chocolate chip cookies, which makes all her stories worth listening to."

"Right?" he whisper-hollered.

"Right!" I agreed, straightening with a grin. "Come on," I said, nodding toward the kitchen. "She left me a plateful, but I'm not going to finish them. I don't mind sharing."

"Yes," he hissed and scampered back through the hallway.

Gram grasped my hand. "I'm sorry for Kurt's ignorance, and thank you for your kindness to DJ," she stated quietly, her tone unsteady, her eyes watery and filled with gratitude.

I squeezed her fingers, having to swallow the thickness from my throat.

Perhaps coming to Pippen Creek wouldn't be a waste of time.

"You shoot hoops?" DJ hollered from the kitchen, the garbled words evidence he'd shoved a cookie into his mouth and attempted to speak around the chocolatey goodness.

"Yeah!" I hollered, expecting he and I would be out in Grams backyard, intent on sinking baskets into the ancient rim still hanging above the shed door.

"You're a sweet boy, Jimmy," Gram said, and for once, I

didn't feel the need to argue what she'd believed of me since the day I'd first walked into her shop.

I'd been hoping to hide from Dad and the frigid air that cut through the threadbare coat from two winters before.

She'd invited me farther into the only consignment store in town, told me to make myself comfortable on an old Victorian couch, a soft throw blanket atop my thin legs and a mug of hot chocolate in my hands minutes later.

I'd fallen in love with her that afternoon and had spent more afternoons there than in my own home. But everything had changed—and continued to with every passing hour.

One day soon, I would be free of Pippen Creek while Gram would be retired, possibly lounging poolside beneath the Florida sun, but I wondered how much happiness either of us would feel considering what we would leave behind.

Her, willingly.

Me, not so much. But I'd learned that worms didn't always get what they wanted, no matter how hard they hung onto the hope of one day being able to bask beneath the sun-flooded sky without drying to an empty husk.

Chapter 11

Sutton

Jamie's first week working at the station started out quiet except for Babs's squeals of delight over learning my son and Chaz had gotten engaged over the week-end. Since she was the town gossip—with only the best of intentions—I wasn't surprised word about their upcoming marriage spread as quickly as it did.

I also found out from her vast knowledge that Jimmy had rented a dumpster to empty out his dad's house.

I'd finally gotten a glimpse of the real man behind the facade, the total lack of the tough front he'd always worn as a kid, and couldn't think about much else. The last time I'd seen past his walls was that September afternoon he'd been crying on the front porch of a house that hadn't ever been his safe place.

He'd called himself a worm, and over his teenage years, I'd heard him whisper the word as though it played on repeat in his head. Made me wonder what else his dad had said to him when he'd been a child.

I expected he hid his true self because he didn't like who he was beneath.

The person under the veneer Jimmy Riley wore like a shield intrigued the hell out of me and was ten times as magnetic as the sassy flirt I struggled to say no to. After that glimpse of the real Jimmy, I'd been even more intent on burrowing into his brain and heart, sifting through the bullshit for the gem of a man I expected he could be given the right support and edification.

After that breakthrough we'd had, I'd felt sure he would reach out and allow me to help, offering me the opportunity to get to know him better even though the idea scared the hell out of me.

He didn't call or text, which suggested he didn't want me around.

I didn't have his number, so I allowed him the space he seemed to want.

Daily, I drove by his neighborhood but stayed far enough away he wouldn't see me or be able to accuse me of stalking his fine ass. Twice, I'd seen Mary's grandson DJ working alongside Jimmy to clean out the house, tossing shit into the dumpster and chatting as though neither had a care in the world. Flashes of a true smile curved his lips while with DJ, and while I was happy to see him lighter in spirit, jealousy roused in me over his easily sharing that part of him with a young boy. My brain acted like a petulant child because I wanted to be the sole reason for those glimpses of truth he unveiled.

Even from a distance, he was sunshine, and I could imagine the sparkle in his baby blues, the hint of peace in them even if only for a moment. Considering all he'd endured as a kid, he deserved to find contentment and happiness in living without a mask of protection.

We often caught sight of each other in passing while

downtown, and I'd soaked in his stare, my body restless as he checked me out, that smirking facade firmly in place.

I'd expected him to hang at Frenchie's, but he kept a low-key profile rather than get into trouble by drinking too much like he'd done as a teenager. Mostly, he was with Mary, accompanying her to get groceries at The Market, taking her to Dig-In, and talking to our town's sole realtor around her shop and his dad's house. I'd heard he'd driven Mary and DJ to the apple orchard, and I'd seen him with the young boy at Scone Haven and the ice cream shop more than once.

Jimmy had been nothing but self-centered and selfish before leaving Pippen Creek, and I had difficulty trusting his intentions that appeared innocent and loving. I hated that my mind immediately went toward deception, that he only invested in Mary's grandson to gain my attention. No doubt, he wished to prove he was a changed man.

I relived every glance we'd exchanged downtown, his smirks and winks, how his gaze trailed over my body, making me heat up and wish for things I hadn't enjoyed in far too long. From a distance, the boy was on his best behavior as he claimed he would be, but I knew it was only a matter of time before his manipulative little ass attempted yet again to get my dick inside him.

The thought of his smooth hands on me, his body teaching me how to please a man when I'd only slept with women, made me shift in my office chair.

"Dad."

Blinking, I turned toward my office door, grinning at my son who held takeout containers from Dig-In. My stomach growled loudly, reminding me the lunch hour had passed without my realizing it, and I appreciated the distraction from my obsession.

"Perfect timing." I stacked folders and shoved them to the edge of my desk as Jamie settled into the chair across from me.

He slid one Styrofoam box to me, and I flipped the lid, breathing in deep, my mouth watering.

We hadn't gotten much time together since his graduation and first day on our tiny force here in Pippen Creek, so I looked forward to sharing our lunch break. As one, we ripped into the ketchup packets, creating piles in the corners of our box lids.

"You seem to be settling in just fine," I said before sinking my teeth into my burger.

He'd already beat me to it and chewed, lips firmly closed, while nodding. "Yeah," he said once he swallowed, grabbing two fries and smearing them through ketchup. "Figured I would since I've known everyone on the payroll for most of my life."

Officer Davidson was the only new hire since Jamie had left for college. He was the single ladies' man around town and was easy to get along with. Like Jamie, he fit in as though family, a perfect addition to the no-drama station I appreciated having.

"Been meaning to ask you about something," I said, wiping my mouth with a napkin.

One of his eyebrows popped up, but he continued eating as though he hadn't a thing to hide—which I would usually believe considering he rarely lied or kept the truth from me.

"What trouble did you get into while down in Boston that came rushing back to haunt you the second Jimmy walked into Frenchie's?" I'd been suspicious over his reaction and had guessed what had caused it but wanted his admission rather than accuse him.

Red flushed up Jamie's neck and stained his cheeks. "Shit." He huffed, uncapped his water, and took a swig. "It's uh...a little embarrassing."

"I figured that from the color on your face, but I won't judge."

Jamie hesitated before speaking. "First, I have to ask what all you know about Jimmy and what he's been doing since leaving here?"

"Everything," I admitted without hesitation.

Jamie's brow rose again.

"I look after our people," I attempted to reason away my stalking of the boy.

"Yeah, but he moved out of town," Jamie argued. "Wasn't your responsibility anymore—not that he ever really was."

I shrugged, wishing I could believe what my son claimed.

"So you're aware of what he does for work." Jamie didn't ask a question, but I nodded while sinking my teeth into another bite of my burger. "That guy Zack—his co-worker..." My son scratched at the back of his neck, his face flushing red. "I, uh...hired him a few times."

"No need to be embarrassed," I promised even though my suspicions had been proven correct. "Don't give a shit about who a man sleeps with. But how did you afford that?" I asked. "Because I've seen what Elite Escorts charges for Jimmy, and my son didn't have those kinds of funds while in college."

"Shit." Jamie eyed his fries and swallowed hard. "I had an OnlyFans."

I might be old but was well aware of what he spoke of. Dex had tried to get me interested in a few younger guys on there he thought might appeal to me.

Jamie glanced up at me. "You really don't care, do you?"

"Of course not," I said, studying my burger for my next bite. "A man's gotta do what a man's gotta do to get what he wants."

"Speaking of." Jamie paused until I met his inquisitive gaze. "What's up with you and Jimmy?"

"Not a damned thing." I took a large bite to give myself a minute to decide how to wade through this topic with my son.

"Liar."

I chuckled while chewing, shaking my head. "Seriously, there's nothing going on between us."

His head cocked to the side. "You wish there was though, don't you?"

Jamie had been honest with me, so he deserved the same openness. I hoped he wouldn't look down on me for my actions since Jimmy had left.

"I kept tabs on him just like he accused me of doing. Even went so far as to hire a private investigator initially, because there was no trace of him online. He lived on the streets before landing the job at EEMM. After that, he was easy to check up on through their website and social media."

Jamie watched me, and I could hear his brain working as long seconds ticked past. "How long, Dad?"

I knew exactly what he asked, even though his tone didn't hint at accusation of grooming and inappropriate actions with a minor. "Something about that boy always made me concerned for his well-being, but I promise there was no interest on my part back then."

He blew out a breath and picked up his burger again. "When did you find out he wanted you?"

"The night he turned eighteen, he stopped by our house before escaping town."

Jamie chewed, still eyeing me. "Where was I?"

"At Chaz's."

He nodded and dipped more fries in ketchup. "So you didn't..."

"No. I didn't want him then like I do now." Well, my body had, but I'd been too confused and gobsmacked at the time to do anything but deny the boy.

A smirk twisted Jamie's lips as he chewed.

"What?"

He shook his head, grabbing for more fries. "I wish I could hate to say it, but Jimmy seems kind of perfect for you."

It was my turn to exhale loudly and study my food that grew cold.

"He hides behind one hell of a wall, and I'll bet you're dying to dive through it and sus out his every secret."

I released a slow exhale. "You would be right."

"So why haven't you given in to his pursuit?"

I toyed with a single fry, eyeing the granules of salt littering its dark tan flesh. Old Man Ron made the best fries in town. Burgers too.

"Dad."

Heaving a sigh, I dropped the fry, wiped my fingers free from grease on my napkin, and sat back in my squeaky chair. "Even though I'm lonely as fuck and want a relationship, I'm wary as hell—as a guy like me ought to be."

Jamie's face grew stormy, his forehead furrowing. "You can't let Darla and what she did to us keep you from trying again, Dad. Not everyone is a manipulative, selfish asshole like she was."

Jimmy had always been devious as fuck, even as a kid, but I wouldn't share his past with my son to justify my fear.

I had every right to be skeptical of his manipulative words and actions.

"He's not planning on sticking around, so why start something that won't last? Why lower my shields and open myself to that kind of hurt?" I shook my head with the excuse I could discuss without uncovering Jimmy's poor choices. "I want connection and love like you and Chaz share, but letting that boy into my heart and watching him walk away one day without a backward glance will hurt even worse than Darla leaving us."

"Damn." Jamie stared at me. "You like him more than you did Mom?"

"Since we're laying ourselves bare," I said, shifting on my seat, "there are some things I never shared with you."

He stilled as though readying himself for what I was about to unload. "I'm all ears."

Feeling confident in my relationship with my only son, I knew I could tell him the truth of how he'd come into existence without him falling into any type of depression. I'd just never had reason to unnecessarily burden him.

"Your mom was abused as a kid and was desperate to escape her parent's house." I kept my voice low even though no one outside my closed door would be able to hear unless they pressed their ear to it. I wouldn't put it past Babs to do so and wasn't willing to take the chance others learned the truth of my marriage to Darla. "We hadn't been dating long when she got into her dad's liquor, and we spent a night beneath the stars. I lost my virginity that night, and I don't remember much because I was also drunk as a skunk."

I could see the lightbulb go off in Jamie's head. "Shit— she did it intentionally, didn't she?"

I nodded. "I didn't find out the truth until you were in kindergarten, but yeah. She'd planned to get pregnant, expecting I would do the right thing, which would save her from her dad's house sooner."

"Because you've always been a caretaker and would insist on marrying her even though you weren't of age."

"Unfortunately, yes. Both of our parents signed papers so we could tie the knot."

"Fucking hell," Jamie muttered, rubbing a hand over his face.

"I wouldn't change the past, Jamie—hadn't ever once wished I could go back and choose differently. You're the best thing that's ever happened to me, the greatest accomplishment I can claim."

His eyes grew misty, causing my throat to tighten. "Regardless, I still believe you should go for what you want, Dad. You only live once."

I grimaced, picking up what was left of my cold burger. "That's true, but I don't want to experience that kind of pain. I might not have been in love with your mom like a husband ought to be, but she still ripped my heart out when she left. I can't let anyone have that kind of power over me."

Jamie didn't argue, and we finished our lunch without mentioning Jimmy again.

"You going to the season opener tomorrow night?" he asked while gathering our trash.

"Wouldn't miss it."

Even though Jamie had hired on full-time as an officer, he still volunteered whenever he could to the high school's football team he'd coached the year before.

"You ought to ask Jimmy to go with you."

I huffed a laugh. "Yeah, I don't think sports are that boy's jam."

"He's not a boy, Dad," Jamie said with a grimace.

"Please don't tell me you're into that whole Daddy thing, because I just *can't*."

Laughter rumbled in my chest. "Jimmy might need a firm hand to set his troublesome ass in line, but I promise you won't ever hear him call me that."

"Thank fuck." Jamie shivered while heading toward my office door. "Because that's...yeah. No."

Grinning even though my heart ached, I pulled those files in front of me again and got back to work, attempting to focus on caring for my town rather than daydreaming about Jimmy lowering his shields and allowing me to love him in the way I longed to.

Chapter 12

Jimmy

Music blasted from the stadium's tinny speakers, probably the same ones from back when I'd been in high school. Close to a hundred cars littered the gravel parking lot alongside the fenced-in field, and the noise from hyped-up voices and laughter deafened.

"This is my first game!" DJ danced like he had ants in his pants alongside me as we hurried toward the entrance, both of us bundled in sweatshirts and beanies on our heads to ward off the slight chill in the air. Gram's insistence, of course since I hated having to smoosh a hat over my styled waves.

I enjoyed how DJ's gaze jumped from here to there as he stared at everything with wide-eyed wonder. I imagined taking him to TD Garden for a Bruins or Celtics game and grinned, shaking my head.

That would be one reason to go to Boston again, but I couldn't come up with another drawing factor. Sure, I had a handful of co-workers I considered friends, but I'd always kept things on a surface level—same as with everyone else around me. Only Gram and Sutton had ever seen the deeper parts of me, and I planned on it staying that way.

Once I paid the small entry fee, I led DJ toward the snack shack. The line dwindled down since both teams were stretching out on the field, and we were minutes away from kickoff.

"Fries, candy, or both?" I asked DJ, sidling up to the shed that had been peddling empty and fat-filled calories for as long as I could remember.

"Both, duh," DJ sassed, dragging out the second word with a roll of his eyes.

Chuckling, I placed his order along with a hot chocolate for myself.

Same as every day I'd walked around downtown, no one gave me a weird second glance even though I dressed to impress with my tight jeans and shimmery gloss. I wondered what the townsfolk would think of the lace panties I wore.

I wondered what *Sutton* would think of them, and my body broke out in goose bumps.

The stands were already packed, but I managed to find a too-small space for me and DJ to jam our behinds into at the far end.

"Hey, Jimmy," the woman on my left welcomed me with a smile, and although she looked familiar, I couldn't put a name to her face.

"How are ya?" I asked with my fake smile before settling DJ in with his boat of fries. Thank fuck he didn't like ketchup, or I feared having a mess on my hands, considering how he squirmed in his seat, trying to peer around the head of the man in front of him.

"Here," I got back on my feet and shifted over. "Trade places with me."

"Thanks!" He grinned and shoved fries into his mouth, chomping away while scooting along the bench, his gaze on the field.

The dude now blocking my view was massive. I wouldn't be seeing much either unless I stood, which I expected would happen more often than not considering it was opening night and everyone was riding a high.

Sipping my tongue-burning hot chocolate, I glanced beneath my feet to the gravel and sparse patches of weeds below the bleachers. A memory ingrained in my brain played out in vivid color. It'd been a Wednesday after school, and one of the senior football jocks had decided to give into my bet that he wasn't as straight as he claimed to be.

His coach had caught me on my knees with the kid's dick down my throat, but Sutton's son Jamie had been lingering nearby without knowing what we'd been up to. He'd been found guilty by proximity even though he claimed to have no idea a blow job took place mere feet from him. Hell, I'd been gagging, the straight boy groaning while gripping my hair—no way Jamie hadn't heard us.

For the first time, I had felt real guilt over the chief being called over my shenanigans. I'd been a minor but admitted to being the aggressor. Seeing as how the guy I'd blown was the town treasurer's son or some shit, he'd walked away with only a suspension. He'd moved to Tennessee for college and hadn't ever returned, so I didn't worry about running into him. Hopefully.

Chief had stepped in to keep me from getting a worse punishment. He'd also never said a word to my dad, but the asshole had somehow heard about it through the grapevine.

He'd labeled me a whore that day, beat the shit out of me, and I'd gone on to prove him right by selling myself for food and then a sweet paycheck that had made me feel as though I'd done a worthwhile service.

Bile rose up the back of my throat, and I forced my focus off the ground. I craned my neck to check for my favorite fantasy who would never treat someone as my father had with me. Sure enough, Sutton had a seat front and center on the fifty yard line.

Good*damn*, the man was fine as fuck in a red hoodie, his gray-speckled hair a mussed mess my fingers itched to sink into and tug while tonguing that incisor that made him imperfectly perfect.

Sighing, I slouched in my seat and stared, completely missing the kickoff. Daydreams of him falling for me and offering the happily ever after I'd always wanted but didn't deserve filled my mind.

DJ hollered along with the rest of the crowd, but I only stood when everyone else did so I could get a better view of the whole reason I'd come to the game.

Sutton was gorgeous no matter the expression on his face, but grinning and laughing with Dexter? The man was absolute fire, burning me up inside. I couldn't begin to imagine what it would feel like to have his hands on my skin. His lips on mine. His wet tongue dragging over my taint, teeth tugging at my piercing.

I shifted on the hard bench beneath me, blowing out a slow, steady exhale.

This wasn't the time or place to get caught up in—

"He scored!" DJ shrieked, but seeing as how no other Pippen Creek fans were screaming, I realized the opposing team had crossed the goal line. DJ didn't care. He was having too much fun, and after checking out the field to confirm, I didn't bother telling him the touchdown wasn't something to be celebrated.

Still, we exchanged high-fives, and the woman on DJ's other side gave me an encouraging smile, which caused my chest to puff up the slightest bit.

I knew I did a good thing hanging out with DJ, loved how Sutton seemed to appreciate my actions from afar, but I hadn't taken the kid under my wing to impress anyone. I honestly enjoyed DJ's company. He made me laugh more than I had in years, and I'd decided after day one of shooting hoops with him in Gram's backyard that I would act as his big brother for the duration of my visit to Pippen Creek. My energy matched his, which made his stays at Gram's easier for her to handle.

The game ended with our town the victor, and the press of people attempting to leave the stadium caused me to lose sight of the chief. The woman on DJ's other side had clued me in to the fact that lots of folks headed to Frenchie's after Friday night home games, so I settled a plan in my head for after dropping DJ off at Gram's.

We hopped in the car, buckled up, and inched our way through the gravel lot toward the exit along with everyone else.

"Dad asked about you and was being all weird."

I glanced over at DJ. "What do you mean?"

DJ peered out his window, unable to sit still as was his norm. "He was drinking. He's *always* says stupid stuff when he's got a beer bottle in his hand."

A shiver of unease slid down my spine. "Does your dad mind that we're buddies?"

DJ shrugged. "He didn't tell me we couldn't be friends, so I don't think so? But he doesn't care what I do. He's too busy daydreaming about his *girlfriend* to pay attention to me." The sarcasm and eye roll spoke volumes.

I'd talked to Mary about DJ's home life, remembering

Kurt only a little from back in school as he was a few years ahead of me. He'd been a hothead and got into a lot of fights, one of which I'd witnessed as a freshman.

Kurt hadn't been great with paying child support after the divorce, and according to Gram, Carrie constantly threatened to take him to court for full custody. It sounded like DJ was nothing but a bargaining chip between them, the constant push and pull taxing on the poor kid as well as Gram. It was why she babysat him whenever she could, the only reason she'd stuck around as long as she had when Florida called her name.

But I noticed how slowly she walked, heard the constant complaints about her brittle, tired bones that would benefit from warmer weather.

What would happen to the boy if she decided to become a snowbird or move permanently out of town where she wouldn't be a short car ride away?

We rolled forward a few more feet and stopped again, but I was in no rush to rid myself of DJ's company for Sutton's. This was the first time the kid had opened up to me, and I loved how he felt safe enough to share his heart. "Who's your dad's girlfriend?" I asked, wondering if maybe a solid relationship would help settle Kurt and create some stability for his son.

"He won't tell me her name, but I know he has one. He's always stinky like a girl's perfume." DJ's nose wrinkled. "But she smells better than that shit Dad drinks."

"DJ," I admonished like Gram would over his language but let it go, my mind full with not only my own issues but the kid's as well.

More than anything, I wanted to hug the boy's hurt away, to protect him from the further trauma ahead of him, but I'd learned from experience that while support might make things better for a little while, the deeper issues had to be dealt with personally.

I wanted to fix myself but still hadn't found the healing I'd hoped for. Walking into Dad's house had proven there was a shit ton more work to do—and not just with the house's rehab.

I dropped DJ off at Gram's, the tug of wanting to escape reality for a while making me refuse her offer to hang out longer. With a promise to pick DJ up again in the morning to help me paint the living room over at Dad's house, I slipped back out into the chilly night, my heart racing.

Frenchie's called out to me from afar, so I slid my confident, laid-back mask into place and headed downtown.

Chapter 13

Sutton

Something stirred inside me, a feeling I couldn't deny—and didn't really want to.

I'd seen Jimmy and DJ enter the stadium, and same as every time my gaze landed on his gorgeous face and glossed lips, I'd lost my breath.

Dex had chuckled at my reaction, teasing me about my eyes waiting on the gate more than the field while the boys had warmed up. I hadn't thought Jimmy would come to the game but couldn't help myself from watching for him. He was a beacon in the night, drawing me in like a moth to dangerous flames. I had no expectation beyond being singed to death if I gave in to the magnetic pull between us.

Jimmy and DJ had sat quite a ways away, closer to the end of the stands, but I'd felt Jimmy's focus like a teasing caress. I'd have preferred a firm grip, and my near-constant state of hardness made paying attention to the game difficult. At least I'd managed to set my gaze forward rather than casting it over my shoulder every other second like I wanted to.

After the game, I lost out on the chance to see or talk to

Jimmy and followed Dex to Frenchie's, which was packed with people still riding the high of our first win of the season. The noise of the crowd in a tight space after being out beneath the stars bothered me more than normal, and I couldn't help but keep an eye on the door, determined to stay put, just in case.

Dex abandoned me for a cute out-of-towner sitting at the bar, and I watched my best friend flirt toward what seemed would be a sure lay considering the small touches between the two and how they intimately shared space and words.

Christian Cole sat at the other end and studied Dex even more steadily than I did, lips in a thin line.

I sipped my beer as the silent drama played out, wondering over the game Dex played.

He leaned in closer to the stranger, mouth moving against his ear. The guy flushed, a shudder shifting him in his seat before the two shared a laugh, all up in each other's spaces.

Cole dug cash from his pocket, slapped it on the bar, and headed toward the exit without giving the two men a second of his time while striding past them. Red flushed his face, his brow furrowed into a deep groove.

Dex watched him go and wilted on his stool. Less than two minutes later, he bid the guy beside him a good night and headed toward the pool tables with a slow, shuffling gait.

I shook my head and sipped my beer again. Hadn't he figured out manipulation wouldn't work?

"They need to just fuck already."

I chuckled at Babs who sidled up to me without my knowing. So much for my usual awareness. "I think it'll be a fistfight rather than fucking," I said.

Babs snorted. "Tell me you don't see and feel the chemistry between them."

I couldn't argue the truth, but Dex was a lover, not a fighter, and that Cole guy brought out the worst in him.

Frenchie and Iris hollered their usual welcome.

"Speaking of chemistry..." Babs's trailed off, and I turned toward the entrance, heart already speeding up.

Swallowing a groan, I drank in the sight of my kryptonite as he strode into the bar, my free hand at my side flexing with the desire to map out every inch of his skin.

"Thought you were straight, Chief."

Blinking, I tore my gaze off Jimmy.

Babs smirked up at me. She clinked her beer bottle against mine while I struggled to find words to come out to the town gossip, even though she'd picked up on the truth without any problems. Was I really as transparent as Dex and Cole?

"Do yourself a favor, Sutton." Babs shifted toward me, her voice dropping. "Life is short, so grab this opportunity by the balls and enjoy the hell out of that boy."

Her suggestion filled my mind with dick-stiffening images I tried to force away by clearing my throat.

Jimmy crowded against me as usual, swarming my nose with something too damned sweet to be a man's cologne. My mouth watered. "Chief," he purred with the low tone I'd come to expect every time he talked to me.

"Looking good, Jimmy," Babs said, and the boy popped his hip out, pert nose with its silver ring wrinkling with his wink.

"Thanks," he said with enough sass that I shook my head, tearing my focus off his slim, alluring form to check on the rest of the bar while Iris poured him a glass of wine.

The stranger had left, and Dex still played pool.

Jamie and Chaz sat cozied up in the corner at a small table, chairs close together so their shoulders and thighs pressed tight. They only had eyes for each other, and that tender yet wrenching heartache over wanting the same slid over my chest at the sight of the engagement ring on Chaz's left hand.

"Don't behave, boys." Babs's teasing suggestion pulled my focus to the temptation inches away from me, but I didn't step back to give myself breathing room.

"Oh, we won't," Jimmy promised her, his baby blues twinkling up at me. "Or rather, *I* won't. Not tonight, anyway. I'm feeling *especially* naughty." He licked the rim of his wine glass before taking a sip.

I clenched my jaw as Babs chuckled and ambled away.

"How's it hanging, Chief?" Jimmy asked, giving my groin a pointed look before flicking his tongue over his shimmery lower lip.

"Uncomfortable and to the left," I grumbled the honest to God's truth.

Jimmy's pupils swelled, and he stumbled into me. His wine sloshed over the front of my red hoodie. "Oops."

Oops, my ass.

I glared at him, thankful the color of my sweatshirt matched his wine so it wouldn't stain. An abrupt spin on my heel turned me away from him without a word, and I strode toward the bathroom, far from his manipulative ass no matter how delectable it appeared in tight jeans. Frenchie's had three unisex bathrooms, and lips in a thin line, I entered the first empty one.

Jimmy slipped in behind me before I could close the door, and I stumbled when I shouldn't have been surprised or caught off guard. That was what I got for being all up in my head over this boy.

The sound of the lock clicking hit my ears like a gong of doom, leaving us in tense silence.

My dick thickened even as my brow furrowed. "The fuck are you doing, Jimmy?" I asked, my tone low and ragged.

He shrugged, a coy smile curving his plump lips.

"You did that on purpose, didn't you?" I motioned at my hoodie while grabbing a couple of paper towels and blotting at the wine.

"Nope." He popped the P of his blatant lie, stepping in close when I had nowhere to go but against the tiled wall, paper crumpled in my fist.

"Conniving little shit," I muttered, and growling, I grabbed hold of his short shirt and stalked forward, pressing his back to the door, my knuckles brushing against the warm skin of his stomach.

He didn't fight, simply melted and peered up at me with needy baby blues as I leaned into him.

My pulse throbbed in time with my cock as I thirsted for a taste of his mouth.

As though reading my mind, he flicked his tongue over his lower lip again in a slow, sensual glide that captured and held my attention.

I swallowed a groan, my dick bucking in the confines of my jeans and making me realize I'd crowded fully against him and could feel his entire body against mine. I had a handful of inches on the boy, but our hard dicks aligned perfectly thanks to his longer legs.

"Please." He whispered with the first honest tone I'd heard from him all night, cracking my walls from the ground up.

But he'd manipulated me to get me to this point.

I wanted to toss him from my path out of the bathroom

that was much too small for the two of us, but I lusted to redden his ass and fuck him raw even more.

A shudder ripped through me, and I tightened my grip on his T-shirt. "You're playing with fire, boy," I hissed, every cell in my body vibrating to connect and merge with his.

He swallowed hard and whimpered, rubbing his cock against mine. "S-Sorry, daddy."

I grasped his neck and squeezed, hissing over the delicious friction that would send me rushing toward climax if I didn't gain control over this situation. "Do *not* call me that."

Chapter 14

Jimmy

"Oh, God." I tried to gulp against Sutton's palm pressing against my throat and ended up moaning like the whore I was. Knees weak, I wanted to drop to the floor and choke on his dick. My eyelids fluttered shut, and I parted my lips in order to breathe, shivering and shaking from ball-tingling lust and the adrenaline rush of the century.

The way Sutton held and spoke to me caused my head to spin. His hard-as-granite, perfect dick grinding against mine proved we wanted the same thing. Straight, my ass. My chest went light as a kite, butterflies erupting in my belly.

Panting, I opened my eyes and stared into his blown pupils eating up the hazel of his irises inches from mine.

Stillness descended, a tension wrought with desire and deep-seated yearning. Want sizzled in my veins as his grip tightened, and I shuddered as pre-cum wet the inside of my jock.

I swallowed hard. "Sutton..." Desperate to get my mouth on him but unable to initiate a kiss due to his grip on my throat, I slid my hand between us, intent on mapping out the length and girth of his cock.

"Fuck." Sutton jumped away at the first brush of my palm on his groin, leaving me sagging against the wall, fighting to get my legs beneath me. He ran a hand through his hair, glancing around as though hoping to escape. "This—this isn't happening."

I winced at his harsh tone but found the strength to stay upright. "Why the fuck not?" I argued, my voice breathless with need.

He jammed the paper towels into the trash bin, another growl rumbling his chest but not nearly as sexy and possessive as the one before he'd crowded me against the door.

A rush of heat that had nothing to do with arousal flushed through me as my brow furrowed. Heaviness replaced the giddiness from seconds before, my stomach tightening into a knot. "Think I'm not good enough for you?"

His brow furrowed. "Why would you say that?"

Because I'm a worm who allowed countless men access to my holes for cash.

I shrugged rather than state the words in my head.

"Trying to manipulate me again?"

"No! I..." Huffing, I pressed my lips tight.

"How are you doing with the house rehab?"

I blinked, my brain needing a second to catch up with his sharp turn of conversation. Did he actually expect me to spill my guts, tell him how often I wanted to puke or scratch the hell out of my forearms when stepping into that hellhole? Not. Fucking. Happening. "It's good. I'm fine."

Sutton shook his head, lips in a flat line. "Why can't you be honest with me like that day I found you in your old bedroom doorway, Jimmy? Why put on a false front to hide behind?"

I couldn't allow him to see my weakness again, but goddammit, I wanted him more than anything. My throat tightened, trapping words down deep where they wouldn't reveal how desperate I really was. Tears welling in my eyes caused the sight of him to waver like water poured over his stoic form.

I spun and reached for the lock with shaking fingers.

Sutton grabbed my forearm, and I hesitated, breath held, pulse thundering in my ears as electrical currents traveled over my skin.

"I'm sorry. Please don't leave." Concern laced his words, the same inflections in his tone he'd always used on me when I'd been a directionless, troublesome kid.

My guts clenched. "I no longer run from my *problems*, Chief," I bit out the words, hating he still saw me in the same light as he had back then.

"You're calling me a problem?"

I turned to face him, his hand falling from my arm. The longing proved to be too much. He wanted honesty? He could have it.

Two steps put me against his chest, but he didn't back away. Rising onto my tiptoes, I got into his personal space as far as I could, my insides as jittery as my voice as I poked him in the hard chest. "*You're* the reason I can't sleep at night. This feeling of unrest...I *hate* that you're the only one I trust to fill up the emptiness inside me. The power you hold over me—" My voice cut out, my hand pressing against his chest.

His heart thrummed beneath my palm, vigorous and steadfast.

I wanted to crumple against him, bury my face against his warmth, draw from his strength, and just fucking *rest*.

"Jimmy," he whispered, but too much resignation coated his tone, making his thoughts toward me clear as he had the night he'd shut his front door in my face.

I needed to escape.

Now.

Unsteady on my feet and emotions, I unlocked the door, slipping out into the hallway while fighting off tears.

Same as nine years ago, Sutton didn't call after or chase me even though I'd given him the truth he'd wanted to hear.

I'd been stupid to believe the chief would ever give me attention above what he showed the rest of Pippen Creek's citizens. Regardless of how I might turn his body on, I was nothing more than another issue he had to deal with.

Worthless worm.

Dad's voice echoed in my head long after I left Frenchie's behind me and buried my face in my pillow back at The Moose's Muse.

Weeks passed, and as though we had an unspoken agreement, Sutton and I avoided each other like the plague.

While warmth still filled the afternoon hours, early morning and evening took on a chill. The leaves started to hint at change, orange and yellow with hints of burgundy teasing the tree lines. My heart welled with nostalgia over my favorite season about to begin, and I filled my lungs with the scent of woodsmoke from chimneys and the final camp-fires of summer drifting through town from Pippen Creek Pond's shores to the west.

I'd stayed away from Scone Haven since it seemed to be

Sutton's favorite place to grab a coffee in the morning, making do with The Moose's complimentary breakfast bar. The rest of the days proved easier.

I cleaned out Dad's house while obsessing over and keeping my head occupied with how I could break down Sutton's walls and get him to submit to his baser instincts since I had no other plans and no wind was blowing me in a different direction. The man was a goddamned oak, and the axe and saws I'd attempted to use to send him toppling were dull as fuck. When would I learn? When would I give up on the pipe dream of having that man loom over me, filling my body and heart up in all the ways I'd dreamed of since my teenage years?

Never.

"What's on your mind, Jimmy?"

I heaved a sigh and grabbed another cookie off the plate Gram had sat in front of me. Her place was where I spent my time between working on Dad's house without puking and heading to The Moose every evening. I felt like I took advantage of her goodness even though she always welcomed me with open arms and snacks while Kendra pushed her homemade muffins on me every morning. Both women were amazing bakers and gave me something to look forward to.

Gram held a steaming cup of tea in her arthritic hands while the coffee she'd poured for me when I'd arrived a half hour earlier grew cold.

"The contractor got the front porch done this morning," I said rather than tell the truth about my feelings for Sutton and how badly his rejection had hurt. "He also patched the holes in my bedroom walls so I can paint tomorrow. The place should be market-ready by the beginning of next week as long as DJ and I can get the yard work finished this weekend. Did you hear back from that guy down in Berlin about your shop?"

Lips pursed, Gram studied me until I shifted on the chair. "Yes," she finally answered, allowing me my secrets. "We are going to meet tomorrow afternoon."

I nodded absently, breaking the cookie in two before nibbling on one corner. Gram still spoke about possibly heading to Florida near the end of October but had only made steps toward selling her store so she could retire. "You're really considering leaving us, huh?" I couldn't help but ask, even though I knowingly did so with the intent to guilt-trip her into staying.

"I thought you didn't have plans to stick around?"

I had no *romantic* reason to, Sutton had made that clear, but no inner urging attempted to lead me elsewhere, no bucket list item called me away from town limits. Talk about a stagnant existence. I hated not knowing my future other than my pipe dream, and I certainly didn't want to discuss my lack of vision for my life other than riding off into the sunset.

"What about DJ?" I asked instead of answering, setting down the cookie and brushing my fingers free of crumbs. He'd become my buddy, and I wanted to offer him the safe place to go that I never had as a kid.

"Kurt and Carrie agreed to let him visit over February vacation and also for a week at the beginning of summer if I decide to move." Gram sipped her tea. "Maybe Kurt would allow me stay in his spare bedroom when I fly up here on occasion too. He can be somewhat decent when he's sober, so I could deal with being at his house for a little while."

I nodded, torn between wishing she could live her best life with the time she had left and selfishly longing to keep her near because I didn't want to have to do without her again now that we'd reconnected.

She eyed me as though trying to map out the roller coaster in my head. "Jimmy—"

Banging on the door cut her off, and I hopped up before she did, striding toward the entryway.

Kurt shoved inside before I got to the door, his eyes bloodshot, and he reeked of booze.

My stomach clenched, brow furrowing as he shuffled DJ in ahead of him with a too-sturdy shove.

DJ stumbled forward, and I knelt to steady the boy, adrenaline rushing through my system telling me to stay still —avoid the danger lurking nearby. "You all right?" I somehow managed to whisper past the tightness in my throat, and even though wetness coated his eyes, DJ nodded.

"Mom!" Kurt shouted, ignoring how I cowered with DJ at his feet, thank fuck.

Gram shuffled our way, and I soothed back DJ's wayward hair with a shaking hand, fighting to find my voice and keep it steady. "Head outside and grab the basketball," I whispered. "I'll be out in a minute, okay?"

He nodded sharply and ran toward the kitchen.

The back door slammed shut a second later.

I barely had an ounce of willpower in order to stand upright. My fingernails scratched down my left arm out of habit, and I swallowed hard, eyeing the two facing off in front of me. Tension radiated through the entryway, and I wished I could sink into the floor and disappear. I wanted to escape like DJ had done but couldn't move my feet.

"How dare you drive drunk with DJ in the car?" Gram hissed at her son, having come close enough she doubtless smelled the alcohol on him.

Kurt grumbled something under his breath, stumbling around to leave.

"You get your act together, Kurt, or so help me God…" Gram called after him.

He paused on the stoop and spun, glowering at his mom. "I have enough shit on my plate. Don't need *you* nagging me too!" His words slurred past curled lips. "Carrie won't shut up about the past child support I owe her, and now—" Kurt shook his head, turned, and stumbled down the stairs.

"You shouldn't be driving!" Gram called after him, but Kurt slammed himself into his truck and tore off up the road.

My breath left in a rush as the negative energy dissipated. "I'm calling Sutton," I informed her with a telling, shaky-as-hell voice while pulling my cell from my pocket.

Lips pursed, Gram nodded, her eyes welling as she glanced toward the backyard.

Cursing Kurt, I hit send, my body trembling from the after effects of too much adrenaline crashing through my blood.

Chapter 15

Sutton

A call from a number I didn't recognize rang my cell while I was on my office phone. I had to let it go to voicemail, and seconds later, a text came through.

Unknown: **Gram's son is drunk off his ass and just took off in his truck.**

Jimmy—it had to be.

"Mayor, there's an emergency, and I have to go." I interrupted the voice droning in my ear, hanging up before he could say goodbye. Grabbing my keys, I sped from my office and rushed past Babs's desk.

"Everything okay?" she called after me.

"I'll let you know!" I hollered while shoving the rear door open and sprinting across the parking lot for my cruiser.

A second later, I turned onto Main Street, and Kurt Wallace's truck roared past me, heading east for Route 16. Radioing Jamie, who was out patrolling, I flicked on my lights and made a U-turn, adrenaline racing but my hands steady on the wheel.

Kurt swerved into The Outdoor Store's parking lot and

managed to get his stumbling ass inside before I pulled in behind his truck, angling my car so he wouldn't be able to drive off.

I hopped out and headed toward the entrance, giving Jamie another quick update through the two-way.

"Be there in a few," my son replied.

Raised voices reached me before I stepped into the building, and I braced myself for whatever drama was about to unfold. The sound of flesh hitting flesh promised a drunken brawl and the need to get physical before I even saw the situation.

Kurt grappled with Stefen Kaufman, the shop's owner, fists swinging, contact being made on both bodies.

Sarah, Stefen's wife, cowered behind the counter, eyes wide and hands over her mouth.

"Hey!" I hollered, rushing forward to grab Kurt's shoulder so he couldn't throw another punch. "Enough!" I wrenched him back, and he stumbled, falling to the floor, which allowed me to easily slap handcuffs on his wrists to keep him somewhat under control.

"You have no fucking right!" Kurt slurred, but at least he didn't attempt to resist my hold.

I stood, yanking him to his feet. He smelled like a brewery and could barely stay upright. "The hell is going on?" My tone was set low and with authority.

"Found out he's been texting my wife, sending her dick pics and shit." Stefen spat, rage mottling his face red. "Told him if he didn't stop sniffing around her skirt I was going to skin him alive!"

"I saw what you did to her!" Kurt yelled, trying to pull free from me. "You fucking hurt her!"

"Liar!" Stefen bellowed, hands fisted at his sides and rage distorting his features.

The two tossed profanities back a few times while I quickly checked out Sarah.

She huddled in on herself, arms wrapped tightly around her core, but there was no visible evidence of bruising from what I could see. But she also wore a long-sleeved shirt as Jimmy had often done.

It was no secret around town that Stefen and Sarah's marriage had been on the rocks since the beginning of the summer, but this was the first I'd heard anyone mention an affair or physical abuse.

"Enough!" I barked out again, and both men went silent.

Jamie walked in behind me, shoulders back and gaze assessing, but kept quiet, seeing as I had things under control.

I handed Kurt over to his care before approaching Sarah.

"Chief—"

I raised a hand, cutting off Stefen, who shifted nervously on his feet as I examined his wife. No hint of marks marred her pale face, but clothing covered her from the neck to her ankles. "Is Kurt speaking the truth? Has your husband hurt you?" I asked quietly.

Twin tears slid down her cheeks, and she glanced at Stefen before dropping her gaze to the floor. The silence was heavy and telling as hell, rousing my protective instincts to take care of my people—especially the vulnerable and more easily intimidated.

"Sarah," I pushed with a gentle voice, but she shook her head.

Fucking hell.

Heart heavy and lips in a grim line, I eyed the two men who continued to glare at each other. "Do I need to arrest you both and drag your asses to the station?"

"He started it," Stefen muttered like a middle school brat. "Came tearing in here with accusations and hit me first. I was just trying to defend myself." He pointed at his cheek, and sure enough, a bruise had begun to discolor his skin.

"You going to press charges, Stefen?" I asked, and it took him a few seconds of glowering at Kurt before shaking his head.

"Get Kurt out of here," I told Jamie, who'd watched on in silence. "He can sleep it off at the station."

Wouldn't be the first time Kurt Wallace crashed on the cot, and I doubted it would be the last.

My thoughts went to Jimmy's dad, then the boy himself who'd always managed to get into trouble. He'd been behaving since coming back, and I hadn't heard a single complaint from anyone about public drunkenness or disorderly conduct on his part. Frenchie said he visited the bar to chat with her occasionally but rarely had more than two glasses of pinot noir.

Perhaps he'd learned his lesson of what too much alcohol did to a man and possessed the self-control his father never had.

I slipped Sarah one of my cards without Stefen being aware and left a few minutes later, my questions over their marriage unanswered and concern for the woman heavier on my mind.

Checking in on Kurt via radio with Jamie, I headed toward Mary's for a little chat.

Jimmy's red BMW sat in her driveway, and I pulled in alongside, my pulse kicking up even though I had expected him to be there. If he wasn't at his dad's place or The Moose, this was where he could be found every damned day, and I would know, because I couldn't help but keep tabs on his daily whereabouts.

I no longer questioned *why*. The interest every part of me took in him was clear as a summer sky and just as alluring no matter the instinct to flee far, far away from the pain that boy would bring me. Sure, he'd gifted me with a bit of truth that had spun my head, but he still hid himself and lied about his emotional well-being. Attempted to manipulate me into bed.

Darla fucking incarnate.

Mary answered my knock on her front door, her eyes harder than I'd expected while glancing behind me at the empty cruiser. "Kurt?" She snipped his name like anger more than worry filled her mind.

"Sleeping off the booze on the comfy cot in our holding cell," I stated sternly, happy to have something other than Jimmy to focus on.

Lips pressing tight, she nodded and stepped back, allowing me inside. "I'm sorry."

"Not your fault, Mary." I peered down the hallway but didn't see or hear Jimmy.

"Coffee?" She headed for the kitchen before I could reply, but this wasn't the first time I'd shown up at her house to discuss her son's issues.

"How much trouble is he in?" she asked while retrieving a mug from the cabinet atop the coffee pot.

"No jail, but it's not good."

She muttered a curse and handed me the coffee but still didn't seem all that concerned for her son.

I sipped, eyeing the window overlooking her backyard. "What do you know about Kurt's affair with Sarah Kaufman?"

"Sarah?" Gram echoed, her tone high with surprise.

"She's a married woman—Kurt would never..." Her voice trailed off, and she sank into one of the kitchen chairs as though exhaustion liquified her bones. "What has that boy gotten himself into?" she muttered to herself, disgust leaking into her voice.

I stepped past her, lightly grasping her shoulder briefly before moving closer to the window.

Jimmy was shooting hoops with DJ. Both were laughing, and Jimmy ruffled the boy's hair with fondness.

He seemed...real in the moment. Pink flushing his face, eyes bright with happiness I longed to see on a daily basis.

An ache spread over my chest, longing to linger in watching this alluring version of my obsession, but I turned away and sat across from Mary, determined to give her my undivided attention. I explained the altercation her son had gotten into and how I had more questions than answers.

Mary studied her arthritic hands, rubbing gently at swelled joints. "Not that it's an excuse for his drinking, but Kurt's got some personal issues going on."

"Can you share specifics so I can figure out how to help?"

"He and Carrie are constantly arguing these days. DJ told me he screams at her over the phone, calls her names." Mary pursed her lips and sighed heavily. "It's not healthy for any of them, and here I am selfishly dreaming about moving to Florida because of my aching bones."

As far as I was aware, Carrie was a good mom and had a steady job in Berlin.

"Maybe she ought to take Kurt back to court for full custody until he gets himself straightened out," I suggested what Mary had told me Carrie had been threatening Kurt with lately. "DJ seems like a pretty stable kid, so perhaps some time apart from the toxicity would be best for now."

Mary nodded even though her eyes remained haunted. "I can't help but believe Kurt's headed down a dark path. I've heard him be unkind with his words, but the thought he might get physical with DJ like Jimmy's dad..."

Something inside me crumbled, causing my eyes to sting.

"And *that* boy." Mary glanced toward the window through where occasional laughter reached us. "Jimmy has seen the world, knows he's not alone, but he still can't accept that he's worth loving. I want better than that for my grandson's future, Chief." Her voice broke, and I swallowed hard as guilt for possibly contributing to Jimmy's words flooded through me.

"You're the reason I can't sleep at night. This feeling of unrest...I hate that you're the only one I trust to fill up the emptiness inside me. The power you hold over me—"

His honesty from that night in Frenchie's bathroom replayed through my mind as it had been doing on repeat, hitting so goddamned close to home it made my eyes sting.

Jimmy was the reason *I* didn't sleep at night, the burr in the back of my mind that didn't allow me rest. Regardless of my fear, I wanted him broken down to his baser self. Raw in his emotion and *real.*

He was a goddamned gift in need of unwrapping so he could see the beauty beneath the facade.

But if I found the balls to be vulnerable, would he even offer me the chance to peel away his layers? Would the possibility of fulfillment in giving that boy what he needed and watching him make gains toward healing be worth the sure heartache when he had enough of this small town and took off again?

"So what happens now, Chief?" Mary asked, pulling me away from my heavy musings I couldn't escape.

My chest ached, and I cleared my throat, having to be the bearer of even more bad news. "I'll have another little chat with Kurt once he's sobered up. This will be his first DWI, but he'll have to pay a hefty fine and lose his license for a while. I can't shelter him from the consequences for his actions this time."

"I wouldn't expect you to, Chief. My son needs to learn a lesson before he makes a choice that has even worse consequences." She spoke as though a premonition hovered over her mind, and I shivered on instinct.

My attempted smile hurt as our gazes met atop the table. "You're a good mother, Mary, and I can't thank you enough for being a safe place for DJ—and Jimmy—when they need you most."

Chapter 16

Jimmy

I'd heard the crunch of wheels on gravel and had caught sight of Sutton pulling into the driveway while chasing after a wayward basketball toss from my opponent.

Butterflies had erupted and continued to swarm in my stomach while DJ and I played one-on-one, teasing and talking smack. He easily outshone me with his natural athletic abilities, and I couldn't use the excuse for my missed baskets because of Sutton's gaze on me for a few brief moments I'd felt his stare.

The warmth of his eyes disappeared, but the cruiser didn't drive off.

I tired long before DJ did, and I eventually managed to talk him into heading in for some lemonade, hating how sweat caused my T-shirt to cling to my body.

When we entered the kitchen, the sound of heavy footfalls up the hallway and the closing of the front door kicked up another burst of adrenaline.

"Gotta head out, kiddo!" I called over my shoulder, leaving DJ behind where he began to rummage in the fridge.

"Bye, bud!" he hollered.

Mary stood in the hallway, and I sidled around her with a quick kiss to her cheek.

"What's the rush?" she asked with a chuckle—and knowing look.

I winked and scurried out the door before shutting it gently behind me. "Chief!" I called out as he reached his cruiser.

He turned, his quick glance over my sweaty body heating me more than the half hour I'd spent shooting hoops.

I stopped in front of him, breathless and flashing a grin, praying my sweat-stained shirt wasn't as disgusting to him as it was to me. "I was hoping to catch you before you left."

"What do you need, Jimmy?" His tone held its usual suspicion, but I couldn't be bothered because those *words*.

God*damn*, I loved when he asked me that, and I had a million and one possible answers.

"How about we meet for dinner tonight and I'll explain every single one of my *needs* in detail?" I suggested with a promising smirk that usually awarded me a mouth or ass full of dick.

As usual, Sutton didn't appear moved by my blatant flirting, his brow furrowing as though annoyed by my flirty behavior. But how else was I supposed to show my interest?

Remembering his hard length grinding against mine gave me the courage to strive onward regardless of the inner sirens warning me of even more impending disappointment.

"Or we could go straight for dessert at my room at The Moose." I flicked one of his buttons while taking in every glorious inch of the chief in his somewhat rumpled uniform.

Shit.

My grin wiped away as I remembered why Sutton

might not be his usual pristine self. "Is Kurt okay?" I asked, all trace of toying with the chief gone from my voice.

Sutton's steady gaze lightened slightly as though he was proud of me for thinking outside of my own selfishness.

"He's sleeping off the booze on your favorite jail cell cot."

I grimaced. "God—don't remind me."

"You've come a long way since then, Jimmy. It's nice to see you investing in DJ's life."

Warmth welled inside me at the words of praise I'd been desperate to hear leaving his lips. I couldn't contain the heart eyes shining from my face as I peered up at him. "So about that dessert..."

Sutton narrowed his gaze even though interest and heat resided behind his stern stare. "Knock it off."

"Yes, da—"

He popped an eyebrow in warning at the same time a voice cut through his radio requesting his presence back at the station.

I squirmed, my backside aching for his hand and hole desperate for the stretching sting of his cock.

"Be a good boy and stay out of trouble," Sutton said, pulling his door open.

Good boy.

Holy fucking hell...

I shivered and stared as Sutton backed out of Mary's driveway, his gaze flicking down over me with definite desire in his eyes before he drove away. "Jesus," I whispered while fanning my face and heading toward my car.

I hadn't lied to Sutton that night in the bathroom—I trusted him.

But I didn't trust who *I* was beneath the exterior I allowed him to see. One moment of weakness had revealed the emotional ugliness beneath. The connection and affection-starved clinger who didn't know how to stop the driving force for attention spurring me on. What man would want to get tangled up with someone as broken as me?

I lay curled in my bed at The Moose later that night, staring off into the darkness, replaying every minute I'd spent in Sutton's presence since returning to Pippen Creek. I was desperate for some sort of assurance, the slightest hint of possibility, he might be swayed toward lowering his own walls regardless of me not being good enough for him.

His body might want mine, but I longed for a hell of a lot more than physical release. I teased him about being a daddy and didn't really have interest in that type of dynamic, but I yearned for the safety of his presence, the quietness in my mind while being wrapped up in his arms. His nature was to protect and nurture—exactly what I craved, a perfect fit for every single one of my needs.

A weight sat heavy on my chest as frustration over my shortcomings ruined every single fantasy I'd built up over the years.

My cell dinged, and I heaved an exhale, rolling to grab it off the bed stand.

A zing zapped straight to my groin at the name I'd given the chief, and giddy bubbles popped in my belly. Breath held, I tapped the text box open.

Daddy McDreamy: **I appreciate you looking out for DJ.**

I nibbled on the inside of my lip. Was he telling me that as the police chief of this town, or was there more behind him reaching out to me for the first time with words he had to know would make my heart swell? I debated on how to reply but decided on a game plan change. Maybe giving

Sutton what he desired from me—honesty—would lead me toward that damned sunset I longed for.

Me: **He's a good kid and doesn't deserve the cards he's been dealt.**

I stared at the screen in anticipation of another ding, proud of myself for not going my usual route even though my libido climbed aboard the flirt and fuck train while waiting for a reply.

Daddy McDreamy: **You're proof that a phoenix can rise above the ashes, Jimmy.**

My throat went tight—if he only knew the truth about where my money had come from, he wouldn't think so highly of me.

Me: **Careful, daddy. Words like that will make me believe I have a chance at getting into your bed rather than the old jail cell cot.**

So much for that change of plans. Deflection and not being able to accept a compliment to the rescue. Even though I was disappointed with what my fingers had typed out, I held my breath, imagining his cocked eyebrow and the unspoken threat of putting me in my place.

Yes, please.

The cell rang, scaring the shit out of me, and I shrieked, fumbling with shaking hands to keep from dropping it. I swiped to answer.

"Do *not* call me that," Sutton ordered with his sexy cop voice before I could say hello.

I took a deep breath to steady my nerves. "But you play the role so well," I murmured, my pulse thrumming as I lay back, my dick going from semi to granite. "And I gotta admit —I'm struggling to be the good boy you want me to be."

"Jimmy." His tone lowered, full of warning.

Unfortunately, I'd had enough vulnerability for the day

and went the easy route. I slid my hand beneath my lace panties to fondle my balls that were creeping up against my groin. "Hmm?"

Silence settled between us as I stroked myself a few times, my breaths growing intentionally louder and shallow. Neither of us spoke, but I could sense the sexual energy rippling through the connection between our ears. I had to believe he'd meant for this to happen—why else would he call me rather than text me to knock it off?

"Sutton?" I breathed his name.

"Yeah, Jimmy?" He sounded on edge but without the usual guardedness—or resignation. He wanted this as much as I did.

I put him on speaker so I had both hands to give me what I needed. A pearl of pre-cum welled at my slit, and I smeared the slickness over my cockhead with a soft whimper. "Feels so damned good," I whispered.

"Are you touching yourself right now?" Sutton's tone hinted at the same desire racing through my blood, and I had more honesty for him as greediness rose up inside me, choking me with its potency.

"I always touch myself when I'm thinking about you," I admitted, my heart racing and voice shaking. "You're my favorite distraction, my ultimate fantasy—but it's never enough."

His low curse reached over the line and sent shivers down my spine.

"I *need* you, Sutton," I begged, my voice breaking from sheer desperation as I fucked up into my fist. "Tell me what to do. *Please.*"

"Goddammit." He hissed a few more curses, and I moaned. "Are you wet for me?" he asked, his voice ragged and sexy as fuck.

"Always," I whimpered as more pre-cum slid down my length, my chest fluttering with the wings of a million butterflies. "Hard and *aching*."

"Is your hole needy too, baby boy?"

"Oh, Jesus—*fuck*, Sutton." I gulped, body curling inward as my stomach tightened. "You're going to make me come."

"Pinch your tip—now," he demanded, and I did as told, cursing him for interrupting the climax of the century. "Jimmy?"

"I—I stopped myself." I gasped, shuddering and wincing over the ache in my balls.

"Good boy."

"Shit." I choked on a laugh while yanking down on my firm sac. "You can't say those words when you aren't in front of me. Makes me lust to fall to my knees and worship your dick, Sutton. God*damn*, I want your cock on my tongue. Your cum coating the back of my throat and filling my belly."

A low growl filled my ear, and shivers raised the hairs on my skin. My eyelids slammed shut as my mind went on a fantasy bender, living out in color where he was and what he did.

"Are you touching your dick?" I asked, praying like hell he was.

He grunted as I imagined his strong grip on his thick length. "Yes."

Curses spilled from my lips at his admission of desire, and I had to squeeze the base of my dick. "Sutton..."

"Slow but firm strokes, Jimmy. Edge yourself for me."

Yes, *fucking*, sir.

"Are your balls tight?"

"Uh huh," I croaked.

"Pull them down and play with them."

I hummed, planting my feet on the mattress and widening my shaky legs for better access. "Wish it was your hands on me, Chief. Tugging on my guiche piercing," I murmured, fingertip flicking over the ring in my taint.

"Christ," he bit the word out, and I imagined him squeezing his cock to stop himself from shooting before I did. "Suck on your fingers."

"Oh God." Heat flushing my body, I did as told, shoving three digits over my tongue and getting them sloppy wet.

"Did you listen like a good boy?"

"Damned right, I did," I replied, breathless and already smearing saliva over my pucker.

"Slide one in your hole, baby boy. Make yourself feel good but don't come."

A low keening noise rose in my chest as I obeyed, but after a single stroke, I added another. "Need more—so much more. Not enough."

"Jesus, Jimmy." Sutton groaned in my ear, sending another shockwave of goose bumps over my skin.

"Please," I whispered, sliding three fingers up my ass, a delicious sting causing my breath to stutter.

"You want to come for me?"

"Yes—*fuck*, yes. So bad." I gasped, gliding over my prostate with steady strokes.

"Shoot all the fuck over your abs, Jimmy. Milk yourself dry for me."

My eyelids flew upward on a gasp, and I watched as spunk laced from my slit clear to my chest. "Ung," I grunted, gulping and gasping as throbs in my groin sent pulses along my stomach. "Sutton..."

My head spun, lungs desperate for oxygen as I panted and slowly settled, my brain blissed the fuck out and extremities tingling with a glorious afterglow I wanted to last for eternity.

I ran my hands through the warm cum on my torso as a shuddered sigh rippled through my lax body. "That had to be the most satisfying orgasm *ever*."

"Mmm," he hummed.

I licked over my dry lower lip, wishing his cum covered my flesh and coated my tongue. "Did you come?"

"No."

My brow furrowed, elation dimming at his firm tone. "Why not?"

Maybe he was saving his load for my ass. Or perhaps he wanted to make that other wish of mine come true—flood my mouth and stomach.

"Good night, Jimmy."

"Wait—"

But he was gone.

I flopped back on my bed, scowling as the sweet tingles from seconds before faded into nothingness. "What. The. Actual. Fuck?"

He'd given me a hint of heaven, how delicious we could be together. No way in hell would I let him regret or forget this deviation off whatever straight and narrow path he traveled.

It's on.

Chapter 17

Sutton

Jimmy told me he needed me, and I fucking caved, having phone sex for the first time in my forty-three years.

Why the fuck had I called him? I'd told myself not to do it while hitting send rather than reply via text. Cursed myself the second he'd answered, but his voice had lacked the usual low coyness. He'd sounded...*real*. Walls down. Vulnerable in his desire.

Exactly as I yearned for him to be with me.

It'd been a long two days since that night I'd denied myself an orgasm, my grip tight as a vise on my throbbing cock's base. I refused to rub one out to thoughts of Jimmy on his knees for me. Letting him into my fantasies might as well be offering him the key to my heart.

Couldn't fucking do it. Didn't trust myself or him, no matter the evidence he'd grown up while away from home.

But a part of me whispered I saved my load for the day I lost the battle with temptation and Jimmy peered up at me from where my cock lodged in his throat, his eyes watering and begging me to give him what he needed—a belly full of cum.

My cell dinged for the third time since I'd gotten into the office on Tuesday morning, and same as every notification, a shot of adrenaline caused blood to rush to my groin where my cock already lay half-hard against my thigh.

"Damn him," I muttered, unable to help myself from opening up the one-sided thread of texts Jimmy had been sending me since I'd talked him through his orgasm.

He'd included a picture of cum-covered fingers teasing his extended tongue with its metal bar.

"Jesus," I croaked, having to squeeze my junk again.

Not even Darla's daily voicemail had deflated my dick fully. The woman ought to take a hint and leave me the hell alone. Hadn't she learned that I wouldn't be manipulated again into putting her needs above my own?

There was that damned word.

My gaze flicked up to the two previous images the neediest person I'd met had sent—Jimmy's hard, pink cock with its dribble of pre-cum oozing down its length, and a close-up of sticky white stripes over his taut stomach and the belly piercing I lusted to lick along with the one in his taint he'd admitted to having.

The boy was such a delicious distraction.

My dick throbbed, and I rubbed a hand over my face but couldn't keep from staring at his wet tongue. Plump lips about to close over his cum-soaked fingers to suck them clean. Memories of his whimpers and moans while finding release over the phone with me flooded my mind, causing my cock to buck in the confines of my uniform pants.

"Christ." I swallowed hard, shut my cell off, and slammed it face down atop my desk.

A knock sounded on my office door, and Officer Jones

poked his head in before I could get a hold on myself. My face had to be beet-fucking-red as I shifted on my chair.

"Hey, Chief—thanks for helping my wife with the flat tire this morning."

I cleared my throat, glad to have something else to focus on other than the blueness of my balls. "Glad I happened to be driving behind her when she hit that pothole."

He grinned, seeming completely unaware of my unease and embarrassment. A detective, he would never make with his lack of suspicion. "She told me the boys called you a superhero."

I chuckled over the memory of all four little noses of the Jones kids pressing against the passenger side windows while I'd switched out the car's tire for its spare.

"Pippen Creek would be lost without its oak," Officer Jones claimed before giving me a two-fingered salute and quietly shutting my door again.

My gaze flitted toward my window overlooking Main Street, and I watched vehicles and people passing by. It wasn't the first time I'd been compared to a towering, strong tree.

Talk about a facade.

I snorted, shaking my head.

Everyone wore a fucking mask. No one made it through life without secret fears, weaknesses, and suspicions that kept them from truly living.

My main reason for squashing the desires deep inside me sauntered past my window, but the rising sun, without doubt, hid me from his curious, searching eyes. Jimmy wore tight jeans and a hoodie, his pale hair a rumpled mess. A flush highlighted his cheekbones from his recent release, a soft curve lifting his lips as though knowing what he'd done to me and finding complete satisfaction in driving me insane.

He stole my goddamned breath and disappeared from sight.

"Fucking hell," I muttered to myself, shoving back my chair and pressing hard against my bulge that refused to relent. Should have jerked off in the shower that morning rather than curse my straining length. What did it matter if I eased the ache to the memory of his beautiful face and the noises he'd made while being a good boy for me?

I snorted.

Oak, my ass.

Babs eyed me as I strode across the entryway. "Let me guess," she said with a glint in her eyes. "Pippen Creek's prodigal son just walked past on his way to Scone Haven for his morning coffee, which made your tongue water for a taste of him—I mean, coffee."

I scowled when she winked. "You see too much, Babs."

"Double shot of espresso in mine, please!" she called as I exited the front door.

The cool fall air filled my lungs as I dragged in deep breaths, trying to calm my racing libido.

What the fuck was I going to do with him?

Order him to his knees.

Choke him with my dick.

Crush him with my weight while flooding his ass with the cum he lusted for.

Cursing my one-track mind, I shoved in Scone Haven's door.

Jimmy leaned against the counter, hip popped out, tight backside as mouthwatering as ever. His eyes sparkled as he murmured something through his coy smirk to Kel, the shop's owner, who handed him a to-go cup and small bag.

My stomach hardened and hackles rose as I sharply stepped across the tiled floor.

"Chief," Kel greeted me with his usual flatlined lips. I'd never once seen the grumpy fucker smile. Good to know he didn't have a thing for Jimmy, but that ugliness in my gut over Jimmy flirting with him remained.

"Kel," I grunted. Jimmy's slow-turning head took me in from head to booted toes and held me captive.

"Chief," Jimmy murmured, his cheeks still a luscious shade of pink. He straightened from where he'd all but draped himself in offering to Kel, rubbing a fingertip over his lower lip to hide his satisfied smile.

He'd done this on purpose. Knew I would follow and had set me up to make me jealous—or at least *hope* to make me jealous. Maybe stake a claim.

Molars grinding, I tore my focus off him for the baker.

"Usual?" Kel asked, already moving to grab enough cups to supply the station like I always did when stopping by in the morning.

"Orange cranberry scones too," I added, my body tensed and vibrating from annoyance and deep-seated desire I couldn't seem to escape no matter how much Jimmy's actions got under my skin.

Jimmy sidled closer—of course he fucking did—brushing his shoulder against my arm in order to get my attention.

I attempted to stare stonily ahead but caved.

Again.

Baby blues peered up at me, alive with light, mischief, and a whole lot of lust, and while that last bit might be real, the rest was a facade as usual. And here I'd thought he had started to lower his walls with me.

Mine had slammed firmly back into place thanks to his attempt to orchestrate a situation to get what he wanted.

"You've been ignoring my texts," he murmured low enough none of the other patrons sitting at small tables around the cafe would hear.

"Been busy." I all but grunted the words.

He flicked at one of my buttons, too damned close to my groin.

A muscle ticked in my jaw as I fought the need to grab him by his sweatshirt and shove him against a wall. Ravage him regardless of onlookers. Tear off his goddamned mask. Make him beg—and give the fuck in until we were both broken down to our baser selves, sticky with sweat and cum.

"Feeling extra needy today, Sutton," he whispered, leaning in too damned close for comfort.

My eyelids slammed shut, nostrils flaring as I fought for control. The boy knew the words that threatened my rigid stance on avoiding hurt.

"Can't stop touching myself, reliving every second of that phone call."

"Jesus, Jimmy."

He smirked, rubbing an inconspicuous fingertip over my shirt. "Wouldn't mind a repeat—or three."

Kel set a carryout tray of coffees and to-go bag on the counter, and I cleared my throat, stepping closer to pull out my wallet, thankful as fuck for my tight briefs.

I paid, too aware of the lustful gaze on my back. Heat flooded through me, and I prayed the pre-cum oozing from my trapped cock didn't leak so much that a wet spot marked my trousers. "Thanks, Kel."

"Anytime, Chief."

Nodding, I turned away, intent on the exit and freedom

from the suffocating desire from sharing a room with Jimmy.

He followed me out into the cool air, and I walked at a brisk pace, cursing myself for chasing after him to Scone Haven in the first place.

"Hey." He scurried to keep up with me. "You ought to take me with you for a ride along like you used to do."

My imagination went straight to road head and how Jimmy's pouty lips would look like wrapped around my dick. Big blue eyes all watery from me shoving my length deep into his throat—

"No." I stumbled to a stop, my groin *aching* as I faced him fully.

Jimmy bumped into me on purpose. "Oops." He flashed a grin at me, eyelids heavy with an obvious invite to do whatever the hell I wanted with his body.

"Jimmy." My tone carried warning.

"Yes...Sutton?" He winked, pretending to have caught himself from calling me daddy.

I wasn't about to *good boy* him no matter how badly he longed to hear those words from my lips. But fuck, did I want to see him melt by giving him what he needed.

"Enough, boy," I hissed, leaning down to get in his face. "We're not doing this."

"There's no stopping that train you put in motion when you made me come so hard I almost blacked out, Chief."

A muscle ticked in my jaw.

"You started an engine that won't quit until I'm bone-less beneath you, my insides coated with your hot cum, my spunk smeared between our sweaty bodies."

I swallowed hard, my cells buzzing and balls drawn up tight. "Jesus, Jimmy."

"I'm so damned hard for you my lace panties are wet."

Fucking. Hell.

I spun on my heel and stormed off as best I could considering the hard bulge between my thighs.

And I'd thought Jimmy Riley was trouble before. He was temptation, the promise of deliciousness beneath.

But I wanted the treasure beneath the pretty package with its tightly tied bow.

Realness twenty-four seven. Raw emotion like he'd shown me his first day back in town, not this coy brat who tried to steer the outcome of our interactions. I'd had enough of that the first time around with my ex.

I desired everything Jimmy hid behind lock and key, but if he couldn't give me honesty, I refused to touch him.

Chapter 18

Jimmy

Chief Sutton was an oak.

How the man could resist my blatant pickups, the dirty talk that caused his pupils to swell and probably his dick in his pants too, I had no clue. Somehow, he managed to avoid me for the rest of the week, but it wasn't like I was actively looking to run into him since I had my hands full.

Dad's place was almost ready to go on the market, but there was one major eyesore parked out back that I hadn't gotten around to addressing.

Henderson Auto's garage doors were down against the chilly afternoon air, but lights still shone inside.

I let myself into the reception area since the front entrance was unlocked. The office door was propped open, and I stumbled across the threshold at the sight of two hot guys sucking face, grasping at each other's groins.

"Oh, shit." I snickered but didn't bother glancing away as Chaz and Jamie tore themselves from each other, hands shoving into uniform and coverall pockets. Both faces blazed red. "You don't have to stop on account of me," I joked, lounging into the closest chair across from Chaz's desk where they stood shuffling on their feet.

Jamie huffed and shook his head, but a smile curved his generous mouth.

I'd always thought he was hot, but his dad was ten times yummier. At least, I expected he would be. I also wondered about Jamie hiring my old co-worker Zack, who was a dead ringer for Chaz.

And while I loved a bit of gossip, I wasn't about to pry into the life of the son of the man I wished would just fuck me already. Fall for me. *Keep* me and care for me until death parted us. A heavy sigh left me at the thought of the happily ever that seemed farther away than ever.

"Can I help you?" Chaz asked, and I sat up straight, turning my mind toward business.

"I wondered if you'd be interested in taking my dad's old truck off my hands—a free fixer-upper or for parts."

"Does it run?" Chaz asked, sitting down behind his desk in attempts to hide his tented overalls, but I didn't tease or mess with him since I wanted to stay in these guys' good graces in case I landed myself in the chief's bed.

"Started it up this morning, but I'll be honest—" I grimaced "—it's a piece of shit that should probably go to the junkyard. Figured I'd ask if you wanted it first before having it towed. I'd rather someone who knows cars maybe make a few bucks off of it."

"I'll swing by later tonight and check it out if that's all right?"

"Sure thing."

Chaz nodded as though he'd already decided to bring the truck to his shop. "The kid who works for me needs a new vehicle, so maybe we'll fix it up, and I'll give it to him as a Christmas bonus."

"I love that," I said, grinning over graciousness that mirrored his father-in-law's.

"How's the house coming along?" Jamie asked.

Warmth filled my chest at his friendly question that didn't sound anything like the interrogation I'd expected, considering Sutton must have warned him about my past. "It should be on the market soon."

"Are you sticking around after you sell or are you heading back to work in Boston?"

I shrugged, wondering what all he knew about me and how careful I needed to be lest I had guessed right and—

My thoughts cut off.

If Jamie had hired Zack, he was definitely aware what I'd done for a living up until a few weeks ago. Which also meant Sutton probably did too since there was no way Jamie would hide from the chief what Pippen Creek's long-term visitor had been up to in his absence.

Was my being a sex worker Sutton's reason for turning me down?

Shit.

Talk about making me feel like even more of a worthless worm.

Was that how Sutton saw me? A whore with a used up hole good only for a cum dump and run? Soiled goods?

God, my heart hurt to even consider what he might think of me.

"You okay?"

I shook myself off the depressing train of my brain and tried for a smile. Definitely failed. "Yeah—sure," I lied, swallowing hard.

"So—are you going to stay?" Jamie pushed.

"There's nothing for me back in Boston, but it depends."

"On?" That one-worded question definitely held some suspicion, but with my current mind frame, I probably read too much into every tiny inflection and twitch of his eyelid.

I shrugged again, my feet itchy to get me the hell out of there. "Waiting to see how the winds of change blow."

He studied me like his dad often did, searching for something I would never allow him to see. A calculated glint filled his navy-blue eyes.

"My dad is having a cookout on Sunday afternoon—the last of the season before it gets too cold," Jamie said. "You ought to come."

I stared at him. No fucking *way* would he invite me if he was aware of the work I'd done while in Boston.

"I...wouldn't want to impose." My words were hesitant as fuck as I glanced between the two men.

Chaz smiled at Jamie like the younger Forrester hung the moon in the night sky. I could understand the sentiment.

While I hated letting anyone past my walls protecting me from criticism or judgment, this unspoken shit between us needed to be aired out or I would fret and worry myself to a stomach ulcer.

"Do you, um...you were in Boston for a few years." I made the statement while rubbing my palms over my jeans.

"Yeah," Jamie said.

"You, um...ever heard of EEMM?"

Chaz chuckled as Jamie's face flamed.

I blew out a heavy exhale. "Guess that answers my question."

Jamie rubbed a hand over his face while checking out the floor. "Yeah, I'm well aware of what EEMM stands for."

"You can tell Zack my fiancé says hi," Chaz said with a satisfied chuckle.

Good to know there was no jealousy, but Jamie's obvious unease hardened my stomach and caused me to stiffen in the chair.

"There's nothing wrong with sex work," I said, my tone low and somewhat haggard.

Jamie's head jerked up, his eyes wide. "No—I'm not judging you." He grimaced. "Fuck—I'm not ashamed about what I did. What you do—did. Whatever. Doesn't matter to me."

"Then why get all uncomfortable when I brought up Elite?"

Chaz chuckled again. "Because I love to give him shit about being so damned desperate for me he was a cam boy in order to afford your friend."

Relief caused me to finally relax a little.

"Asshole," Jamie hissed, crossing his arms, making the muscles of his arms bulge in his uniform as his fiancé barked a laugh.

"You love me." Chaz tossed a dirty rag at him, which Jamie batted away.

"Fucking right, I do," Jamie grumbled, but he couldn't hide his smile.

They shared a heated stare, the air in the office zapping with sexual energy enough that my own dick twitched even though giddiness over the entire exchange had allowed my guts to settle.

I glanced between the two men, jealous of their connection and ability to find joy in each other's pasts that weren't exactly...savory. An ache spread over my chest, and I rubbed at it.

"About that invite." I spoke quietly, not wanting to interrupt their hot moment but desperation for a chance to be in Sutton's space spurred me on, and their non-judgment offered me a little hope the chief might be of the same mind as they were.

"A handful of friends usually show up—it's not a family thing," Jamie said, giving me his attention again. "The door is always open, and you're welcome to join us."

Even with the lack of judgment, why was Jamie being so nice to me? Pity was the first thought I had, causing me to frown, but I was starved for attention and inclusion, a sense of belonging.

"You sure?"

"Yeah," Jamie replied to my hesitant question.

"Maybe you ought to run it by your dad first," I suggested, my tone still wary in wondering if the chief knew about my past.

Jamie huffed a laugh. "I'm sure he'd love to see you."

I wasn't so sure, but I wouldn't pass up an opportunity to step inside Sutton's home and breathe in the scent of him that doubtless covered every inch of the house. Just daydreaming about it made me half hard.

"Does he know about..." I waved a hand, too damned worked up to ask outright.

Jamie's gaze softened. "Yeah. He's been stalking you ever since you left."

"He—" I snapped my jaw shut, blinking hard.

Sutton's son chuckled. "Yeah."

"Holy fuck," I whispered, my heart racing at the possibilities... "Why?"

"*That*, you'll have to ask my dad."

"I'll be there," I stated, hopping up, my pulse thrumming, limbs twitchy as fuck. "What time, and what can I bring?"

"Two and a six-pack of beer—Dad likes Stella."

I bid the guys a good rest of the day and headed into the reception area on light feet.

"What are you doing?" Chaz asked Jamie quietly, but I had ears like a hawk and slowed my steps because I needed the answer to that question too.

"Dad has been saying since I got home that he wants someone to take care of. According to him, Jimmy's always been a needy handful, and considering he's been pining for the guy for a few years..."

I could imagine Jamie's shrug as his voice trailed off.

But was *I* the one he'd said pined, or did he mean Sutton?

"They kinda makes sense," Chaz mused while I stood on the edge of hyperventilating.

"Yeah," Jamie agreed without a hint of judgment in his voice.

Butterflies fluttered in my belly.

Sutton was looking for a man to "take care of", and he wouldn't find someone better than my desperate ass.

Hope like I'd never experienced flooded through me as I snuck out the shop's door.

Sunday afternoon couldn't come soon enough.

Chapter 19

Sutton

"You did *what?*" I frowned at my son, who wore torn jeans, a red flannel, and a backwards ball cap as he waltzed into my kitchen like he still lived here.

I missed having him at home but wouldn't change our living arrangements for the world. His and Chaz's house on Pippen Creek Pond was nicer than mine a little north of downtown, and they had each other for company.

Envy, my faithful companion whenever the boys were around, slunk into my chest and settled atop my heart, making it feel heavier than usual.

"I invited Jimmy," Jamie repeated what he'd said the second he walked in, his fiancé on his heels. "The guy could use a friend, and I see the way you look at him."

"Ha!" Dex barked a laugh from the living room, and I rolled my eyes. The guy had superhuman ears.

I set aside the tongs I'd retrieved to put steaks on the grill and turned toward my son, arms and ankles crossed as I leaned my back against the kitchen counter. "The age difference doesn't bother you?" I asked what I expected everyone to have issue with even though I and Jimmy certainly didn't.

Jamie shrugged. "Just want you happy, Dad. You deserve it after all the shit you went through with Darla."

"Goddamned right!" Dex hollered and muttered under his breath what sounded a lot like *psychotic bitch*.

He didn't lie, and to this day, I couldn't stand fake people or their underhanded methods of getting what they wanted—Jimmy to an absolute T.

But fuck, the draw toward him was real. Sleep-depriving and ball-aching in its intensity. And he *had* shown a shit ton of signs of having grown up since leaving but not nearly to the level I needed to trust him with my heart.

"What about you, Chaz?" I asked.

"What about me?" he asked while setting a container of store-bought potato salad onto the table.

"What do you think about me getting involved with a younger guy?"

"Couldn't care less, Chief." He pressed against Jamie's side, and my son slung his arm around Chaz's shoulders.

Dex sauntered into the kitchen, and they all glanced at one another before turning their gazes on me. The sudden silence made my skin itch.

"What?" I asked, feeling like a bug under a microscope.

"Jimmy needs a guy like you," Jamie said. "He doesn't have the cleanest record or prettiest past, but I don't believe a single one of us—you included—gives a shit about what he's been up to."

I rubbed a hand over my mouth, my freshly oiled beard soft on my palm while glancing at my best friend.

Dex nodded, his dark eyes offering encouragement. The

asshole loved to tease the shit out of me, but in this, I knew he would have my back no matter what.

"We talked about Elite."

My focus jerked toward my son. Since he didn't keep secrets from Chaz, same as I didn't from Dex, everyone in the room was well aware of the escort company my son spoke of.

"He seemed uncomfortable," Jamie continued. "Probably thinks you'll judge him for what he used to do for a living."

"Past tense?" Dex asked before I could question what I'd also zeroed in on too.

"He didn't come right out and say he quit, but that's the feeling I got," Jamie said, and Chaz nodded his agreement.

A knock sounded, and as though of the same mind, Dex, Jamie, and Chaz hightailed it toward the slider leading onto my small deck.

Dex snagged the tongs and bag of marinated steaks off the counter on his way past me. "I'll put these on the grill. You go greet your new boy toy and maybe let him talk you into allowing him to hang around after the rest of us leave."

I growled beneath my breath at his back as he snickered and left me alone. The last thing I wanted was another situation where fake Jimmy attempted to steer the outcome of our interactions. Heaving a heavy breath in and out, I started toward my front door. The twitch of my cock over the prospect of Jimmy being in close proximity made me remember I wore sweats, and I wondered if I had time to quickly change.

Jimmy knocked again, and there was no way I could have him driving off thinking I didn't want him here because it took me too long to let him in.

"Fuck." Steeling myself, dick mostly soft, I pulled the door open.

For a brief second, gorgeous hesitancy and insecurity radiated from Jimmy's tired eyes, but after a quick glance over my choice in clothing, that goddamned mask slid into place. His lips curled upward, and a twinkle lit in his baby blues, erasing the truth he hid from the world. The sly smirk did nothing to dissolve the obvious exhaustion on his face though.

"Chief," he purred in that low, sultry voice I hated to love—the same exact tone and word he'd greeted me with when he'd stood on my stoop all those years ago.

Unlike that night, a shiver licked down my spine this time, and I stepped back, motioning the devilish angel into my space. "Jimmy."

A sweet yet musky scent filled my lungs as he brushed past me, the mere touch of our clothing heightening my pulse. I wondered if he wore lace panties beneath his skintight jeans, and I bit my tongue to keep from groaning—and outright asking if that particular fantasy of mine was true.

He cast a quick glance around the kitchen before handing me a brown paper bag. "Jamie said you like Stella."

My lips twitched as warmth spread through me over Jimmy's thoughtfulness. Had he asked my preferred drink, or had Jamie suggested it? Either way, Jimmy had gone out of his way to stop and get something for me. "Yeah—I do."

Jimmy beamed, a real smile that lit him up from the inside out. He was so goddamned beautiful with his walls lowered and made my nerves dance with anticipation. The blood in my body sped south faster than if he'd popped his hip out and winked at me.

"Thanks," I said, more for his genuine smile while taking the beer off his hands.

Cock thick and somewhat hidden behind the bag I clutched with both hands, I cleared my throat and nodded toward the slider. "Guys are outside. I'm going to throw on some jeans real quick."

Jimmy glanced down at my groin. "Hiding something from me, Chief?" He reached out to push the gift away from what he wanted to see.

I fucking let him, my arms dropping to my sides, bag fisted in my right hand.

His pupils swelled at the sight of my tented sweats, and he licked over his lower lip. "I think you look mighty fine as-is, Chief. Perfect, actually. Don't change on account of little old me."

"It's *because* of you I need to put on jeans," I muttered, my face hot, feet on unsteady ground.

He snickered from behind me as I set the beer on the counter and strode toward the stairs to escape to my bedroom. "Need any help?"

Yes. Fuck, yes.

"No!" I barked instead, knowing that once I gave that boy an inch, he'd take everything I had, and we wouldn't come up for air anytime soon.

My company out on the deck might be fine with me falling into bed with Jimmy, but I had self-control, dammit. Proper priorities in seeing all of the boys fed like I'd promised to do.

Responsibilities came first. Always.

Afterward? Who knew. A few more real smiles, a bit of vulnerability on Jimmy's part...

It was only a matter of time before the axe he'd taken to

my legs made me topple over, no matter how badly my suspicious nature insisted I stand firm.

Somehow, I managed to talk my dick down, tugged on tight briefs I usually wore beneath my uniform pants, and stepped into well-worn, baggy jeans that would hide whatever boners Jimmy's fine ass made me pop in front of the guys.

"Don't fantasize about his ass right now, for fuck's sake," I grumbled to myself while heading back downstairs and into the kitchen.

Jimmy had joined the guys out on the deck, so I finished getting out the rest of the food I'd prepared, setting up a buffet on the island.

Dex came in, platter of grilled T-bone steaks in hand. He leaned against the counter sipping a Stella while I tented foil over the meat to let it rest. "He looks tired."

"Yeah. From what I've heard, he's been running himself into the ground every day to get that house fixed up and on the market."

"The kind of work he's not used to."

I nodded, snagging a beer from the fridge and guzzling a few swallows. "What do you think, Dex?"

He glanced out the slider to where the three younger guys stood against the railing, overlooking the woods and mountains beyond. "He's got a fine-as-fuck ass, I'll give him that."

Scowling, I elbowed my best friend, and he chuckled, clinking his bottle to mine.

"You want more than a hookup, but that boy would agree to anything you want to try. Don't pass up the opportunity to figure out what being with a man you're into is like before it's gone."

"Yeah, but that's only part of the problem," I muttered,

gaze on Jimmy's bubble butt. "I want the boy beneath the fake exterior. Can't stand how he tries to manipulate me into sex like Darla did." Another sip of beer cooled my esophagus, and I could feel Dex's stare.

"Have you been honest with him?"

I snorted. "Of course, I have."

"So you've shared your fears. Your dislike for his actions? Maybe telling him the truth would give you both what you want."

Lips in a thin line, I sighed heavily. Dex had a point, but I had to consider what *after* Jimmy was gone looked like too. Loneliness tenfold, my heart without a doubt shattered. "He doesn't plan to stick around. Why lower my walls and open myself up to that kind of hurt?"

"Because life is short and you never know which breath will be your last."

"Morbid," I muttered, my forehead furrowing again.

"It's the truth," Dex assured me, having seen devastation alongside me as a first responder for our town and the area surrounding us.

The war between desire and better sense continued to rage, worsened by calling the guys in to grab plates.

No one touched Jimmy's past with a ten-foot-pole while conversing, but I learned all about the work he'd been up to since returning home, the truck he'd gifted Chaz, and the contractor he'd hired to fix the things he wasn't sure how to do.

"So are you heading back to Boston once you sell?" Of course, Dex had to ask the question that lay heaviest on my mind while we sat around my fire pit in the backyard, after-dinner beers in hand.

I held my breath, ears ringing to hear Jimmy's voice assure me he wasn't going anywhere.

He cast a quick glance at me, the silence heavy with longing.

I kept my feelings locked up tight—same as he did.

Jimmy tore his gaze away first, taking great interest in the dying flames while lifting his shoulder in a shrug.

Did he wonder if I wanted him to stay, or was that wishful thinking on my part?

Either way, I needed to dig out the truth, because Dex had been right. Time could be shorter than hoped for or expected.

I would have answers before Jimmy left tonight so I could move forward—heart broken or not.

Chapter 20

Jimmy

Exhaustion from the long week had me sagging in the seat by Sutton's fire pit, but the butterflies that had been with me long before arriving still fluttered in my chest, making me feel half-high with elation.

The guys had been really nice to me, no judgment in their eyes or dirty looks over my obvious interest in Sutton. Out of them all, I'd expected Jamie to corner me and ask me my intentions toward his dad, and even though he'd had the opportunity a couple of times, including at Chaz's shop, he'd didn't speak a word.

Maybe he assumed I was just a flirt and *had* no intentions.

But I couldn't keep my gaze off the chief. His broad shoulders that could carry the weight of the world. His strong jawline covered in a soft-looking beard that stated he could take whatever shit someone threw at him. The sure, steady way he moved, the confidence that oozed from him. Everything about the man was sexy as fuck, including the interior package that attracted every cell in my body like a magnet.

Kindness. Compassion. His nurturing soul I craved to have intertwined around my broken one. I longed to be pressed against him, to soak in his nature until I was healed. We would meld together and never be separated.

Deep yearning flooded through me, and I slouched farther into my seat, focused on glowing red embers that weren't doing much to ward off the chill of the September evening. I huddled in my sweatshirt, wishing I'd worn a fleece jacket or something heavier.

"Not really sure what I want to do after Dad's house sells," I finally answered Dex. "There's nothing for me in Boston." I glanced at Sutton again, desperate for a hint of what he thought about my future plans.

Legs stretched out and crossed, he scanned the darkened horizon, always on the lookout for danger that might threaten his town.

Warmth filled my chest over his protective instincts, making my eyes sting.

Fuck, did I want him.

An owl hooted, a soothing sound I hadn't heard in years, causing a small smile to rise through the welling wetness coating my vision.

"What's up with DJ?" Jamie asked, poking a stick into the dying fire and causing embers to rise with the smoke. "You've been spending a lot of time with that kid."

"He needs a friend," I answered quietly, watching as the sparks faded into the night sky.

"He's lucky to have you," Chaz said. "I know what it's like not to have the best relationship with your dad, and if it hadn't been for Jamie and Sutton..." His voice trailed off, and Jamie entwined their hands together in my periphery.

"But there's hope things could get better between them," Chaz continued. "Not sure if you knew, but my dad was a major asshole to me up until the beginning of this year. We've both been going to therapy and are working to better ourselves and our relationship."

Therapy.

Inwardly, I shivered. No fucking thank you.

"*You're* lucky," I suggested. "Not many guys get a second chance like that."

None of the men around the fire offered condolences for my loss. I guessed they were well aware I didn't mourn my dad's passing. There had been no apologies from him, no forgiveness from me, but I didn't carry a burden of weight over that part of my life. Yeah, my childhood had sucked ass, but even if he had crawled to me on hands and knees, wallowing and horrified over how he'd treated me, I would have turned my back on him.

Boundaries and all that shit.

Just because he'd been blood didn't mean I owed him a goddamned ounce of affection or moment of my time.

Dex slapped his thigh, pulling me into the present. "Well, I have to be in at the station early tomorrow. Gonna call it a night." He stood, and Jamie and Chaz did the same.

Sutton didn't argue their leaving earlier than I expected they usually did but pushed up to his feet to hug his friend and family goodbye.

Jamie was the last to walk away, clasping his dad's shoulder with a wink before glancing at me. "'Night, Jimmy."

"Thanks again for the invite."

"My pleasure."

I stared after the three guys as they made their way around the house toward the front.

Was Jamie...*encouraging* his dad with that little wink?

My gaze fixed on Sutton's back as he shoved his hands

in his pockets. His shoulders hitched near his ears, and he took a steadying breath before turning toward me.

Our gazes clashed over what was left of the fire, and heat sizzled through my blood.

Car doors slammed, and seconds later, engines roused to life. The crunch of gravel faded as the two vehicles drove off, leaving me and the chief alone.

Fucking finally.

"Sorry I don't have any wine. Want another beer?" Sutton asked, his voice a little hoarse, and I wondered whether his tone hinted at desire or fear over my still being there.

I didn't care either way. He hadn't suggested I leave—and he'd offered me a reason to stay.

"Sure." My voice shook, and I slid damp palms down my chilled jeans.

"We can go inside if you're getting too cold."

I nodded, and after he set a screen lid over the fire pit, I followed him into the house.

The silence felt heavy but not stifling, thick with tingling anticipation as we cracked open our beers and headed into the living room.

Sutton sat in the corner of his couch, and I settled not quite in the center but close enough he could touch me if he wanted to.

Arm across the back of the cushions, he angled toward me, gaze sliding over my face as though searching out all my secrets. But I didn't take his suspicion personally. Chief gave everyone that inquisitive look—it was his damned job and probably deeply engrained in his brain to root out any possible danger to his community. Naturally, he would do the same with his heart.

"What's on your mind, Sutton?" I asked without the usual sass or suggestive smirk.

"What kind of trouble did you get into down in Boston?" He asked the question carefully, and I recognized the test for what it was.

I could lie and prove myself to be a man he couldn't trust, or I could be honest. Vulnerable. Give him what he wanted that could very well make him grimace even though Jamie's stance on sex work gave me hope he might not hate that part of my past.

My heart raced from both arousal and fear, causing my stomach to curdle. I set the full beer on the coffee table.

"I had just over a hundred bucks to my name when I left here that night," I said, and Sutton seemed ready for whatever tale I would weave, gaze unwavering.

I went with the truth because I was that desperate, that needy for the man to let me in past his own walls. Maybe he would allow me to love him—and gain his in return. High stakes, but the possibilities of good overshadowed getting hurt. Fuck knew I'd dealt with plenty of that and would find a way to move on even if Sutton was disgusted by how I had supported myself.

"I lived out of my car while delivering for a pizzeria for a few months. But the piece of shit died on me, and I had to abandon it on the side of the road where it had left me stranded." I stared at Sutton's knee while telling him about how cold it had been attempting to survive on the streets in a cooler than normal spring. How cardboard boxes didn't really help a whole lot other than to keep the biting wind off my body.

"I lost my job," I said and swallowed hard, my muscles tensing in readiness to leave. "Ended up giving blow jobs in back alleys so I could buy myself some food."

Sutton didn't speak, didn't move.

I glanced up to find him watching me, his expression void of both revulsion and judgment like I'd expected. If anything, his hazel eyes encouraged me to continue in the path I'd chosen that wasn't complete bullshit like I'd have spewed as a teen.

Clearing my throat, I rubbed my palms down my thighs *again*, and shifted my focus back to his knee. "Shit escalated from there. I was stupid. Wasn't safe. But I escaped that time of my life without any lasting health issues. Met this kid named Sean Fox at a party one night. He wasn't into pretty twinks, but he said he had the perfect job for me if I was interested."

I hesitated, unsure of how to continue even though I'd already told Sutton I'd become a hole for pay.

"Elite," Sutton filled in when the silence grew to be too much.

My focus jerked toward his face, and I swallowed hard. "Did Jamie tell you?"

He didn't exactly smile, but he wasn't scowling either. "No. I've been keeping watch over you for years."

"Because I'm a part of your Pippen Creek flock?" I held my breath.

"No—because I care." The warmth of his tone slid through my veins. "I appreciate you telling me the truth, Jimmy."

"You expected me to lie." I didn't ask a question. I could read it on his face clear as the green glints in his kind eyes.

"I hate to say that I did, but yeah," he said before releasing a heavy sigh and sinking into the couch. I hadn't realized he'd been tensed, waiting for me to pull my usual shit.

"Because I cried wolf one too many times as a kid." I

supplied yet another truth he was well aware of. "It's a part of my past," I stated quietly, studying his face for a hint of his thoughts and desires, coming up empty as usual. "I'm not getting paid to fuck for money anymore."

Sutton nodded as though he was already aware I'd quit Elite before returning to Pippen Creek.

"My ex-wife manipulated me into sleeping with her in high school. Some might even call what she did to me rape."

My brain scrambled to navigate the sharp turn in conversation along with him. His honesty acted like helium to my hope, but the words he'd spoken made me crash and burn just as quickly—I'd attempted to do the same as his ex but without the non-consent. I'd wanted him willing. As desperate for me as I was for him.

No wonder the man stood like an oak against my flirty onslaught.

Sutton eyed me, watching my rolling emotions probably play out on my face since I no longer had the energy to hide from him. "She hoped to get pregnant because she knew I would marry her and save her from her father, who was a lot like yours."

"Shit," I muttered, my eyelids fluttering shut. I was doomed. It was no wonder Sutton had turned me down and pushed me away every time I'd tried to get my hands on his body.

"You're not her."

My eyes popped back open, and my pulse stuttered, breath held as I waited for him to continue.

"Since you've been home..." Sutton's gaze flitted over my face but without the calculating type of investigative interest as usual. He seemed to study my features for further reflection or maybe to think on later. Spank bank material?

A boy could hope.

I sat still when I would rather have climbed onto his lap and begged him to take whatever he wanted from me—because everything he embodied was exactly what I needed.

"You've grown up, Jimmy. Learned some hard lessons while away. I'm damned proud of how you've been looking out for both Mary and her grandson."

Tears stung my eyes again as a sense of having accomplished *something* good swelled inside my chest.

Sutton blew out a heavy exhale and finished off his beer, the bob of his Adam's apple making me want to lean in and lick a stripe along his skin.

My mouth watered as my gaze slid down over his chest with the dark blue shirt clinging to his pecs and draped casually over the waistband of his jeans. The bulge below, along with those tented sweats earlier, promised he packed a perfect dick.

"I wasn't trying to trap you," I whispered, swallowing at the rush of saliva coating my mouth over the thought of sucking him off.

"I know."

"You always made me feel safe, and I may have had a slight crush on you."

He chuckled, one eyebrow raised.

"Okay, so I still do," I admitted and shrugged. "I'm needy, what can I say?"

Sutton's eyes darkened far beyond the hint of interest I'd seen before. His pupils swelled as his gaze dipped, roaming slowly over me.

Whatever walls had stood between us no longer existed.

Fuck, honesty was a beautiful thing.

Goose bumps scattered over my skin, causing me to

shiver. The memory of what I'd overheard Jamie tell Chaz about Sutton's desire spurred me on, desperation dictating my actions. Heart racing, I slid off the couch onto my knees.

Sutton's breath hitched, but he didn't speak or move as I crawled the short distance between us and settled onto my heels in front of him. I'd tossed the facade aside, but rather than be honest with what I truly wanted from him, I shamefully chose manipulation, using the exact word that would get me what I hoped for tonight.

"I *need* to taste you."

Chapter 21

Sutton

The boy had to go and say the one thing that would crumble my walls, but it was the raw desire in his eyes that assured me his tactics to get at my dick went beyond trickery. I bet my life that what he craved ran close to what I did.

Emotional connection.

Affection and affirmation.

Dark pupils ate at the blue of his irises as he stared at my groin, my cock, which had been half-hard all damned evening, thickening beneath his gaze. He licked his lower lip, but the action seemed instinctive rather than tactical, like a child filled with anticipation over a tasty treat that would be sweeter than any chocolate bar on his tongue.

He and I had been on a crash course since the night he'd shown up at Frenchie's in August. There was no denying the magnetic pull between us, the connection of puzzle pieces created by different yet perfectly aligned needs.

But how long would this last?

My pulse hummed with steady thumps beneath my skin that had become overly sensitive to restrictive material, but I wasn't about to rip off my clothing and fulfill my lust. This boy had been through the fire, and he deserved the satisfaction of unwrapping the gift he viewed me as.

Even if I ended up trampled beneath his heel, my heart nothing but a bruised lump in my chest.

Choice made, I spread my arms across the back of the couch and widened my legs to ease the ache growing in my groin.

Jimmy took the action as the invite I'd intended, sliding into the space between my knees, trembling hands landing atop my thighs, the warmth of his palms searing me through the denim separating us. He tore his focus off my dick and stared up at me. Masks and walls had shimmered out of existence earlier, and vulnerability flared to life between us in the most honest, silent communication we had ever shared.

"Take what you need, baby boy," I murmured.

A shudder ripped through Jimmy's entire frame as a whimper leaked from his pouty lips, causing my dick to buck inside my jeans.

Jesus, he would be the death of me.

His hands fumbled with the button, and I lifted my hips slightly to make the dragging of my zipper over my aching cock easier.

He huffed over finding restrictive briefs in his way, but that didn't cause him a second's hesitation. Warm fingers fished me free from my briefs, balls and all. My shaft throbbed in his grip, and I hissed as he tugged down on my foreskin, revealing the swollen, leaking tip.

"Oh, God, I knew it," he croaked, eyes wide as he stared. "Your dick is *perfect*." He licked his lips. "You could stuff me full twice a day, every day without a problem."

I gripped hold of the couch to keep from taking over and

making him be my good boy. "Jimmy," I rasped his name, my voice betraying how he'd already wrecked me.

"Yeah, Chief," he whispered—and fucking jammed me straight into his throat.

"Fuck!" My hips jolted up on their own, my hands clasping around Jimmy's head.

He didn't gag but swallowed, the wet heat of his flesh tightening around my cockhead with welcomeness I'd never experienced before.

"Jesus *fucking* Christ." I hissed, gyrating my hips to fuck deep into his throat, my focus on his gorgeous lips wrapped around me, the metal ball through his tongue gliding along the back of my dick. "Beautiful boy—fuck." I pulled him off me, and he filled his lungs before whimpering, trying to go at me again, mouth open, pierced tongue searching. "Jimmy. What the hell?"

I gave him control and stared as he loved on my shaft, licking and sucking, lavishing kisses along my saliva-soaked length, burying his face in my balls and sniffing. Fucking nibbling and leading me to the edge. The boy was a blow job god, worthy of worship.

"You're gonna make me come," I warned, and he closed his mouth over my tip, sucking hard while playing with my sac. "Fuck." I grasped his head and shoved him down while thrusting up. Slick heat enshrouded me, and I cursed as my taint throbbed.

Cum shot through my shaft, and Jimmy shuddered as the first spurt erupted into his throat.

"Fuck yes." I grunted, stabbing into him again, loving how having control over his body caused him to shudder, eyes rolled into his head. "Jesus, you're so good for me, boy —perfect mouth." I thrust, giving him another spurt. "Talented tongue—goddamned piercing—Jesus, boy."

Curses and praise continued to spill from me as he greedily gulped every dribble of my cum as though he'd been starved of sustenance. Satisfaction rose up inside me like I'd accomplished my life's purpose, and I choked on a laugh over the absurdity of my thoughts while releasing my hold on Jimmy's hair.

But he stayed on my dick, slurping and sucking me until I softened.

Shuddering, Jimmy finally lay his cheek on my thigh, eyes closed, a smile curving his generous, reddened mouth.

I soothed my shaking hand over his head, fingers sifting through his soft waves of pale gold. "Such a good boy." I murmured what would fill his heart with happiness.

He shivered as I continued to pet him, releasing a slow, contented sigh when I'd been the one who'd come so damned hard my vision had gone black.

Had he...

I pulled Jimmy off the floor and onto my lap where he curled up, nuzzling his face into my neck. He fit perfectly in my arms as though he'd been made for me. I glanced down at his groin...

Wetness coated the front of his jeans.

"Jesus," I whispered, sliding my fingertips over the evidence of the pleasure he'd derived from me giving him what he'd been after since coming back home. What he *needed* from me.

Another shuddering sigh sank him deeper into my arms, and I wrapped him up tight, kissing his hair and closing my eyes while basking in the rightness of this moment. The fulfillment I'd always longed for but had never felt.

Jimmy had owned me for years, but tonight, I had submitted myself to the sure doom that awaited me.

Sassy, coy Jimmy caught my breath.

Sleepy, sated Jimmy hurt my heart in the best way possible.

I carried him to my bed and stripped him bare. Finding piercings through his nipples then the sight of cum-soaked, lace panties clinging to his skin brought a groan from deep in my chest. And the ring through his taint? Although I'd had the climax of the century minutes earlier, my spent dick twitched, and my tongue tingled over temptation to flick the metal and maybe even tug a bit.

Next time.

Soft puffed exhales escaped Jimmy's parted lips as I used a warm, wet cloth to clean between his lax thighs. I loved how his instincts allowed him full rest while I cared for him so intimately. I longed to map out every inch of his skin, memorize every hidden freckle, *own* him.

I'd given into temptation, hoping I could maybe keep my desire for something more on lockdown while enjoying a physical connection. What a joke. I wanted Jimmy now more than ever, right where he lay passed out and lightly snoring. I would fulfill his every whim, whatever need drove him, until he had his fill. Pain waited around the corner, but I would wait to deal with it rather than be burdened by its weight.

I stared at him as I stripped down to skin, leaving my clothes where they dropped. Breathed in the sweet scent of him while big-spooning the hell out of his limp form, sliding one of my legs between his and wrapping him in my arms. Nuzzling my nose in his hair, I sighed, sinking into warmth and satisfaction.

I'd failed in helping Darla find healing and become a better person, but I'd been offered a second chance with someone who'd been proving to me since returning to my town that he wasn't all selfishness and coercion.

I would be *Jimmy's* oak for as long as he allowed—and pray like fuck he never took that metaphorical axe in hand.

A handful of soft warmth, a twitch of my middle finger sliding over metal, made me aware of how I held Jimmy before I even opened my eyes.

He still nestled against my chest, breathing deeply even though I cupped his groin as though that part of him belonged to me.

I should have removed my hand from his dick, didn't have consent to fondle his balls or the ring through his taint while he slept.

But I knew this boy, and he'd made his desires *beyond* clear. I could lube up my dick, slide balls deep inside his ass, and his greediness would have him begging for more.

Squeezing his junk lightly, I ran my nose along his neck, nipping at his shoulder. A gentle roll of balls more pliant than mine caused a moan to rumble in my chest, and I pressed my morning wood against the most perfect, luscious bubble butt on earth.

I'd never buried my dick in a guy, but I'd done my research and felt somewhat confident I could give Jimmy what he needed. Might not be the best at nailing his prostate, but practice made perfect.

His inhale stuttered, and he whimpered while coming awake, shifting to press his thickening cock into my hand. "Am I dreaming?" he whispered, all sleepy and sweet.

I kissed beneath his ear while wrapping my hand around his shaft.

He mewled, the sound going straight to my groin. Wetness slipped from my slit, and I rubbed against his ass cheek, smearing my pre-cum over his skin. "No, baby boy," I murmured against his ear.

He shivered, entwining his fingers with my other hand that rested atop his chest.

"Love these." I flicked over the rings in his nipples and taint while nibbling on his lobe.

"Feels good," he whispered, shifting his backside so his crack cradled my shaft.

I hissed, clutching him tighter and thrusting along his supple flesh.

"Can you get off like this?" he asked, his hips moving perfectly to rub me through the crevice of his backside. "Or do you want my ass?"

"Fuck." I groaned as he squeezed his cheeks around me. "This," I forced myself to say since I would rather take things slow. Enjoy the hell out of every step we could until penetration.

"Do it, Chief. Shoot your cum all over me. Make a mess out of me."

We moved like a well-oiled machine, the timing of every shift of our muscles leading toward completion. My pre-cum slickened his crack, and my hand pulled some from his shaft until the squelching sounds fought for dominance with our heightened breaths.

I closed my eyes. Rested my forehead on the back of Jimmy's head, and gave over to chasing my orgasm.

"Sutton," Jimmy gasped as I smeared my thumb over his slit.

"Come for me, baby," I ordered. "Soak my hand."

He shuddered and gifted me what I'd asked for, the first throb of his cock in my palm causing my balls to pulse with release. I cursed and painted his skin with sticky spurts of cum, stroking him through his pleasure until we both lay spent.

"Definitely dreaming," he said with a soft chuckle, his chest heaving for breath.

"Mmm." I could stay right there wrapped around Jimmy until the sun fully rose and fell again, leaving us in darkness until light once more flooded the sky.

Would he allow me to have him for more than a day?

How long before he stripped me of every ounce of love I had to give and took off to his next conquest like Darla had done?

This thing between Jimmy and I wasn't forever—couldn't possibly be, I reminded myself as a means of protecting my heart. History had proven to repeat itself, and it would be best to remember that fact. But fuck, did yearning to cling to him and this feeling of rightness, of *completeness*, cause me to hope otherwise.

The overthinking was making my stomach roil, but Jimmy shifted before I could, sprawling onto his back and stretching like a satisfied cat who'd lapped up all the cream in its bowl.

Would he hunger for more?

Or sashay away with a sly smirk on his mouth over having gotten what he'd needed from me?

Jesus.

I scrubbed a hand over my face and rolled out of bed, my throat suddenly uncomfortable and dry over the expectation and surety of the latter.

"Where you going, Chief?" he asked with that lowered voice full of mischief and sexual intent, the same slyness that had tried time and again to coerce me into getting naked with him.

Manipulation at its finest. I mourned the vulnerability we'd shared moments before.

His tone caused unease to slide down my spine regardless of what my aching heart wanted, and I strode toward the bathroom, my feet itching to distance my heart from Jimmy's clutches before it was too late.

"Shower," I rasped without looking over my shoulder because I was no goddamned oak when it came to him.

I assumed he would ask if I desired company—or maybe just follow me in because he knew he owned my personal space as much as I did.

Jimmy did neither.

And I stepped beneath the hot spray, eyes closed, head hanging, not sure if I wanted him waiting for me when I finished or already long gone so I could attempt to get on with my life. One taste of realness from that boy had ruined me—I'd taken the goddamned axe to my *own* legs, severing my ability to draw strength when I needed it most.

Ten or so minutes later, I pulled open the bathroom door.

My bed sat empty, sheets rumpled.

Jimmy, along with his clothes, was gone.

I didn't have to check the rest of the house. I could sense his abandonment as clearly as the water droplet that slipped from my wet hair and trickled down my spine. I swallowed hard as a crack split my chest in two regardless of how I had steeled myself in readiness to be proven right about him *needing* me.

Jimmy had gotten what he'd wanted and no longer had use of me.

"It's better this way." I tried to tell myself the truth, but every part of my body disagreed, leaving me shattered and empty.

Again.

Lips in a grim line, I rebuilt the walls around my heart

while putting on my uniform. Set my emotions behind lock and key while buckling on my belt. Shoved the heartache deep as I holstered my gun.

Work and the citizens of Pippen Creek waited on their chief, and no matter how my legs felt chopped out from beneath me, I would not fail in my responsibilities to keep them safe.

Chapter 22

Jimmy

There had been no affectionate cuddles after our release, no murmured good morning, no soft, first kiss against my mouth like I'd hoped for.

Sutton had walked away from me like a paying customer always did—without a backward glance at the escort who'd only been hired to get his rocks off. He'd rutted against me until he climaxed, but at least he'd been kind enough like some of my past experiences to help me get there as well.

Sure, he'd left the bathroom door cracked open, but I hadn't seen the action as an invite considering the utterance of where he'd headed to wash the feel and stench of me from his skin.

Sutton regretted what we'd done. Him leaving me behind was all the evidence I needed, his tone about showering as dismissive as anything I'd heard when working for Elite.

I'd gone on to become that whore Dad had accused me of being when I'd gotten caught on my knees for that jock back in high school. He was probably right about me being a worm too, good only for wallowing in the dirt, living beneath everyone else where light that offered warmth would never reach me.

Pulling on my clothes that Sutton had taken off of me the night before had been a struggle. Stepping out of his door into the bitter cold morning had caused me to hunker further in on myself as I wallowed in self-pity and heartache.

I should have known better than to pursue a man like Sutton. I wasn't enough for him, and he was too well-respected to be in a relationship with a person like me.

The following hours proved me right.

He didn't text.

Didn't call.

Avoidance at its finest, but I willingly—*gladly*—repaid the favor in kind since the entire affair embarrassed the fuck out of me. Who the hell was I thinking I could land a man of such standing? Someone as highly respected as Sutton Forrester?

I made it through the day by finishing painting Dad's house with music blasting to keep my mind from spiraling and contacted the realtor.

Tuesday, we did a walkthrough and talked numbers, deciding on an open house Saturday and Sunday.

With nothing to do on Wednesday, I stayed in bed until close to noon and drank coffee from The Moose rather than walking downtown past the station for one of Kel's scones and a latte. I drove down to Berlin to do a little shopping and ate at a restaurant's bar by myself, ignoring the guy who'd hit on me.

Thursday, I slept even later, my mind nose-diving to the point I didn't even want to get out of bed, but Gram called, telling me DJ had gotten in trouble at school. Kurt hadn't been able to leave work, so she'd picked up her grandson and had taken him back to her place since she couldn't get a hold of his mom either.

I agreed to hang out with them, try to get the boy out of his petulant funk, as she'd called his attitude.

DJ sat on the couch, arms crossed and scowling when I arrived at Gram's.

"Good luck," she whispered and left us alone, heading to the kitchen to make us a batch of chocolate chip cookies.

"What's going on, buddy?" I asked, ruffling DJ's hair and sitting beside him.

He jerked away from me, but wetness filled his eyes.

"Gram said there was some trouble at school," I said. "Want to talk about it?"

"Why? So you can be like Dad and tell me how I need to *wise up or else?*" The kid even made quotation marks with both hands.

I sagged into the couch. "I would never say something like that to you."

DJ hung his head, a tear sliding down his cheek. He sniffed and swiped his shoulder over his face. "Austin said my dad's trying to steal his mom from their family."

I had no fucking clue what the hell he was saying.

"I called him a liar and punched him in the nose."

I had to admire DJ for sticking up for his dad even if the asshole didn't deserve his son's loyalty or love.

"Dad's gonna be pissed that I got in trouble—won't even care that I had his back!"

Unsure what to say, I tugged DJ into my side, and he huddled close, reminding me so much of myself when clinging to Sutton in my childhood that my throat tightened, and I had to blink against threatening tears.

We sat in silence together, and I wished I had the

perfect advice to give DJ, but all I knew how to do in the face of danger was freeze like a coward. At least I now had control over my bladder unlike when I'd been a kid.

"Want to try to defeat Dr. Eggman?" I suggested a distraction.

"Yeah!" DJ hopped up to turn on the TV and Xbox. "Dibs on Sonic!"

"I'll be Knuckles," I said with a chuckle and settled in to keep DJ's thoughts from the day's not-so-great events or possible fallout after Kurt found out about the altercation.

Gram offered to cook dinner for us, but I told her not to bother, deciding to take DJ to Dig-In for a burger and fries. She opted to stay home—the cold made her bones ache—so the two of us boys drove downtown and parked in the lot.

DJ scooted on antsy feet to the diner's red door, chatting about the boat he'd built on Roblox while at his mom's over the weekend. His detailed descriptions about redeeming codes, getting gold, and using portals baffled me, but the excited waving of his hands instead of tucking into his food a short while later kept a smile on my face.

Jamie walked in halfway through our dinner, screeching my mind to a halt like a needle over a vinyl.

Sutton followed, and like he wore a honing device, his head snapped our way, gaze landing on my face. As usual, I couldn't read a single one of his thoughts because he didn't react to my presence. Of course, he'd seen my car out front, but I had no such heads up and couldn't help the jolt that ripped through me or the widening of my eyes before I could settle myself and fix my own mask firmly into place.

DJ spun in his seat to see what had caught my attention. "Chief!" He waved, ants in his pants again.

A gentle smile curved Sutton's mouth for the boy as he

lifted his hand in return, and I couldn't help the jealousy that snaked through my guts.

Stars lit DJ's eyes when he turned back around. "I'm going to be a cop just like Chief Forrester when I'm older," he said, grabbing a fry and dunking it in ketchup. "I'll put bad guys in jail where they can't hurt anybody."

"Cops are the best thing ever," I said, fighting to keep my attention on DJ as Jamie and Sutton sat at the opposite end of the diner. Awareness of Sutton being in close proximity caused the hairs on my arms to stand at attention, even if he ignored me as I attempted to do with him. "They're protective," I whispered past the tightening in my chest. "Helpful. Kind."

Everything I had always wanted but couldn't have.

Worm.

Whore.

Clearing my throat, I took interest in the few, cold fries on my plate and the tomato I'd removed from my burger and left beside the limp pickle.

"Dad said Chief's a punk," DJ continued, "but he had too many beers that night. I know he didn't mean it."

Ever the faithful son making excuses for his asshole father.

"He talks all sorts of bullshit when he drinks," DJ continued, and I didn't bother chiding him for the swear word.

I understood Gram's reluctance to move to Florida, her concern for DJ not having someone in his corner like she and Sutton had done for me.

If she decided to go—I would stay. Even if my heart shredded every day from having to see the chief while out and about downtown.

The door opened again, letting in a blast of cold air, and

I glanced up to find DJ's dad scowling and scanning the restaurant. His focus landed on our table, and he attempted to walk our way, face growing more thunderous with every step.

I cowered into my seat, eyes locked on the man whose instability suggested he'd been at the bottle, the frown furrowing his brow and red-rimmed eyes promising shit was about to get ugly. The sensation of things moving too quickly slammed into me, but I couldn't control my brain or body as he stumbled to a stop beside our table, hands fisted at his sides.

"That's *my* son!" he slurred, and all I could do was stare up in horror at the man who looked like he wanted to smash my head between his meaty palms.

"Hey, Dad," DJ said, his voice wary, limbs still for the first time since entering the diner. "What are you doing here?"

"Did you hear me, you fucking fag?" Kurt hissed rather than acknowledge his son, leaning down to get in my face.

My breath exited my lungs in a rush, and I cringed deeper into the booth.

"Dad!" DJ slid off his bench and tugged Kurt's arm, pulling him upright. "That's not a nice word! And Jimmy is my friend! I heard Gram on the phone say he's a good influence on me."

"Fucking groomer," Kurt sneered, ignoring his son. "You need to stay the *fuck* away from my boy, you hear me? Don't give a shit what Mom says—you keep your filthy hands off him!" He grabbed hold of DJ's wrist, and the boy winced.

Adrenaline raced through my blood, causing my heart to palpitate and extremities to tingle. A lack of oxygen made me lightheaded, and I swayed in my seat.

I saw bruising on my arms from harsh fingertips. Felt

the sting of a split lip. Heard the ringing from having my ears boxed. Remembered the warm wetness when I peed myself while Dad beat on me.

"Kurt!" Sutton barked, coming to the rescue, but I was too far gone in my panic to appreciate him being a hero like he'd done for me countless times in the past.

A whimper slid across my lips.

Fuck you, Dad. I hope you're burning in hell.

Chapter 23

Sutton

I recognized trouble the second Kurt walked into the diner, but Old Man Ron's daughter Addy stepped in front of me, full tray of food in hand, blocking my view of the entrance. Considering Kurt's son was sitting with Jimmy, I expected him to head their way.

"Thanks." I smiled up at Addy as she set my burger in front of me.

"Enjoy, boys!" she chirped at us and headed off to the next table to check if they needed anything.

My gaze shot across the restaurant.

Kurt towered over Jimmy, shoulders bunched, fists hanging low. Anger vibrated off him, and I found myself on my feet as he grasped his son's wrist in a vice grip.

"Addy, call Mary Walker—tell her to get down here ASAP," I ordered, moving past her.

"Yes, Chief." Addy scuttled toward the kitchen, sneakers squeaking on the laminate floor.

Jimmy, blank-eyed, as though reliving every moment of physical abuse from his father, cowered in his seat.

Heat erupted inside me, and I strode forward, pulse

thrumming and muscles quivering. "Kurt!" I hollered, and the man stumbled around.

Red-rimmed eyes met mine, the scent of booze leaking out of his pores. "This doesn't concern you, Chief," he sneered, giving me his back again.

"You cause any sort of ruckus in my town while drunk, and you better believe I'll be stepping in to make sure things don't get out of hand," I warned, my hand falling to the butt of my gun on instinct.

"Got what I came for—my kid," Kurt snarled over his shoulder. "Order that fairy over there to keep his hands to himself and to stay away from my son, or so help me God..."

Ignoring Jimmy's trembling form in my periphery didn't come easy when all I wanted to do was wrap him up in my arms and assure him everything would be okay—if he would even allow me to hold him like I used to.

"Did you drive over here, Kurt?" I asked, needing to stay focused on the task at hand. My body tensed, ready for whatever shit the drunken fool might pull. "Because last time I checked, you no longer had a license."

Kurt glanced out the diner's front windows overlooking the gravel lot. "I'm not stupid, Chief."

"Then what's your truck doing out there?" Jamie asked from behind me, and my shoulders lowered slightly at the knowledge he had my back.

"Friend drove me—he's at Pedro's picking up a sub."

Sure he was.

"Keys." I gestured with my hand.

He eyed me. Glanced out the window again as though weighing his options.

"Don't make this uglier than it already is." I spoke quietly, my tone conversational and unthreatening. "You know you don't have a leg to stand on, so just give 'em over.

Your mom will come pick DJ up, and Jamie can run you home since you've clearly had too much to drink. I'll bring your truck along in a little while, all right?"

Kurt hesitated another minute before slapping his keys into my outstretched palm.

"Come here, DJ," I held out my other hand, and the boy sidled away from his dad, who released him without argument. The boy tucked himself against me. "Jamie?"

"Let's go, Kurt." My son motioned Kurt toward the exit, and the drunk asshole thankfully shuffled from Jimmy's booth without a fight.

I released a heavy exhale, my hand tight on DJ's shoulder. "You okay?" I asked once the door shut, leaving the restaurant in stifling silence. I could feel every set of patron's eyes, their ears straining.

"You're my hero."

My heart ached over DJ's whispered words that sounded too damned familiar. I glanced at Jimmy.

He still huddled in the booth's corner, arms wrapped around himself, eyes glazed over as though lost in the past.

A quick scan of the half-full restaurant revealed every gaze plastered on us as I'd expected. I waved my hand. "Go on back to your meals. Show's over."

Murmurings slowly broke out but not loud or intrusive.

I crouched in front of DJ. "You head to the kitchen with Miss Addy. She's going to dip you up a scoop of ice cream while we're waiting for Gram to come get you."

"Yes, sir!" Tears wet DJ's eyes, but he saluted me and took off through the swinging door.

Turning toward Jimmy, I found him mute and unmoved.

Yet another asshole dad had created tension in my town —Kurt had triggered Jimmy, and I wasn't sure what to do.

The desire to be a better man and therapy had helped heal Mr. Henderson and Chaz's relationship, but if a problem wasn't openly acknowledged, change wouldn't happen. The town's lone accountant was evidence that even the worst people could turn their thoughts around and better themselves. Jimmy's focus on nurturing DJ like a big brother, showing kindness to a boy who he wasn't even related to, proved the same.

There was so much more to Jimmy than met the eye, and I yearned to know everything in his heart and mind, learn if I had maybe been wrong in assuming the outcome of getting involved with him.

I'd seen glimpses of his true self here and there, enough to whet my appetite for another taste of his sweet surrender. Right now, the boy needed me more than ever, even if he didn't recognize the truth. But I didn't want other townsfolk watching us like a bunch of rubbernecks, desperate to gobble up the next bit of gossip to spread around to their neighbors.

At least no one sat at the table backing against his, so we had a little space for privacy.

"Jimmy?" I kept my tone low, hoping to ease him gently from whatever nightmare he relived.

He blinked a few times, sucking in a rattling breath. A full-body shudder shifted him on the bench before he straightened. "Wh-Where's DJ?" he asked, his voice haggard as though he'd been crying for hours.

I held his gaze, pouring all my concern and encouragement from my eyes. "Safe in the kitchen with Addy."

"K-Kurt?" He still clutched his arms around his body.

"Gone. Jamie took him home. He can't hurt you," I assured him with the firmest tone I could muster. "Won't ever if I have any say on the matter."

Jimmy's chest seemed to collapse, and he swallowed hard, his stare dropping to the table.

"Jimmy."

He shook his head, slipped out of the booth, and stumbled for the exit.

"Jimmy!"

The door closed behind him, and heaviness settled in my chest, tugging my chin downward until I closed my eyes. I stayed put, reminded yet again that I wasn't wanted. No longer needed even for soothing his nerves.

The kitchen door swung open, and I turned to find Addy sticking her head out, checking if the coast was clear.

Lips in a grim line, I strode toward her, digging a few bills from my pocket to cover both Jimmy's and my bill. "Thanks for looking out for DJ."

"Of course, Chief," she whispered, accepting the money with shaking fingers. "Mary should be here—"

"What trouble has Kurt caused now?" Mary grumbled, shoving into the restaurant. She clutched her cane in a white-knuckled grip, eyes blazing as she shuffled my way. "If I could still take him over my knee, Chief, I promise I'd set him straight. Should have done more of that when he was younger."

"Wasn't your fault, Mary," I assured her quietly, leading her to an empty booth by a touch to her elbow. "He's a grown-ass man who's making his own choices—poor ones for sure."

She sat, and I perched on the bench across from her.

Concern lined her face, her eyes wary. "Was he behind the wheel?"

"According to him, no. He said his friend drove him down here."

Her lips pressed tight briefly. "Don't believe a single thing that boy tells you. He's full of lies and deceit."

I didn't bother arguing. "He spewed some homophobic bullshit, Mary—I won't put up with that in this town."

Her gaze narrowed as though momma bear had awoken —and not for her son. "What did he say?"

"Called Jimmy some not so nice names."

"In front of DJ?"

I nodded.

"I'll whip that boy's ass!"

Leaning onto the table, I held her blazing stare. "Think he would be open to going to therapy? Mr. Henderson has become a changed man because of it—might do Kurt a world of good."

Mary shook her head. "Unfortunately, no. I've already tried to talk to him about getting some help, but he's stubborn as his old man was. There won't be any change in his heart or mind until something terrible happens. I'd thought the DUI would be enough but clearly not."

I hoped Mary's prediction about her son's behavior didn't come true. The "something terrible" lay in the back of my mind, and I kept my fingers crossed that whatever it might be took place outside of Pippen Creek, far from my jurisdiction.

Chapter 24

____

Jimmy

Sutton texted to check on me. Again.

Tossing my cell onto the mattress beside me, I stared up at my rented room's ceiling, thankful as fuck the Coles had soundproofed the walls at The Moose's Muse. Silence surrounded me, same as it had Thursday when I'd returned from Dig-In and lost my shit.

I had cried myself dry, my nose a runny mess, my screams muffled by the pillow beneath my head. My reaction to Kurt at the diner had embarrassed the fuck out of me. Revealed to every single person in Pippen Creek's diner how broken I was inside.

I couldn't imagine the gossip about my weakness spreading up and down Main Street.

Poor little boy didn't know how to deal with his emotions. Couldn't stand up for himself in the face of a bully's verbal attack. Froze in the face of danger. Took off without thanking their beloved chief for stepping in to save the day.

Couldn't even find the gumption to look out for DJ when his dad had gotten handsy and hurt the boy either.

Worthless coward.

My face burned and throat tightened over what Sutton must think of me. I'd proven how much of a child I still was, and I hated myself for it.

Since returning, I had been triggered a handful of times, which had nearly flattened me, reminding me that I wasn't any more cured of my childhood trauma than I'd thought while living in Boston.

Being away from where I'd endured unimaginable pain had made it easy to distract myself, set my emotions to the side where they wouldn't be bothersome. With every passing year, I'd thought I was healing—days passing, distance, and all that shit.

But nope.

I continued to be controlled by fear responses deeply ingrained in my psyche.

Coming back here had been a mistake. A whim that had landed me in a pile of shit I'd been desperate to leave behind, revealing my deepest insecurities to people— someone in particular—I'd hoped to prove my worth to.

The open house later this morning had better end with a bid so I could get the hell out of this town and focus on finding a sense of peace I'd experienced in Massachusetts. But, I expected my reawakened nightmares would follow me no matter how much distance I put between myself and the past.

Maybe I would move to Washington, the farthest west I could go.

Spend a few months abroad, even. Tour Europe and immerse myself in history of those who had suffered before me.

Would running away again be the answer I searched for though?

I could hear Dad in my mind calling me a fool, and growling, I tossed the blankets off and climbed from the bed. A hot shower and little bit of pampering were in order since I had about two hours before the open house began. While I hadn't been invited to hang around and witness the hordes of people checking out the house—dreaming about the numbers—I was going to park a bit down the road and watch, fingers crossed.

I'd originally planned to hang with DJ at Grams, but after Kurt's homophobic slurs, I agreed with Gram's suggestion I stay away for a bit. We'd spoken on the phone Friday night, and I'd bawled my eyes out, her attempts to soothe me appreciated but ineffective.

She'd had it out with her son earlier in the day while DJ had been at school, and she threatened to cut him off and out of her life completely if he didn't agree to get some help. He'd supposedly started AA meetings after the DUI and some other program that would allow him to get his license back sooner, but she'd told him he needed therapy too.

Didn't we all?

But no way in hell would I subject myself to reliving what I'd been desperate to escape for more than half my life. I wondered if Kurt was in the same headspace as me, which allowed a bit of empathy for the man.

Didn't make the thought of running into him again any more tolerable, that was for damned sure.

My cell dinged as I descended the stairs to the lounge.

Daddy McDreamy: **Good luck today.**

I huffed under my breath, grumbling. Why couldn't Sutton leave me the hell alone?

Because he cared, just like he did every other goddamned person in Pippen Creek. It would be best to remember I wasn't special.

"Good morning, Jimmy!" Kendra called from the front desk as I hit the landing.

"Morning." I cast her a quick smile even though I didn't feel an ounce of joy over the new day. My face probably revealed that truth, but I couldn't rouse a single fuck to give of my mask slipping.

"There's a fresh pot of coffee and some goodies from Scone Haven this morning. I didn't have time to bake muffins."

Kendra made the best banana chocolate chip muffins *ever*, and some mornings, I'd been seen smuggling an extra to my room to save for a nighttime snack.

I sweetened my coffee and nearly swooned at the sight of Kel's orange cranberry scones. Two found themselves wrapped up in a napkin and tucked into my hand as I approached the front desk.

"Open house is today," I told Kendra, cradling my to-go cup in my other hand.

"While I hope you get an offer, I'll be sad to see you leave us," she said, her tone definitely downcast. At least no pity shone in her eyes. "It's been a pleasure chatting with you every morning."

Guess she hadn't yet heard about the showdown at Dig-In the other day. Thankfully, she'd been back in the kitchen when I'd stumbled in with tears coursing down my cheeks and hurried up to my room on Thursday.

"I'm not sure when I'm heading out of town, but I'll let you know when I do." I doubted I would stick around until the closing. That could take a month or two depending on a bunch of variables. I wouldn't subject myself to more of this misery while waiting to scribble my name on a bunch of papers.

"The room is yours for as long as you need it," Kendra assured me.

A few hours later, I sat in my idling car at the end of Dad's street. While a handful of people had done a walk-through of the house, my phone sat silent in my clammy grip. No bids yet. It was too early for me to fall into despair, but I couldn't help how my chest attempted to cave in on itself. Fatigue settled in my limbs, exhaustion in my bones, causing my eyes to sting.

Would I ever be free of this damned town and its bad memories?

Was peace even possible?

My cell rang, jolting my heart into my throat, and I swallowed hard, fumbling with my phone. I recognized my realtor's number, but that didn't lessen the rush of adrenaline or the thrum of my pulse.

"Hello?" I squeaked.

"Great news, Jimmy!" The guy's chipper tone said it all.

Shoulders relaxing, I closed my eyes.

Two bids.

Two *fucking* bids.

Shaky laughter left me as I hit end to hang up a few minutes later, giddiness causing my hands to tremble.

"It's five o'clock somewhere," I declared to my car's interior before turning in the nearest driveway and heading downtown.

Frenchie's had just opened, so I pulled in and parked, my steps lighter than they had been in days. Not even the thought of gossip over what a coward I was would keep me away from a celebratory glass or two of wine. I would leave my car and walk back to The Moose if I got too buzzed. It was time to let loose and celebrate the first bit of good news I'd so desperately needed.

"Welcome to Frenchie's!" Iris called out with a wide grin when I stepped inside.

Only a handful of people sat at the bar, and the sight of Babs, Chief's secretary, at a far table stalled out my lungs for a few seconds. She was the gossip queen, and while I usually would have loved to sit and hear all the dirt about shared acquaintances, wariness crept through me.

She smiled, friendly as could be, waving me over to sit with her and Coach Bernard, her husband.

Whatever actions I took would be repeated to Sutton, and while he'd hurt me, I still found myself wanting to please him. Be a good boy.

Ignoring her would probably be frowned upon.

There was no way in hell she hadn't heard about the Dig-In incident, and I slid onto the seat beside her, trying to brace myself for the inevitable grilling for information, the delving into my emotions over the matter.

"Afternoon, kiddo," Babs said, rubbing my back with a soothing motion, her gaze filled with warmth and concern.

My smile wobbled at best, but at least I was able to relax into the chair.

"What can I get you?" Iris asked, her eyes as sparkly and bright as ever as she approached the table.

"A glass of pinot noir, please."

"Anything to eat?"

"Nothing for now, thanks." I wanted the wine to hit my empty stomach and give me a decent buzz before I fed my body the fuel I needed.

"I heard from a little birdie that you did a great job fixing up the house," Babs said once Iris walked off to retrieve my drink.

A slow exhale of relief over her chosen topic allowed my

shoulders to unhitch even further. "It looks a lot better than it did when I left town, that's for damned sure. Just found out two offers came in during the open house this morning."

"Congratulations, and I'm not surprised. Property out here has been going for a mint," she said, stirring the thin straw in what appeared to be a Cape Cod.

"Interest rates are low—it's a seller's market," Coach Bernard said, lifting his beer as though toasting what was a sure thing. "You'll get top dollar."

I couldn't care less about the money, since I had more than enough already in my bank account to see me through the next ten years if I chose a frugal lifestyle. Which, considering my childhood, I knew how to do like a pro. My days of acting like a hole for hire were over, which meant no more gifts to myself like my BMW.

But I was okay with that, was all done with cold transactions that didn't fulfill what felt like a massive crater inside my soul. I'd hoped for Sutton to offer the connection I craved, to help heal the hurt I'd been lugging around with me from childhood, but I was too much—or not enough, more like it.

Nothing but a worm.

Setting aside depressing thoughts was easier than usual thanks to joining the town gossip for a drink. While I sipped my wine, Babs caught me up on the Pippen Creek going-ons then we returned to property values, how Pippen Creek Pond lots had been a hot item the previous two to three years. Out-of-owners had been flocking in, trying to escape the bustle of the city to live a simpler lifestyle.

The Coles had been one such family, bringing along their adult son, Christian, who'd been hired at the fire station.

Mention of him opened another can of stories about Dexter, Sutton's best friend, and how whenever he shared a room with Cole, sparks flew. A hint of violence simmered between them, Babs swore with a twinkle in her eyes, but a whole lot of lust too.

She looked forward to the day those two firemen got their hands on each other and extinguished the sparks between them. I hoped they burned themselves to the ground then found a way to rebuild in order to do it all over again.

Melancholy crept back in as Iris handed me a third glass of wine.

We'd been sitting at the table for a few hours, during which time I'd had a plateful of wings and a basket of fries. Not exactly a good pairing for my favorite wine, but the food hit the spot and silenced my growling stomach.

A dozen or so people had also flocked in since I'd arrived, another group packing in for after-dinner drinks. I'd become downright comfortable while sitting with Babs, chatting on occasion with others as they paused to say hello.

"So what are your plans after you sell?" Babs asked.

"Welcome to Frenchie's!" Iris hollered yet again as the door behind me opened, letting in a blast of air smelling of fallen leaves and woodsmoke.

In my mind, my future remained as dark as the inch of wine left in my glass. "There's nothing left for me here, so..." I shrugged.

She glanced over my shoulder. "You sure about that?"

Babs's tone hinted at devilry, but I didn't look over to see who had walked into the bar behind me. I could feel his presence as though Sutton had laid a hand on me. An immediate craving tore through my body, causing the hairs on my arms to raise and my pulse to kick into high gear.

I didn't want the reminder of him turning away from me the other morning but couldn't help myself. Longing for him, the merest hint of his attention, shifted me in my seat.

My gaze clashed with Dex's dark eyes rather than the concerned hazel ones that scanned the bar's far side. Dex stood between me and his best friend, and with a grin, he slung his arm over Sutton's shoulders.

A burning sensation in my chest caused my face to heat, and I muttered a few curses under my breath, eyes narrowing at the asshole teasing me.

"That's what I thought."

I tore my focus off the two men heading to the bar to find Babs smirking at me with a knowing grin.

"What." I muttered, not exactly asking a question while slumping in my chair and grabbing up my glass to suck down the last of my wine.

"He's running scared, Jimmy." Babs leaned into my space, her tone low and eyes intent. "Don't stop your pursuit—he needs you as much as you've always needed him."

Shit.

If anyone had insider info into what was going through the Chief's head, it was the woman he spent almost every single day with over at the station.

"Grab hold of that pissiness you better believe Dex caused on purpose, and go claim your man, Jimmy Riley."

Liquid courage...a blessing or a curse, time would tell.

I pushed up onto shaky legs, and Babs nodded with encouragement.

If Sutton turned down my last attempt at trying to talk him into me, I would be leaving Pippen Creek in my rearview soon anyway.

The truth did little to comfort my lack of high hopes,

but I was stubborn if nothing else. I would hold my chin up and walk away with tears streaming down my face and a barely beating heart inside my chest.

My lips never having tasted the one man who'd made me feel any semblance of peace.

Chapter 25

Sutton

Dex was handsy as fuck, snagging my focus and suspicion as he led me toward the bar with a firm steering of his arm over my shoulders.

A quick scan to the left revealed Christian Cole at the bar's far end, which clued me in on what my best friend did.

Shaking my head, I sat on the stool Dex had led me to. "What the hell is up with you two?" I asked after Iris poured us both a beer.

"He's an arrogant know-it-all. Cocky shit who needs taken down a peg."

That wasn't anything Dex hadn't already told me. "Sounds like someone I'm well acquainted with," I said, a smile in my voice.

Dex muttered a curse my way before sipping his beer.

"Just fuck him already and get it out of your system," I suggested what I'd said dozens of times already, picking up my beer.

He clunked his glass back on the bar, lips downturned. "He's the last man I'd stick my dick into."

I almost snorted my mouthful of beer across the bar top. "All you do when he's around is stare at his ass."

Dexter had nothing to say on that matter because I didn't lie.

"He's refusing to drop his bid for the job I deserve," Dex grumbled. "Trying to wear my ancient ass out and force me to quit. Says I'm getting old."

"You've got what? Eight years on him? Not much of an age difference if you ask me." A hell of a lot less than the years between me and Jimmy.

Dex glanced at the mirror behind the bar, and a grin split his face. He rubbed my sagging shoulder with a weird, lingering touch.

"The fuck?" I muttered, jerking away from him. "Haven't you figured out manipulation isn't going to land you into Christian's bed?"

A throat cleared behind me.

"Hey, kid," Dex said to the mirror as I turned, a shot of adrenaline racing through me at the sight of scowling blue eyes filled with murderous rage.

"Not a fucking *kid*," Jimmy muttered at my best friend.

Dex held his hands up in mock surrender, making it abundantly clear what he'd been playing at since we'd walked into Frenchie's.

He'd seen Jimmy upon entry when I hadn't because the way he'd steered me after I stepped in behind him.

Bastard.

I finger tapped the bar in annoyance as my clenched jaw began to ache.

"Dex was just leaving," I stated through gritted teeth, the command in my voice more than a hint while spinning my stool to face my best friend.

"I was?" Dex attempted an innocent voice, but his smirk betrayed him.

Jimmy continued to glare at him, giving off possessive vibes that sent blood rushing to my groin.

A jolt of hope caused my breath to bottle up in my chest. "Yes, you were. Are. *Leave.*"

Chuckling, Dex slid from his stool. "Mission accomplished," he murmured and sauntered toward the bathroom.

This bit of manipulation I wouldn't complain about because he'd gotten me the attention I'd been trying to gain.

In my periphery, I watched Christian set down his beer and follow after Dex, but I couldn't tear my focus off Jimmy's slender form as he perched his plump ass on Dex's vacated stool. Mere inches separated our knees, but I kept still rather than shift forward on my seat to touch him like I longed to do.

Baby blues latched onto mine, the raw emotion in them yet another gift to my aching heart.

"Why haven't you texted me back?" I asked, keeping my voice low since people bracketed us in on both sides. "I've been worried about you since that run-in with Kurt."

"I don't want a hero, Sutton," Jimmy said, brow still furrowed. "I'm not some little boy in need of a savior anymore."

"I never believed you were—and you're all man, Jimmy. I've been well aware of that fact for years."

He stared at me, the wrinkle between his troubled eyes slowly smoothing out.

"I thought we shared a pretty special moment on Sunday. More connection than I've felt with anyone—ex-wife included," I said, determined to be vulnerable even if he refused to be in return. "But you walked out of my place like you got what you'd wanted and had no further use of me."

So much for that relaxed expression. A dent marred his forehead again. "Because you went to shower off the stench of me without a backward glance. No different than a paying customer!" He kept his voice lowered, but the hiss, the hint of pain in his voice, hit my gut as if he'd hollered the words.

Jesus fucking Christ, I had messed up. So many assumptions had cost us what could have been precious hours. Growing together. He'd given me vulnerability, and I hadn't considered his emotional state while trying to protect my own.

I'd been the selfish one this time.

Fucking bullshit pasts had influenced us both, and that shit needed to be taken care of so this didn't happen again.

"I'm sorry," I said, imploring him to believe me. "I got caught up in my head, imagining you sashaying away from me at the end of this. Then you used the flirty tone of voice you do when trying to manipulate me—just hit me the wrong way, making me fear the worst."

Jimmy nodded as though he understood. "That side of me always comes out to play when I'm uncomfortable."

I flinched at his word choice, my eyebrows drawing together. "I made you feel *uncomfortable* while we were—"

"No!" Jimmy shook his head, eyes wide. "No. *After*," he emphasized with a soothing voice. "I didn't know what to expect, and I was flying higher than any kite, waiting for a burst of wind to rip through me and send me tumbling to the ground."

I could see the picture he'd painted of his emotions and shifted closer in my desire to connect with him. Our knees bumped, and his breath caught as though feeling the same electrical zap to his nerve endings as I did.

We stared at each other, his skin flushing, my fingers tingling to touch his warm, soft flesh. Pull him toward me. Hold him. My heart beat heavy in my ears. Frenchie's and its other patrons faded in my periphery as I focused on the alluring, needy boy peering at me.

Maskless.

A heady desire radiated from his eyes. "I got two offers on the house."

My shoulders hitched, and my stomach turned to a rock at his announcement that sounded more like a question. I swallowed audibly. "Will you leave town after the closing?" I asked, my tone already broken from yet again assuming the worst.

He lifted and dropped one shoulder, gaze never shifting off my face as though hoping I would answer for him. I opened my mouth to tell him exactly where I wanted him.

A clattering of plates jerked my focus from Jimmy's expectant face.

Someone had knocked their dinner off their table.

A quick scan of the bar's interior revealed no sign of Dex or Christian. Were they still in the bathroom? Slipped out together without my knowing?

Babs raised her drink my way with a smirk and wink.

Iris glanced between me and Jimmy with an encouraging smile while drying a glass.

The warmth of Jimmy's knee against mine, the sweet scent of him wafting beneath my nose reeled me back in.

I'd swallowed down the bait he tempted me with, hook, line, and sinker, years ago. There would be no protecting my heart—he already controlled my desire. He *owned* me with his neediness.

I faced him head-on, mouth drying and heart racing. "Come home with me."

His pupils swelled, and he licked over his lower lip but without his usual cunningness. "Yeah?"

That was yet another question, not an answer. "Do I have to talk you into it?"

"No!" Jimmy rubbed his palms over his jeans and swallowed hard. "Just...uh...you're sure you want me?"

Insecurity bled from his tone, and I realized that I held the string to that kite tied to his heart as he did mine. My craving to acquaint myself with every facet of him tripled without an ounce of fear.

Uncaring I hadn't told many people about my being bisexual, I threaded our fingers together, hoping to assure us both that I had us well in hand. "I want every part of you, sweet boy. The good, the bad, and everything in between."

Tears welled in his eyes. "Even the ugly?"

God, this man made my chest ache. "There's nothing ugly about you, Jimmy Riley. You're beautiful inside and out."

He inhaled a shaky breath, a dazzling smile lighting me up like the first rays of sunshine after a dark night. "You're blind."

"I'm *observant*," I corrected him and continued, not giving him the chance to argue. "Ready for me to love on you all night long, baby boy?"

"Fuck, Sutton," he hissed, shifting on his stool. "Yes—a million times *yes*."

I stood, discretely adjusting my stiffening cock while pulling him to his feet and lacing my fingers through his, uncaring what others would think. I would finally have what I wanted, and Jimmy's happiness meant more to me than any supposed reputation I held.

"Took you two long enough!" Babs hollered, and more than one of the other patrons let out a whoop as we headed for the door hand in hand.

I guessed people had already been talking.

Heat rushed to my face, and I shook my head, exiting the bar without a backward glance. Let the gossips have their fun.

I was going to have mine with the man bumping against my side as we strode toward my Bronco.

"Mind leaving your car here until tomorrow?" I asked.

"Nope. It can stay until next week for all I care."

"I like the sound of that," I said, squeezing his slender fingers.

"Yeah?"

"*Hell* yeah." I tucked Jimmy into my passenger seat like he *was* a kid, and he didn't argue, letting me care for him like the sweet boy he was. I climbed into the driver's seat. "Do we need to stop at The Market for condoms?"

While we had to talk, no fucking way would this night end without me being balls deep in this man, hopefully experiencing the connection we both longed for.

Jimmy turned to face me in the dark, gaze searching in the light afforded us by Frenchie's sign atop the entrance. "My bloodwork before leaving Boston came back clear, and I'm on PrEP."

I nodded and started the engine, turning us toward home. "Haven't been with anyone since my ex."

"You've never..."

"No." I answered the pitiful truth of my sex life for the past decade. "I've done a little...research, but will you teach me how to please you if I don't get it right the first time?"

"God, yes," he whispered, breathless while fidgeting in his seat.

"Are you wearing lace panties again?" I asked, remembering how gorgeous he'd been in them when he'd been in my bed what felt like ages ago rather than days.

"Yeah—and they're already wet for you."

"Jesus, Jimmy." I gulped, shaking my head in attempts to clear it so I could focus on getting us back to my place in one piece.

My foot wanted to press harder on the gas pedal while pulling out of the parking lot, but I refrained for two reasons. One, as Chief, I had to obey the in-town speed limit law. Two, because we needed to clear the fucking air before I laid my hands on this boy.

"I believe it's safe to say we both made a few assumptions about each other," I said.

Jimmy angled to face me, his gaze warming me clear through to my toes. "I have a lot of shit in my past that tends to control my head—and body's—reactions."

I nodded, having seen evidence of both. "Understandable, Jimmy. You've been through the wringer and have gained maturity you lacked as a teen. The selfishness that used to rule you no longer does. I see evidence of your growth in how you care for Mary. Make yourself available for DJ—you're a good man, Jimmy, and no whispers from before should have the power to tell you otherwise."

He exhaled heavily. "Next you'll suggest I go to therapy," he mumbled.

"Nothing wrong with getting help," I argued kindly. "Jamie has. Chaz and his own father have."

"Don't want to relive that shit." Jimmy stated exactly what I'd expected. "Been trying to escape it my whole goddamned life."

I reached out, beckoning with my fingers.

Jimmy slid his palm against mine, sending a jolt of

desire up my arm, and I laced my fingers through his. "I'm sorry for thinking I knew your mind. For making assumptions about your intentions."

"Same," he whispered, and I tightened my grip. "And I'm sorry for being so...extra. Too much."

"Don't apologize for those parts of you," I stated firmly while turning onto my street. "You're a perfect fit. I want to give you all the attention and love you need."

"Love, huh?" His tone held a teasing lilt again, but I recognized the defensiveness now, the attempt to protect his heart.

"Well on the way, yeah." I glanced over to find his baby blues wide and vulnerable. "We've both have walls up, but in order for this to work, we need to be completely honest from here on out. Open our mouths if shit from the past starts to muddle either of our thoughts toward each other."

"I'd like that," he agreed with his soft voice I wanted to hear whispering against my ear every morning and night.

God help my soul, I was gone for this man.

Chapter 26

Jimmy

ell on his way, Sutton had said.

Fucking hell, I was *done* for, because yeah. I'd loved the chief since forever ago.

Sutton ordered me to stay put when he parked in front of his house, and I watched him circle the front of his Bronco to open my door like the fairy tale prince he was. Apparently, the time for talking was over.

He held my hand while walking me to his front door. In silence, he knelt to take off my shoes in the entryway. Laced his fingers through mine again to lead me to his bedroom, where he dimmed the lights to a romantic setting.

Shivers slid down my spine, my pulse racing beneath skin that felt exposed even though clothing covered my body.

Our heightening breaths sounded loud in the stillness, a sense of peacefulness surrounding me even though sexual tension raised the hairs on my arms.

Holding my gaze, Sutton brushed my wavy locks back, cradling my head in his hands. He stared at my mouth.

Old me would have flicked out his tongue to entice the man into finally kissing my lips, but I refrained, showing him I really could be a good boy for him. That I would attempt honesty as he'd requested in *every* way between us.

I wanted him desperately, but I could be patient and allow him to take charge and love on me however he wished. There was no doubt in my heart that he would give me everything I needed and more.

"So beautiful," he mused, rubbing his thumb over my lower lip to the ring in the corner. "Pillowy soft—pouty. Been dreaming about this mouth for years." A shuddered sigh panted his exhale over my face. "I've never kissed a man before."

Pre-cum seeped from my slit as my dick attempted to buck from its lace and denim prison. I would be his first kiss. His first fuck.

I, Jimmy Riley, would own those parts of Sutton.

My throat tightened, eyes growing wet over the gifts he wished to give me.

Sutton's gaze lifted, searching my face, a slight frown marring his brow. "You okay?"

"Better than." I breathed the words, my smile trembling.

He tugged on my lower lip. "Jimmy..." He snaked an arm around my waist and pulled me flush against him before grasping the back of my neck. "Hold still. Let me taste this luscious mouth."

Swoon. Fucking. City.

My knees went weak as he closed the distance between us, and I whimpered at the press of his lips against mine. We both panted, and being a good boy, I didn't move. Soft, gentle kisses peppered over my slightly parted lips from corner to corner, his tongue flicking over my piercing.

A low rumble in his chest caused my already thrumming pulse to throb in time with the ache in my balls.

He suckled on my lower lip, drawing it into his mouth, his tongue soothing over my flesh.

Weak knees caused me to sag against him, and I clung to his shirt with a death grip. Our hard dicks pressed tight, and I fought my lust to grind all over him like the needy whore I was—

No.

Sutton found me worthy enough to bring me into his bedroom, and I would *not* allow echoes from the past to take me out of the moment.

He slid his tongue into my mouth, exploring and tasting. Probing. Licking and sucking however the fuck he desired, and I let him carry me away from the shit in my head. Sutton had owned me since my teenage years, and almost a decade of needing this intimacy with him had finally come to fruition.

A slow retreat, a chaste press of his lips to my lip ring, and Sutton stepped back.

I whimpered, trying to chase after him because I wanted my tongue on that incisor, goddammit, but he held my upper arms in a firm grip.

"Stay still."

Swallowing hard, I stared up at him, nodding, hands dropping to my sides.

"Let me unwrap the gift of you," he murmured, gaze sliding down over me from the throbbing pulse in my neck to my toes curled from his kiss.

Butterflies fluttered in my chest causing a whine to rise up my throat.

"I've got you, baby boy."

I trusted him.

He gathered the edge of my shirt and tugged upward, encouraging me to lift my arms so he could strip my torso bare. A low groan rumbled in his chest as the material dropped to the floor, and he palmed my pecs.

"Love these," he murmured, thumbing over the rings in my nipples. He leaned down and licked, flicking the metal with his tongue as he'd done with the piercing in my lower lip.

I hissed, my balls tightening against my groin. "Keep at it, and I'll come from that alone," I warned.

One of his brows lifted as he peered at me. "Seriously?"

"Fuck yeah," I breathed. "Super sensitive there."

"I'll remember that for next time." Sutton knelt—fucking got on his knees.

For me.

A worthless worm so goddamned far beneath his station—

A sob caught in my throat, and I bit my lip to keep tears from slipping over my cheeks.

"Jimmy?" he questioned, looking up to study my face.

Swallowing hard, I nodded.

Sutton gripped my hips as though aware I needed to be grounded. "I want you," he declared, attempting to right all the wrongs in my head.

"Want you too, Chief," I whispered, my smile wobbling.

He might not be experienced with men, but Sutton knew how to open my jeans with deft fingers and slide the denim down my legs like *he* was putting on a striptease for *me*. His gaze never left my lace-covered cock while stripping my lower half, one leg then the other, socks and all.

"Jimmy," he murmured and nuzzled his face against my damp panties, breathing me in. "You smell delicious. My damned mouth is watering." He ran his hands up my thighs. "You shave your legs?" he asked, peering up at me again, pupils now dominating the hazel of his irises.

Lust hit me low, causing my dick to leak. "I've waxed my entire body so many times that hardly any hair grows anymore."

"Satiny smooth," he murmured, touching me from knees to waist but not where I needed him most. "Turn around."

I did as told.

"Jesus." Sutton gulped while lifting my cheeks and squeezing them. "I hope you own stock in these lacy boy shorts because holy fucking shit, do you make them look good."

I twerked my backside in his face—couldn't help myself.

He groaned and slid my panties down. Warm exhales ghosted over my cheeks, causing goose bumps to lift along my legs as he removed the scrap of wet material from my body.

Soft kisses pressed against each globe before he spread them wide.

"Of course you're beautiful here as well. Pink and pretty." Warm wetness laved over my pucker, and I gasped, falling forward to grab the edge of the bed.

"Fuck, boy." Sutton grasped my cheeks and kneaded. "You're gorgeous like this, bent over for me."

"Please," I croaked, trying to hold still and not shake my ass to encourage his exploration.

He gave me what I wanted as though knowing my mind yet again, long licks and probing tongue, flicking over my guiche piercing. Nibbling and sucking at my tender flesh until saliva dripped off my balls.

"Sutton—*please*," I begged, whimpering like the needy little—

He swatted my right cheek enough I flinched, the damned word I hated ripped from my thoughts. My dick loved the impact of his palm, even more pre-cum oozing from my shaft. Sutton yanked the comforter off the bed, tapping my backside a little more gently. "Up you go."

I crawled on shaking limbs and put my ass on display with spread thighs, chest on the mattress. Heartbeat pounding in my ears, I struggled to expand my lungs, fingers gripping the sheet beneath me.

Sutton hummed in appreciation at the sight I made with the deep arch in my spine like a cat in heat.

"While you look like an absolute treat like that, I want to see your eyes when I fill your hole with my cock."

"Fuck. Yes." I spun and flopped before grabbing the backs of my knees and pulling them to them to my chest.

"Such a good boy," Sutton murmured, his focus on my hole, hand squeezing his bulge.

Those *words*.

My heart fluttered.

"Lube up and shove that perfect dick inside me, Chief," I demanded, breathless for what only he could give me.

Sutton slowly unbuttoned his shirt and slipped it off his wide shoulders. Then he unbuckled his belt and jeans before sliding them to the floor and kicking them off. He stroked himself while peering at me in heady, thick silence that made my blood burn.

I clenched, winking my hole in attempt to get him moving and that perfect dick so far up my ass I could taste him in the back of my throat.

He groaned, shaking his head. "The things you do to me."

"I'm so empty—fill me up, Sutton. Need you." Zero trace of manipulation coated my pleadings. I simply spoke the truth.

His gaze darkened, and my dick tapped against my taut belly, ready to erupt the second he slid inside me. "Don't move."

I stayed put, lips parted as I panted, my skin hot and flushed.

Sutton rounded the bed, retrieved lube from the side table, and climbed between my spread thighs.

I bit my lower lip to stop from begging and whining for him to fuck me already.

He seemed intent on drawing this out, and I wasn't about to mess up his first time by taking over when he wanted to love on my body all night long. Smoothing his hands from the backs of my knees to where my legs met my groin, he hummed.

"Perfection."

Words of denial rose up, but I clamped my lips shut to stop myself from ruining the moment.

As though sensing my mind's too active state, Sutton lifted his focus to my eyes.

We stared at each other as he rubbed his thumbs up and down my taint, toying with my piercing. "Will you tell me how to make you feel good?"

I huffed a small laugh. "Just being here with you is like heaven, Sutton. You could get halfway in my ass, blow your load early, and it would still be the fuck of my life because it's *you*."

"I'm going to make this last, and I promise you'll be wrung out and wasted once I'm done with you." Sutton's declaration made my heart race. "The best thing about being my age is I've got stamina, boy, so hold on tight."

He settled on his stomach and licked from my pucker to my leaking slit, growling. "I could eat this ass all night long."

I choked on a moan that abruptly cut off when he shoved his tongue into my hole. "Oh God—fuck!" Clutching at the backs of my thighs, I tried to fuck myself on his probing flesh, but he clamped his hands atop mine and held me still.

He rimmed me for what felt like hours, slurping and groaning over how much he loved the musky sweet scent of my groin, the smooth, hairless skin he glided his tongue over. Once he closed his mouth around my cockhead, I was half out of my mind, delirious with desire, my balls tight and ready to erupt.

"S-Sutton," I gasped, finally grasping at his hair. "Too close."

He hummed around my length, playing with my goddamned piercing, his other fingertips trailing over my saliva-soaked pucker.

I tapped on his head when he ignored my warning. "You're gonna make me come."

Pressure—a finger slid knuckle deep into my ass.

"Fuck!" I convulsed, cum shooting up my shaft and onto Sutton's waiting tongue.

He swallowed, seemingly unconcerned about having a mouthful of bitter spunk. The man sucked. Me. Dry. Rubbed over my prostate he'd managed to locate, enticing me to give him every last spurt I had.

"God." I groaned, swallowing hard and gulping oxygen while going limp. My skin tingled as I lay spent, and euphoria lacing my system caused a grin to etch on my face.

Sutton slid his finger free and took another long taste of me from hole to slit.

"Fuck." I shuddered, a little too sensitive. He grasped

my shaft and gently squeezed, attempting to rouse me to life again. "Need a minute." I groaned as he tugged on the ring below my sac. "Sutton."

"Hmm?" He shifted upward, planked on an elbow, half-atop me while working my dick. His lips were swollen and red from the meal he'd made of me, and I clasped his whiskered jaw in my hands, tugging his face down. He smelled like me, and I whimpered.

"Kiss me."

He did.

Lazily and thoroughly, every gentle stroke of his musk-laced tongue inside my mouth shifting blood back to my groin.

And this time?

I didn't stay passive, letting him explore. Sliding my tongue between his lips earned me a groan from his chest, and I licked over that tooth that had always intrigued me, a reminder that no man was perfect, no matter how much he appeared to be.

"Such a good boy," he murmured against my mouth, and my chest swelled, flying like a kite.

But I didn't fear the crash and burn this time.

I clung to him and wrapped my legs tight around his hips, forcing his hand from my dick.

Sutton gave me his weight, sliding his arms beneath my shoulders and holding me while we exchanged exhales and slow, searching kisses. His hard cock pressed against my taint, and I moved, grinding myself against him.

His saliva had wet my pucker enough that if I could only scoot just so...get his tip against my entrance...

"Ung." I groaned along with him, bearing down to let him in—but he didn't push. Simply rested his thick cock-head against my hole.

A slow leaked exhale left his lips as he pressed his forehead against mine. "Lube."

"Don't need it," I assured him, but Sutton backed off, grabbing the bottle from where he'd set it on the mattress by my hip.

"You might enjoy the sting of being fucked without lube, but I want you wet. Soaked and so slick that I can sink into you without marring your beautiful face with a grimace."

My throat tightened, and I nodded, watching him as he dribbled lube onto his fingers. He circled my hole with two before pressing. Both digits eased in without difficulty, and yeah, he was right. Lube was the better option.

He gathered my shaft in his hand again while stretching me open, gentle, slow glides when I was at my wit's end again already. Biting my tongue, I let him have his fun as he added a third finger and eventually toyed along my stretched rim with his pinkie, teasing the hell out of me.

"Put it in." I pushed against him to prove myself capable of taking whatever he would give me.

"Mmm." He leaned down and kissed atop my heart but didn't penetrate me further. "Some other time. Need inside your little hole, Jimmy. Want to feel this heat swallowing my dick," he murmured stroking over my prostate.

"Fuck, Sutton—*please!*" I undulated, fucking myself on his thick fingers.

He sat back and slowly withdrew from my ass, leaving me empty.

I whimpered, and he made shushing noises while soaking his shaft with lube.

Flutters attacked my chest like a million butterflies, and I panted, licking over my lips to ease the dryness.

Shifting atop me once more, Sutton held the base of his

dick and lined up as I clutched at his ass with my heels. "Okay?" he whispered, pupils blown but full of concern.

This dear, sweet man.

I pulled him closer, holding his face again so he could clearly see the truth in my eyes. "Yes."

He pressed in, filling my ass, my heart, and my soul, with one slow glide that felt like coming home.

Chapter 27

Sutton

This.

Right.

Here.

I groaned, forehead against Jimmy's, luxuriating in how well he fit around me, how perfectly his body had welcomed me. Tight heat sucked at my granite-like cock as he clenched and released around my shaft.

While finally being inside him had my instincts roaring to fuck and mark him with my cum, I'd waited too long. Wanted to draw out this moment, make it last. Physically being one with Jimmy after fantasizing and dreaming about him for the past couple of years soothed me as much as it excited me.

I could sink my cells into his, become a single entity with him, and I wouldn't feel close enough to the sweet boy trembling beneath me. His hot skin rubbed against mine as he wiggled in attempt to make me move.

"Sutton—*please*. Fuck me already," he begged, fingernails digging into my shoulders.

Flicking my tongue over his lower lip, I finally backed out, then rocked forward again while licking into his mouth.

He groaned and shuddered.

"We've only just begun, sweet boy of mine," I murmured with a chuckle against his panting lips.

A sob ripped from his chest, and I clutched him tighter, gently loving on him with all my body, with every thought focused on showing him how special he was, how desired and appreciated.

He cried as I gently thrust in and out of his slick warmth, kissing the tears off his cheeks. "So good for me, Jimmy. Beautiful. Perfect boy." My whispered words caused more salty droplets for me to lick from his flushed skin.

Lust demanded I spur us onward toward completion, but I reveled in the act of slow lovemaking, the type of intensity where emotions ran high and drew us together. Connected our hearts as firmly as it did our bodies.

I closed my eyes and rested my forehead against his, burying my cock deep in his greedy clutches. "Never knew it could be this way."

"Need you, Sutton," he croaked, pressing his face in my neck, clinging to me.

"I've got you, baby. Always. Promise." Lifting onto my knees caused his hips to angle upward, and I added a snap to my hips I'd been holding back.

"Yes," he hissed, his heels clenching my backside, ass spasming around my girth. "Right there—Jesus, Sutton—right the fuck there."

I repeated the motion, watching his face.

A gorgeous grimace of the best kind of pain marred his brow. "Again."

I gave my boy what he needed, thrusting against his prostate until he shuddered beneath me.

He gasped, blinking up at me. Wonder filled his eyes, baby blues darkened with desire. "You're gonna make me come untouched, Sutton. Oh God—don't stop."

"Never." Our gazes held, the connection between us deeper than anything physical. "Soak us both—"

Whines rose past his lips as his dick throbbed, spurting wetness.

"Fuck yeah, just like that," I crooned, grinding against his prostate as his hole pulsed around me, creating a sticky mess between our stomachs. "So good for me, baby boy."

He shuddered, gulping and whimpering until the milking around my cock ceased.

"Fuck yes." I thrust hard a few more times to make sure his balls emptied.

"Sutton," he murmured, his grasp on my body relaxing.

Pulling out, I placed us both on our sides, tugged him against me, and slid my dick back home where it belonged.

He groaned, clasping his hand on mine atop his lower belly. "You're gonna *kill* me," he complained.

I hummed an agreement, nuzzling against his hair, kissing his neck. "You're going to give me another before I'm done."

Jimmy whimpered, shaking his head. "You already wore me out."

"One more, baby—I believe in you." I took his soft cock in hand, chuckling when he tried to escape me. "Tell me to stop and I will."

"Never!" He grabbed hold of my wrist, keeping my hand on his dick even though he had to be sensitive as hell. "Never. Don't ever stop."

I loved on my boy, whispered against his ear how

perfect he was for me, how much he pleased me—how badly I needed him, slowly coaxing his shaft to hardness again.

"Arch for me," I said, "help me stroke into you just right."

Jimmy obeyed, shifting slightly, and—yep. That was the spot.

His low groan, the shudder that rippled over his sweat-slickened skin, told me I'd hit the bullseye.

I gave over to lust, rutting rather than holding back this time.

"S-Sutton!" He cried out, my slamming hips causing him to stutter.

Grasping hold of his waist, I rolled him onto his belly and fucked him into the mattress.

"Yes. Oh God, your dick—perfect. Want to marry it." He continued to whimper gibberish while clutching at the sheets beneath him, head to the side, panting for breath.

Pink flushed his cheeks, his lips swollen from being bitten and sucked on.

He was beyond beautiful.

And finally mine—

My balls spasmed, and I thrust deep, burying my face in his neck as I did my shaft in his decadent heat.

He cried out beneath me, his hole clenching around my dick in pulsing tugs.

Spurts of heat shot through my dick, coating his insides, claiming him.

"Jimmy," I murmured against his slick skin before suckling and marking him outside as well.

The seed I'd been storing up for days eventually ran dry, and I rolled onto my side, keeping him against me, my dick still buried in his ass.

We lay silent while catching our breath, our heartbeats slowing. A sense of pride welled inside me for having accomplished what I'd set out to do—wear Jimmy's ass out until he turned pliant.

A mess of wet and tangled sheets rumpled around us, but I couldn't be bothered to separate our bodies and clean either of us up for a proper spooning. I'd gotten Jimmy right where I wanted him, and I wasn't yet ready to let him go.

Arms wrapped around his torso, I squeezed him tight.

A shuddering sigh rippled through his frame as he laced his fingers with mine atop his heart. "Hold me forever?"

"Anything for you, Jimmy."

I blinked myself back to awareness to find Jimmy breathing heavy in my arms where I'd tucked him. I had no clue what time it was, but the tip of my dick remained lodged in his ass as though reluctant to leave his wet warmth, same as I was the bed I vowed to myself we would share from here until death parted us.

The sweat between us had dried, so I assumed we'd slept for a while.

Having been roused to wakefulness also sent blood to my groin cradled by his plump ass cheeks.

Could he be any more delectable?

A hint of his musk coated my tongue, and I ground my hips against him, coaxing my semi deeper into his stretched-out hole.

I hissed, holding still while my dick thickened, the growth of my erection pushing into his guts. Rolling my hips brought me to full mast, and I groaned, biting where his shoulder met his neck.

Jimmy shivered and let out a pleased sigh, reaching back to grasp my hip. "Fill me up again, Chief. Want another load in my ass so I leak all day long."

"Jesus, Jimmy." His sleepy yet sassy tone was a shot of adrenaline to my bloodstream, his hole clenching around my shaft the perfect enticement.

And I thought I'd caught feelings on our first go-round.

There was nothing better than waking up with my dick tucked in heaven, having that part of my body make itself at home in his body while we'd slept.

I gave my boy what he'd asked for, managing to coax a few more spurts of cum from his balls along with mine.

We both groaned once finished, our bodies sweaty and sticky as fuck.

Somehow, I managed to get him into the shower, washed his exhausted form from head to toes, making quick work ridding my own skin of the evidence of our love-making before climbing out. He stood still and allowed me to dry him then swayed in place while I stripped the bed and remade it as quickly as possible.

We collapsed onto the mattress, and I pulled the comforter high around his chin as he snuggled against my chest.

He sighed, rubbing his face against my pecs. "Love that you're hairy."

"Love that you're not."

We cuddled in silence, and I expected us both to pass out, but his exhales remained steady, my fingertips trailing over his spine.

I shifted, sliding one of my legs between his so his soft cock and balls rested against my thigh.

He huffed an exhale. "My dad called me a whore after I

got caught with that boy under the bleachers. I went on to prove him right."

I frowned wondering where the hell that thought had come from. "Don't say that shit about yourself."

"It's true."

"Fuck that." I pulled him away from my chest so I could search out his eyes in the dimmed bedroom. "You did what you had to survive, and I won't ever judge you for that."

I could feel Jimmy's stare more than I could see his baby blues latched onto my face. "You really don't care that I've been passed around from bed to bed, used and discarded?"

"Nope." I yanked him back where he belonged, nuzzling against his hair. "You're sassy and sweet, bold and beautiful. There's a treasure beneath that facade you wear to protect yourself, and I'm enamored over the idea of rooting out every single facet of who you are."

Jimmy clung to me. "Could you be any more perfect?"

I had my flaws and plenty of them, but I kept silent, allowing Jimmy to believe whatever he wanted for the time being. We both needed to sleep.

Talking could wait.

Closing my eyes, I gave over to the exhaustion from making love and fucking with the small respite in between of what had only been an hour, according to the clock.

In the morning, I woke to find either Jimmy or I had moved during the night. I sprawled on my side facing him, same as he did with me, but space now lay between us. While I hated the distance of those few inches, I wasn't yet ready to disturb his rest.

Besides, he looked like an angel in the morning light pouring through the blinds. Glints of gold shone in his mussed hair, cheeks still pink from the night before, parted lips letting out tiny puffs of air with each exhale deflating his chest.

The comforter rested along his waist, allowing me an unhindered sight of the metal rings through his pink nipples.

My mouth watered for a taste, but I continued my perusal of his smooth, pale skin, noting the purplish bruise I'd left on his neck.

A slow smirk curled my lips, and I couldn't help myself. Had to brush a fingertip over my mark on him.

He was my sweet angel while asleep—but a devil when awake.

I loved how Jimmy kept me young and on my toes. Being in my early forties had played into my favor last night, allowing me to outlast and bring Jimmy pleasure three times before I'd found mine. Life stirred between my thighs as my mind replayed loving on him—his ass especially. Yet another first of mine he owned.

"You're staring," he murmured, a soft smile curving his lips even though his eyes remained closed.

"Damned right I am." I reached around his trim body to grasp his plump ass and tugged him closer, kissing his forehead.

He nuzzled my neck and snuggled lower, rubbing his face against my hairy chest.

My heart beat heavier as he grew handsy, reaching between us to weigh my morning wood.

"Perfect cock," he whispered as though to himself, and I let him have his fun and his opinion because he, of all people, had every right to judge a man's anatomy.

Why didn't that truth flood me with jealousy?

Dexter would be ripping mad over thoughts of another guy touching Cole—and they weren't even fucking.

Or maybe they were. Who the hell knew where they'd gotten to last night.

"Hungry, baby?" I asked, soothing a hand along the curve of his spine.

"Mmm. Yeah, I think so." He wiggled from my grasp and shifted deeper beneath the comforter, intent on my cock.

He swallowed me whole, taking my dick down to the root.

"Jesus, Jimmy." I groaned, clutching at his hair. "I'd meant food—breakfast. Eggs and bacon. Pancakes or waffles—whatever you want."

"Mmm," he hummed before popping off. "Right now, I want this juicy cock."

I gave over to his lead and let him edge the ever-loving shit out of me before I filled up his belly with my cum.

Chapter 28

Jimmy

We spent all day Sunday in Sutton's bed, learning each other's bodies and partaking in the fuck fest of a lifetime. He'd promised stamina, and he didn't lie. The man had control like none I'd met before, wearing me out so I slept through the night.

Monday, he called off work, and although we rested more than messed around, I'd never felt more fulfilled in my life.

Boston became a blur in my past, and Dad's usual negative whispers never once roused in my head.

While I didn't believe in magical dicks that could heal a man's trauma, Sutton's proved to be pretty damn close.

I blinked my eyes open to sunlight peeping over the horizon through Sutton's bedroom window. The warmth of his chest against my back and his possessive arms clutching me close kept me lax and lazy even though my bladder urged me to move. Sighing, I snuggled against him, wiggling my hips the slightest bit to rouse his morning wood.

"Minx," he muttered sleepily, his breath hot in my hair.

But, he ground against me, his cock thickening between my thighs.

He'd already warned me he had to go into the office this morning, and he'd insisted I stay put. He wanted me to be the first thing he saw when he walked in after his shift, so who was I to argue?

He groaned while nuzzling my hair and slowly thrusting his uncut cock over my taint and balls. "Mmm," he hummed and tweaked at my nipples. "Need to wake up like this every morning."

My heart fluttered, and my eyes stung. Yet another suggestive comment that he hoped this for real—for good. "Want to fuck my hole, Chief?" I asked, tone breathy.

"Don't have lube on hand. Don't feel like rolling away from you to get it either." He rubbed between my thighs, and I squeezed them, giving him more friction.

"Too much?"

"No. Fucking hell, baby." He squeezed me tighter. "Wrap your soft hand around your cock—get yourself off with me."

I did as told, a shudder rippling through me at his whispered, "Good boy."

We stroked together, but I needed wetness to get me there. I spat on my palm and reached between my thighs to give Sutton more than his pre-cum to ease his thrusts. Spat again so fucking my hand wouldn't chafe.

"Yes," I hissed, angling my head to reach his mouth, morning breath be damned.

Our tongues tangled in a messy kiss, and I curled an arm behind him, holding onto him as tightly as he did to me.

Pre-cum leaked from my slit, making for an even easier glide over my hard flesh, and Sutton's persistent poking over my piercing and along my balls caused my eyes to roll.

"Gonna come, Sutton—fuck, you know just how to stroke me."

He hummed his agreement, sliding his hand up my torso to pluck at one of my nipple rings.

"Fuck!" I bowed, cum shooting from my shaft, spurting over the sheets.

"Jesus, boy." Sutton thrust hard and held still, his shaft pulsing, wetness soaking my balls. "So good...why is this so goddamned *good*?" He shuddered, and we clung to each other as our hearts slowed.

Sutton shifted away first, and I lay like a limp noodle sprawled out on his mattress while he retrieved a warm, wet cloth. He cared for me with tenderness, ridding my skin of sticky cum. "I hate having to leave."

I nodded and sat as he headed for his closet.

Drawing my knees to my chest, I stared as Sutton slowly covered his body with briefs, his uniform, and eventually his belt, holster, and badge.

He was the epitome of strength, a champion worthy of worship.

I love you.

Finished, Sutton turned to face me, and I swallowed down the words wanting to escape my lips. His hazel eyes flitted over my body atop dirtied sheets, but he didn't speak. Didn't move.

"What are you doing?" I asked when the silence grew too heavy.

"Memorizing the sight of you in my bed so I have something to look forward to returning to."

Heat singed my skin, and I flicked my tongue over my lower lip.

He hissed, narrowing his eyes. "Don't tempt me, Jimmy."

"But—"

Sutton held up his hand, chin lifting. "Be a good boy for me."

"Can I touch myself when I get lonely five minutes from now?"

A low curse caused me to bite back a smirk.

"Yes, but no coming," Sutton stated in his chief's voice as he turned for the door. He paused, glancing over his shoulder, the desire in his warm gaze causing my dick to twitch. "And send me pics. Want to see how needy you are for me all day long."

Groaning, I slumped to my side, cursing as he walked away.

Was this my life now?

I star-fished, avoiding the damp spots from earlier, giddiness making my chest flutter.

Never before had I wished to be a pillow princess, but if Sutton insisted I stay put, edge myself for him, and welcome him home with a stretched and needy hole, I was game.

I showered and toyed with my ass, getting a pic of two fingers shoved as deep as they would go. Breakfast came next where I took a teasing picture of me licking a sausage link. Then I switched out the sheets and sprawled atop the clean ones to get a full-body image, my cock leaking a droplet of fluid toward my belly button ring.

Sutton never responded, but I could imagine the curses he spilled from his lips whenever his cell dinged with an incoming photo.

I kept at it all day, making myself at home in his house but not going so far as to be nosy and search through every drawer like I really wanted to do.

By late afternoon, I'd grown bored and curled on the couch, cell in hand, scrolling through social media I rarely visited. I wore one of Sutton's button-down shirts and nothing else.

An old image of the Elite gang slid through my feed, and I realized I hadn't checked in with Sean, my former boss, in far too long. When I'd left, he'd told me to keep in touch even if I didn't change my mind about returning to work for him and his brother.

I pulled up his number and settled into the couch.

"Jimmy!"

"Hey, Sean."

"How are things?" he asked, his tone happy as always. "Still up north?"

"Yeah. the chief of police isn't going to let me leave anytime soon." Wishful thinking perhaps, but a boy could hope.

Sean snorted a laugh. "Can't keep from getting into trouble, huh?"

"It's what I do best."

"I have a feeling this means I need to stop putting off deleting your profile from Elite's site."

I wanted to be sorry but couldn't find an ounce of regret in my heart for following the winds of change. "I'm done with my whorish days," I said, and Sean snorted again minus the laugh.

"Nothing wrong with sex work."

"Never said there was, but I'm ready to move on." From Dad's voice, from the trauma of my past, from the insecurities that had held me back for far too many years.

"We'll miss you, Jimmy, but I get it. If you ever decide you want to return..."

"Thanks, Sean. You guys were family when I didn't have any."

He was quiet a moment. "Take care of yourself, Jimmy,

and if you're ever in Boston again, let me and the boys know."

"Will do." I hung up a few seconds later, soaking in the stillness of Sutton's home. Peace lay like a weighted blanket, as comforting as his presence even though he wasn't here. That whim and daydream had brought me home, and I was ready for my new beginning to unfold. I closed my eyes, exhaling until my lungs emptied completely.

The sound of the front door unlocking pulled me from sleep, and I rubbed my eyes, cursing beneath my breath.

I wouldn't make it to Sutton's bed where he'd requested I be without him seeing me hightail it from the living room.

So much for being a good boy.

Sudden inspiration had me shifting onto my belly, yanking his shirt up to my waist, leaving my ass bare, one foot hanging over the couch's arm so he wouldn't miss me. Hands beneath my head, I feigned sleep, my pulse thrumming like mad in my ears.

Keys clinked while being hung up.

Shoes dropped.

Soft footfalls started toward the stairs but paused.

"Jimmy?" Sutton called quietly, and I held my breath, trying to stop my eyelids from fluttering. He approached on near silent feet, and I felt rather than saw him round the couch by my feet. "Fuck," he murmured, and I heard what sounded like his palm rubbing over whiskers.

I struggled to contain my smile.

"Little devil," he whispered, running cool palms up the backs of my thighs, causing goose bumps to rise. He bit my ass cheek, and I yelped, flinching. One hefty swat on my other cheek had me jolting the opposite way.

Sutton stood beside me, yanking at his belt buckle— ripping the leather free from his slacks. Heat radiated from his narrowed eyes, and my backside clenched with need. Would he use the belt on my ass? I wouldn't mind more handprints, but—

He tossed it aside, thank fuck, and I licked over my lower lip, staring as he shoved his pants and briefs to the floor. His hard dick bobbed up to slap against his belly, and I moaned, my fingers twitching to grab him.

"You teased me all day long."

"You asked for it," I whispered as he worked his shaft, pulling upward to bead wetness at the tip.

He hummed agreement, smearing the slickness down his length.

"Can I suck you?" I begged, offering him my best puppy eyes and pout.

His gaze narrowed but not with annoyance over my being coy. "Do you want it or need it?"

"Need," I rushed to say.

Chuckling, Sutton sat beside me, spreading his thighs wide. "Get me good and wet, boy, then settle that pert peach of an ass over my dick where it belongs."

I scrambled to obey, dropping to the floor, salivating and so damned empty I whimpered.

"That's it." Sutton hissed, hand on my head as I sank over his shaft until his cockhead slid into my throat. "Fuck, boy—so perfect for me."

I swallowed before backing off, licking and suckling, then taking him deep again.

"Fuck yes."

Saliva dribbled past my stretched lips, dripping down his balls to the couch below.

More than wet enough.

I climbed onto his lap and grabbed his base to hold him upright.

"Okay?" He checked in, hands grasping my waist.

"Yeah," I breathed my answer, popping his cockhead through my ring. "Been stretching myself all damned day." I groaned, sinking as far as I could go. "Still have lube inside me—was ready for you."

"Shit, baby." Sutton's grip tightened as I lifted and sat fully atop him, settling my ass against his groin. "Jesus." He groaned, facial hair twitching as though he clenched his jaw.

Smirking, I leaned forward, draping my arms on his shoulders. "Good, Chief?"

"More than," he stated through gritted teeth.

"Mmm." I swiveled my hips, dragging his length through my pucker and shoving it in again.

"Fuck." Sutton tipped his head back against the couch and met my gaze.

All trace of teasing left my face as he held me captive, emotions alive and thriving in the energy between us.

"Sutton," I whispered, and he ran his hand up along my spine, pulling me closer until our mouths clashed.

So much for showing him how well I could ride a dick.

We fucked like a couple of horny rabbits, the buildup from the day taking us to the edge in mere minutes.

"Jimmy. Baby." He clasped my face, devouring my mouth, hips lifting to meet my every downward thrust.

"Fill me up," I whispered against his lips, and he grunted, shaft pulsing deep in my ass.

I erupted hands-free, wetness spurting between us.

We both laughed once I slumped against his chest, his wide palms rubbing soothing circles over my back.

"Better than I fantasized."

"Yeah?" I asked, my exhale hot against his warm neck.

"Mmm." He reached down and slid a finger inside my

ass alongside his softening cock. "Couldn't stop thinking about your hot hole all day long. Couldn't wait to bury myself inside you where nothing matters but making you come."

Heart light, I clenched around him, and he groaned, holding me tighter.

Chapter 29

Sutton

I longed to hide away and never come up for air, but real life kept interrupting the bubble of happiness I'd gotten caught in.

Jimmy made my head spin, oftentimes causing me to forget about reality. He distracted me in the best ways possible, and I fell harder with every passing minute we shared together.

He finally agreed to get a change of clothes from The Moose, and while I wanted to tell him to let the room go and stay with me until he decided his long-term plans, I feared opening a can of worms I wasn't yet ready to face. The discussion of what we were doing and for how long hovered like storm clouds, suggesting slashing rain would leave me out in the cold. Alone.

But the warmth of his lithe body, the twinkle in his eyes, the laughter we shared while doing a whole lot of nothing made it easy to ignore the warning signs.

I didn't want anyone intruding in on our peace, but I'd already invited Jamie and Chaz over the following Sunday afternoon. While my son and I had chatted throughout the week at work, I'd kept personal shit on the quiet side, but Babs clued him in on the fact that I'd taken Jimmy home with me last weekend and that he hadn't left.

Jamie showed up with a six-pack of Stella, Chaz on his heels.

I gave them both a bear hug, clapping them on the backs while welcoming them in out of the cold. October had brought in fall and the smell of decayed leaves and woodsmoke from those around town heating their home with firewood.

My favorite time of year and the best scents to fill a man's nose.

"Jimmy's still upstairs getting ready." I made the excuse for my perpetually late lover.

"It's just us," Jamie said, putting the beer in the fridge.

"Yeah, but he likes to get all pretty for me," I said, heat settling in my cheeks.

Chaz snickered. "And you love it."

"Goddamned right I do," I said with a sigh and smile.

Jamie clasped my shoulder but didn't speak as Jimmy flounced down the stairs.

"Hey," he said, breathless, blue eyes sparkling, pink staining his cheeks. He'd slickened his lips with gloss, and I drank in the sight of him in his tight maroon crop top and skin-hugging jeans.

Jamie and Chaz greeted Jimmy while I swallowed back a groan, turning toward the oven.

I seriously needed to get to the store for groceries, but those damned distractions lately...

Pulling a tray of frozen dough rolls from the oven, I glanced over to find Jimmy reaching into the overhead cabinet for bowls and plates.

His shirt rode high, teasing me with a swath of pale skin,

his plump little ass making my mouth water more than the scent of fresh bread and the stew I'd had in the crockpot all afternoon.

My son and his fiancé made Jimmy feel as though he belonged, neither of them asking any hard questions or prodding into personal territory.

It was Chaz opening up after dinner while we sat in the living room that erased any questions in my mind over their acceptance of Jimmy possibly becoming a part of our small family.

"My marriage had been on the rocks even though I denied it," Chaz said when the topic of how he and Jamie got together came up.

I hadn't shared the heartache Chaz had gone through with Jimmy since it wasn't my story to tell, but reliving it now hurt almost as much as it had the day I'd gotten the call about his wife being in the car accident that had claimed her life.

Chaz left out the part about her being pregnant with another man's child, and I had to respect him for looking after the memory of her even though she'd betrayed him. But he hadn't been an angel either, having an affair with Jamie behind her back.

Tears slid down Jimmy's cheeks over the story, which caused my heart to ache.

I tugged him against my side, kissing his temple when Jamie did the same to Chaz. "Anyone want another beer?" I asked, pushing to my feet. The heavy talk had made me thirst for another.

No one did, so I went to the kitchen, popping the cap and enjoying a cooling swallow.

"Did your dad ever blame you for your mom leaving town?" Jimmy's quiet question drew me up beyond sight of the living room entryway. While I wasn't one for eavesdropping, I wondered where this topic had come from—or why Jimmy would even wonder such a thing.

I hadn't told him the reasons behind Darla's taking off, so he'd probably only heard the gossip that had littered the town.

"Never," Jamie stated. "I had nothing to do with her shitty choices. Neither did Dad."

I moved into the room, settling into my vacated seat.

Jimmy sidled up against me, and I gave him the arm around his shoulders he needed. He studied his hands clasped atop his lap. "My mom died in childbirth. Dad said it was my fault." Tears laced his voice, but none of us interrupted. The fact he opened up with my son and Chaz with what he'd already shared with me caused gratitude to swell in my heart and made me hopeful our future was cementing together.

He explained why he'd always gotten into so much trouble with the law and, most importantly, why he'd never returned for his father's burial.

Chaz nodded, understanding in his dark eyes. "Ever consider talking to someone?" he asked, leaning forward, elbows on his knees.

Jamie ran a hand over his back, gaze glued to Chaz's profile, the love in his eyes no longer causing jealousy to stir inside me.

"No." Jimmy cleared his throat. "I—I don't mind you guys knowing, but to really dig deep and relive that shit?" He shivered and shook his head.

I soothed my fingertips along his forearm that used to be streaked red from scratching.

"Talking about it hurts," Chaz stated, glancing between us, "but it's so goddamned worth it. Even though you can't set shit right with your old man, you can still figure out a way to move on. Find peace of your own."

Jimmy shrugged, and I recognized him shutting down.

"I don't have anything but a couple of Snickers bars for dessert," I announced.

A soft laugh left Jimmy, and he glanced at me, his eyes wet.

"The first time I remember seeing Jimmy was a hot September afternoon," I said, not taking my eyes off him. But rather than focus on the trauma that had brought me to the Riley home all those years ago, I told the tale of how we had shared a chocolate bar, how over his teenage years we'd often done the same.

I'd kept a box in my bottom desk drawer for the nights he hung out on the jail cell cot and a few stashed in my glove compartment during the cooler months for whenever I ran across him in town.

Twice in the week we'd been holed up I'd tasted chocolate and peanuts on his tongue, licking deep and trying to swallow him whole.

That led to the story of two best friends lying beneath the stars, admitting their feelings for each other, which brought up the topic of Dex.

"I have a love/hate relationship with that man," Jimmy muttered, his forehead dented. "He's so...*handsy* with you. Can't stand it." His pout had me chuckling.

"He's a manipulative little shit," I stated, eyeing him with an intentional stare.

Jimmy huffed, crossing his arms with a petulant scowl, and I chuckled.

"He got what he hoped for though, didn't he?"

"What's that?" Jimmy muttered.

"The two of us together."

Jimmy whipped his head toward me, studying my face. "That's what he's been playing at?"

"He wants what's best for me," I assured Jimmy, hoping he would read between the lines—that he would offer me something in return.

"Well." Jamie shot to his feet, pulling Chaz along with him. "We've got that...thing to take care of at home, right?"

Chaz gave him a strange look, and Jamie rolled his eyes. "Oh. That." Chaz huffed a laugh, and five minutes later, Jimmy and I were alone in the entryway after seeing the two boys off.

"So," I said, checking out the bumps of rings through Jimmy's nipples. "Want to share that Snickers bar?"

"Only if you'll let me suck the cum from your balls afterwards to help wash down all that sugar."

I grabbed Jimmy, tossed him over my shoulder, and strode toward the stairs. "Deal."

Chapter 30

Jimmy

"You haven't been around much the last two weeks." Gram's observance made my face grow hot, and I glanced around her consignment shop that hadn't changed much in my long absence. Because of her declining health, she'd shortened the hours of operation and rarely went in to oversee it herself, leaving one of the two high school seniors who came in after school and for the weekend hours in charge.

I'd swung by a few times since my return, but she was right.

For almost two weeks, I'd been living in absolute bliss in a haze of orgasms, snuggles, and candlelit dinners where Sutton showed off yet another thing he excelled at—cooking. If he hadn't already owned every inch of me, I'd have fallen in love with him for his ability in the kitchen alone. I was all heart eyes and butterflies.

This man took *care* of me, and I couldn't get enough of him.

"You're digging, Gram," I said, "but there isn't much to tell."

"Liar. You and Sutton are the talk of the town right now. We all know you're shacking up with that man." Zero trace of judgment laced her tone, and I grinned, my chest swelling. "Mmm hmm," she hummed with a smile. "I see what you think about the gossip."

"It's nice that everyone is aware he's no longer on the market," I stated, wishing I had more evidence of that truth than us just fucking like a couple of sex-craved teenagers.

"But for how long?"

My smile faded, and Gram eyed me for a few brief moments from where she rested on an armchair behind the counter I leaned on.

"Has the chief made his intentions known?"

"We haven't labeled what we are, but both of us have kinda dropped hints about wanting this for the long run." At least, I'd thought so. Was I reading into our conversations? Wishful thinking again?

Hell, every other topic other than what we were had been covered at length over the dinner table, while snuggled on the couch, or in bed after we wore each other out. From our favorite bands to bucket lists to the one place we could vacation given the chance. Both of us had suggested a tropical island full of sun and sand, but he'd imagined a beer in hand while I envisioned a fruity drink with a cute, little umbrella.

Sutton had to put in quite a few hours at the station but enjoyed a few personal days to lounge around naked with me, answering whatever questions I had for him and vice versa. I learned about his upbringing here in Pippen Creek, his time away from his wife and child while at the police academy.

The day after Jamie and Chaz's visit, he told me all of the details about his ex-wife, who'd cleaned him out and almost ruined his name. While zero hint of bitterness laced his tone while speaking of her, I held enough jealousy and anger in my heart toward her for the both of us.

Thank fuck for the forgiving people of Pippen Creek, who adored their chief regardless of the money she'd stolen from the town.

"So you're sticking around, I take it," Gram stated rather than question.

"Until he no longer wants me."

Gram huffed, tapping her cane on the floor twice. "That man hasn't dated since Darla left, which says a lot. He chose *you* after over a decade of being single, Jimmy. If anyone changes their mind in this relationship, it won't be him."

"*I* certainly won't.." I frowned as goose bumps rose along my arms, causing the hairs on my nape to stand on end. "You're well aware I've had my heart set on him since before I was too young to even know what people got up to in a bedroom. Once I figured that out, I was even *more* determined to get him right where I wanted him."

She smiled.

Arms slid around my waist, tugging me against a hard chest and loaded police belt, and I melted, glaring at Gram. She'd set me up in the hopes I would make a declaration he would overhear.

The front door had been propped open this afternoon because of the abnormally warm October afternoon after a weeklong cold snap, so the bell announcing customers hadn't alerted me to Sutton's arrival.

So that was what had shifted awareness over my skin— I'd thought it was annoyance over her suggestion that I'd end whatever was going on with me and the chief.

"You did that on purpose," I accused her as Sutton kissed my neck.

Gram chuckled and didn't bother arguing. She was almost as bad as Babs at playing matchmaker.

"How's Kurt?" Sutton asked her while holding me tight. I clasped my hands over his atop my stomach and tipped my head back onto his shoulder.

"I think he's depressed, Chief." Mary's eyes flooded with concern. "He's lost weight and has been isolating himself lately."

"How's the drinking?"

"He's attempting to get sober but is fighting me on seeing a therapist. Says it's too late for him."

Sutton made a noise beneath his breath. "And DJ?"

"That boy is doing okay, but he misses his friend." Gram's lips pursed for a moment before she continued, her eyes troubled. "He doesn't understand why his dad doesn't care for him spending time with Jimmy. What does it matter who a man loves?" Gram shook her head. "I'm working on him though, and I promise to call you the minute he gets his head screwed on straight."

Hearing again that I wasn't welcome to visit with Gram while DJ was in her care caused my heart to ache. I missed my little buddy, shooting hoops, playing Xbox, and laughing like I hadn't done as a kid. I'd never had such a friend when I was younger, and being with DJ felt like I got to experience the childhood I'd always wanted but was denied, thanks to Dad.

"Let me know if I can do anything to help, Mary," Sutton said, stepping to my side and taking my hand in his as though he felt my pain.

Gram smiled as our fingers laced together. "I'm happy for you boys. Don't let anyone steal this from you."

Conflicting emotions weighed on me as Sutton and I stepped outside beneath the sinking sun. Joy attempted to bubble up inside me over being out with him in public, but disappointment over the entire Kurt/DJ affair kept popping it with a sharp pinprick.

Rather than tuck me into the cruiser parked alongside Gram's shop, he tugged me toward the grocery store next door.

I'd walked the distance from his house north of town since the day had been so gorgeous. Probably our last taste of summer before the cooler season set in for good. I had told Sutton my plans but had intended to make my way over to the police station once I'd finished my visit with Gram.

"You skipped out early?" I asked, bumping into his shoulder as we ambled along the sidewalk.

"Yes. Thought we could go to The Market and restock the fridge and pantry we've emptied. Need another box of Snickers too."

I grinned, joy winning in that moment. "Our first official outing together, and it's one of the most mundane, domestic tasks—I love it."

Love you.

Sutton's gaze softened as he glanced over at me as though hearing the words I'd left unspoken yet again. We shared the sentiment in silence, our eyes saying everything we both felt deep in our souls. I could have sworn he'd held the same emotion in his heart and mind every time he slowed down to make love to me.

No man had done so before.

Every sexual encounter in my twenty-seven years had been nothing but transactional. There had been no sharing of something other than orgasms, no fulfillment emotionally.

With Sutton, a connection had blossomed, and his

constant affection and attention was like rainwater and sunlight to the flower of my soul.

My chest lightened, and I snuggled into his side while heading across the parking lot toward The Market's automatic doors.

Gram thought I might be the one to walk away from this.

I huffed beneath my breath.

No. Way. In. *Hell*.

Beside Sutton was where I'd always longed to be, and no person, no circumstance, would ever make me run again.

The grocery store's doors swished open before we got there, Georgie Ellis slipping out with a cart full of stuffed, brown paper bags.

His family owned the only grocery store in town, and according to Gram, he'd been delivering to the elderly and too-busy townsfolk for years.

"Hey, Chief!" he called, his dark eyes bright as always, his grin infectious. "Jimmy."

"Hi, Georgie," I returned his greeting with a small wave.

Of course, Sutton paused to help Georgie load up the delivery van. We saw him down the road before our hands came together again like magnets.

"He's a good kid," Sutton said, and while I didn't know Georgie that well, I trusted the chief's discernment.

Georgie was cute as hell, I'd give him that. Had a great body beneath those snug jeans and form-fitting Henley. I bet he had the single folks in town salivating at his feet, but I had found my prince and didn't have wandering eyes or a cheating heart.

I hadn't lied to Gram about my desire for the man ambling along beside me up and down the aisles while pushing a cart and telling me what to retrieve off the shelves.

While The Market was no full-sized store with all the bells and whistles of the bigger shops down in Berlin, they carried most of what the townsfolk needed, and I happily filled Sutton's cart to overflowing. He hadn't been lying about the empty fridge and cabinets.

Other than his going to work, we had pretty much been holed up in his house, neither of us wishing to leave the world we'd wrapped ourselves in. Better than any vacation I'd ever taken—not that I'd gone farther south than Rhode Island before, but I'd driven up to the Maine coast twice on a whim. None of those excursions had gifted me the possibility of a happily ever after like this trip though.

"Coming back was the best spur-of-the-moment decision I've made," I said while standing in front of the ice cream freezer section instead of doing what Sutton suggested and picking out what flavor I wanted.

"I agree wholeheartedly." A smile rested in Sutton's voice, and I grinned, going for Rocky Road. He grabbed my ass and gave it a healthy squeeze when I put the box of ice cream in the cart.

A throat cleared, and we both turned.

Kurt Wallace.

My hackles raised, and Sutton stiffened slightly beside me.

"Kurt," Sutton greeted him, tone wary.

Like Gram had said, Kurt appeared gaunt, his posture saggy. Purple bruise-like smudges sat beneath his eyes.

He nodded at both of us before glancing around uneasily. "I, uh...wanted to apologize for the other day."

The cramp in my stomach eased, shoulders lowering as

hope sprang to life inside me. I was dying to spend time with DJ again and wished Kurt would allow me to do so.

"I'd been drinking." Kurt made the excuse I expected, checking out our clasped hands. His brow indented for a split second but immediately smoothed out. "Didn't, uh, mean those words I used. Hard liquor makes me a different man." A too-quick smile flitted over his lips before a small huff left him, sounding like a depreciating laugh.

Neither Sutton nor I spoke as he continued to avoid our gazes.

"Trying real hard to stay sober," he continued, shifting on his feet and moving the basket he held from one hand to the other. He scratched the back of his neck while staring at the floor. "Mom said you're a good friend to DJ, Jimmy. He doesn't have many of those."

"He's a sweet kid," I stated quietly. "Deserves the world."

Kurt nodded and glanced up at me but quickly looked away again, shoulders up near his ears. "Sure does. Now more than ever. You, um...can hang out with him over at my mom's whenever you want. He really misses you."

The tension in my chest eased, my throat tightening. "Thank you, Kurt."

He turned to go.

"You need anything, you let me know," Sutton stated, his tone firm. Commanding.

Kurt paused to nod. "I will, Chief." He half-waved over his shoulder before shuffling away.

Sutton watched after him, eyes narrowed, a deep furrow between his brows—being his usual suspicious self.

"That was...unexpected," I said.

"Mmm," he hummed an agreement and nodded toward the front of the store. "Ready to head home?"

Home.

My feet barely felt the tiled floor. "Yes."

We snuggled on the couch after dinner, Sutton propped in the corner with me sprawled between his spread legs. His arms wrapped around my core, keeping me tight against his chest, a lone fingertip absently rubbing along my stomach where my shirt had ridden up. Food Network played on the TV, the *Chopped* show Sutton got a kick out of watching. I enjoyed just sitting against him and soaking up his attention that held no intention of fucking, the TV nothing but noise in the background.

Affection from Sutton was life-giving. Affirming. I could stay right there without issue, but I could admit to feeling *too* much like a pillow princess. While I wouldn't turn away a sugar daddy of love since I had plenty of money for the time being, a sense of purposelessness had begun to creep into my mind some of the longer days while waiting for him to return.

"I should get a job," I said to see what Sutton would think.

His finger on my stomach stilled for a second before starting up again. "I'll admit, I haven't thought about your financial situation."

We hadn't discussed my bank account—one of the few, if not only, topics left uncovered in our lazy days together.

"I've got a lot of money in the bank, but when you're not around, I'm bored."

He reached for the clicker and muted the TV. "What would you like to do?"

I shrugged. "All I know is sex work, but that's no longer

an option since I quit Elite. Not that I was thinking of going back to it," I hastened to add in case he assumed I was missing variety of the dick sort. His was perfect, and I didn't want any other shaft to suck or fuck for the rest of my life.

Sutton didn't say anything, and my brain went straight into negative mode. Shifting slightly, I wondered if he thought about the guys who had access to me before he did. Twice, he'd had to reassure me he didn't care about my sexual history, but I didn't understand the lack of jealousy.

I considered Darla who'd had him first, and I grew hot and stabby, fingers itchy to knife a bitch for even looking at what was mine.

"What?" I bit out the word. "You seem mad about my past right now."

Sutton snorted and swatted my thigh. "Far from it, baby boy. I was thinking that all those men had you for an hour or two, but I get to have you in my bed every night. I'm one lucky man."

I slumped against Sutton's chest, not having realized my body had tensed. A heavy exhale rid my gut of its ugliness.

"Sorry," I muttered, closing my eyelids, telling myself I had to do better or Sutton would get sick of me. "Insecurities again."

He kissed the top of my head before grasping my throat to pull my face toward his.

I peered up at him with an odd angle to my neck, and the adoration in his gaze, the complete lack of any negative emotion caused my eyes to sting. "Kiss me," I whispered before he could speak, so damned needy for him that my chest wanted to crack open.

He lifted me, situating me atop his lap, and framed my face with his hands. "I wouldn't change a damn thing about you, sweet boy. Would move the mountains surrounding this town to give you whatever you need."

I didn't have the guts to speak up about how long I dreamed of him feeling that way toward me, and Sutton took my mouth, keeping me from begging for the word *forever* whispering in my mind.

I sank into him, wishing I could curl up inside him where no one would ever be able to tear us apart.

Chapter 31

Sutton

The days ran together, and I couldn't ever remember ever experiencing such contentment. No amount of angst around town, Kurt stumbling drunk off his ass again on Main Street and needing a ride home, or having to hand over a speeding ticket to a newly licensed driver could take away the lightness in my chest or the bounce in my steps.

Even when exhausted some mornings while heading into the station from having stayed up too late loving on Jimmy, the feeling of weightlessness remained. Jimmy claimed he was blissed out, and I agreed with his description.

Halloween was now only two weeks away, and my boyfriend? roommate? helped me decorate the front lawn even though I would be out on patrol that night and he would be handing out mini Snickers on his own. We'd driven down into Berlin for some extra skeletons and fake tombstones to prop up in the yard. We also had a massive bowl of candy, which both of us couldn't keep our hands out of. Every night, we fed each other tiny chocolate bars before kissing the sweetness left behind on our tongues.

Next year, I'd told him, we would be buying two bags earlier in the month because I couldn't get enough of him.

His eyes had lit up, and I'd thought about having the little chat about our future that I'd been putting off until after the closing on his dad's house in November.

I hoped he would stay. Move out of The Moose he hadn't slept in for three weeks, pack up all his stuff at his condo in Boston, and come home for good. I felt sure he desired the same but I didn't want to jump the gun or push him into making a decision until the responsibilities that had brought him back to Pippen Creek were taken care of.

"You about ready?" I hollered up the stairs, having already done so fifteen minutes earlier. The boy took forever to get pretty for me even though I told him every day he was beautiful to me sleepy-eyed, fresh out of the shower, or sweaty after playing basketball with DJ.

It was Friday night, and the football game for the week was at the home stadium south of town, so I'd expected Jimmy to primp more than usual.

"Two minutes!" Jimmy called, and I pulled my winter coat and the one I'd bought for him while we'd been on that shopping spree down in Berlin out of the entryway closet. I'd gotten him a navy-blue hooded jacket he'd turned his nose up at, but the freezing temperatures the past three days changed his mind about it not being flattering. The coat brought out the blue in his eyes though and kept his trim body warm, both wins in my mind.

He skipped down the stairs, cheeks pink, a light sheen of gloss on his lips, and my pulse thrummed, pumping blood straight to my groin.

I groaned, shaking my head and holding out the jacket for him to slip into.

His knowing wink and blown kiss had me fake glowering. "No teasing," I ordered. "I promised Jamie we'd be there tonight."

"Wasn't my fault you couldn't control yourself and we missed last week's game," Jimmy sassed while zipping up.

I lingered in checking my boy out from head to toes. He'd put on baggier jeans because I'd insisted on him wearing thermals underneath since his usual skintight ones wouldn't do a damned thing to keep the cold from his smooth skin. Wool socks and fur-lined boots covered his piggies, ugly troll feet, he'd claimed when I'd purchased them to ensure my baby boy stayed warm.

"Hat and gloves?" I suggested, and he grumbled something about messing up his hair that had taken an hour to tame.

I stood unmoved.

Jimmy rolled his eyes. "*Fine.*" He snatched the hat I'd lain out for him and jammed it atop his head, sticking out his tongue. "Happy now?"

"I will be later once your ass is properly reddened," I promised, tugging on my own beanie and grabbing the keys off the hook by the door.

"Don't threaten me with a good time, Chief."

"Mmm," I hummed, steering him out into the cold with a hand on his lower back.

We climbed into his BMW I'd started by remote a few minutes earlier.

"Thank fuck for heated seats," he said while buckling in.

The boy was spoiled. My Bronco didn't have a remote start or fancy butt warmers, so that vehicle was off-limits until at least May, according to him.

Even though breath fogged and noses turned red, the small set of bleachers at our town's football field was jam-packed as usual with faithful fans of our small school's team.

Jimmy sat huddled against me, my arm around his shoulders, tucking him in tight. He shivered but was a trooper in encouraging our high schoolers along with me.

Jamie was helping out again tonight since he wasn't on patrol. He caught sight of Jimmy and I front and center at the fifty-yard line while the boys had warmed up out on the field pre-kickoff.

Dex used to be my partner in crime at these games, but he'd declined the invite to go with me and Jimmy. Said he was busy.

Probably fucking Christian.

Dex had been cagey and secretive the few times I'd seen him lately, but I had my own full plate with this new...whatever it was between Jimmy and I. Dex and I would catch up eventually, and even though I'd been enjoying the hell out of having Jimmy by my side, I missed my best friend.

I hoped he played it safe both physically and emotionally while doing whatever he was up to with that Cole guy. He tended to get a little rough in the sack, had a definite kink for domination without the pain aspect. Cole didn't seem to be submissive in any way shape or form.

They would be incendiary, no doubt, and I kept my fingers crossed they didn't burn Pippen Creek to the ground once the gossip erupted into flames. Surprisingly, Babs knew nothing about the current state of affairs between the two men, so I was in the dark as well.

After our team's loss, we helped pack out Frenchie's. Jamie and Chaz had gone home rather than hang out, and while Dex and Christian were absent, The Moose's Muse owners were both sitting at the bar.

"Jimmy!" Kendra stood from her seat and hugged him,

squeezing tight. "I've been missing you!" She motioned toward the empty stool beside her, and Jimmy slid onto the seat.

I greeted them both and shook hands with her husband Harry before settling on Jimmy's other side.

Kendra leaned forward to see around him. "So you're the one making my favorite renter stay out all night."

She didn't ask a question, and I was well aware of the rumor mill's current focus.

"What can I get for ya?" Iris asked, keeping me from having to respond.

"Stella and a glass of pinot noir."

Jimmy squeezed my knee, and I slid my arm around his shoulders, reminding him with touch that I knew what he wanted and was more than willing and happy to provide for him.

"So your room is up for renewal on Monday," Kendra said, and I stilled, eyeing Jimmy in my periphery. "Seeing as how leaf peepers are hanging around, I'll have no problem filling the vacancy if you're ready to give the room up."

He glanced at me.

I turned so he would have my full attention, hating that this discussion might happen in a public place.

Baby blues implored me to answer Kendra's question for him as Iris set our drinks in front of us.

"Want something to eat, Chief? Jimmy?" Iris asked.

"I think we're good," I answered.

Iris ambled off.

"We'll swing by tonight to get the rest of Jimmy's things," I told Kendra, and she beamed, her eyes alight with excitement knowing she had a golden nugget to start sharing around town.

Jimmy relaxed at my roundabout way of speaking my

intentions toward him, a soft smile curving his mouth. I wanted to lick the taste of cherry off his glossed lips before probing my tongue inside to enjoy his natural sweetness.

"How's your son doing?" I tossed out as my dick twitched, ready for the focus to be elsewhere until me and my boy got home for the night.

Kendra cleared her throat and exchanged a long look with her husband.

"Anything I need to be concerned about?" I asked, hating the current of unease they both radiated.

Both were tight-lipped, and I wasn't about to probe for information on my best friend since he wouldn't appreciate me getting involved. He and Cole were grown-ass men. Unless their combative natures caused issues for the town, I would stay on the sidelines.

The Coles kept to themselves after shaking their heads in answer to my question, and Jimmy and I moved off with our drinks to mingle. We received a lot of attention, Jimmy got a few congratulations on the upcoming signing for his dad's house—and inquiries of his future plans. He claimed he was waiting to see where the wind blew, glancing at me when answering.

"Toward me," I informed him the second I buckled into the driver's seat a half hour later.

"Huh?"

I turned to face Jimmy, studying his half-shadowed face in the neon lights atop Frenchie's door.

"The wind you're waiting for," I reminded him, smoothing my thumb over the furrow in his forehead. "I'm hoping it blows you *toward me.*"

His eyes darkened, a slow, sly smirk curling the corner of his lips.

Shaking my head, I chuckled and started his car. "Don't

even go there," I muttered, knowing exactly where his mind had wandered.

"I can't *blow* you when we get home?"

Home.

That was the first time he'd called my house that word, and my heart soared.

I reached over and grasped his hand, lifting its back up to my lips. "Don't think you're escaping my promised hand-prints on your ass, boy."

He shuddered and squeezed my fingers. "I want it—want you."

I nibbled lightly on his knuckles while parking in front of Pippen Creek's only lodge. "Want you too, Jimmy, so let's do this quick because I can't wait to get you home where you belong, stripped naked on our bed and my mouth on every inch of your soft skin."

He groaned my name while adjusting himself. "You're mean."

"You're just impatient, but I promise I'll make it worth the wait."

"I trust you, Sutton."

My heart squeezed at the most honest words I'd ever heard on his lips, and I tugged him against me, kissing the top of his head before we climbed the stairs up onto The Moose's porch to gather his things and check him out for good.

Chapter 32

Jimmy

I stood beneath the hot spray, eyes closed, my entire body tingling from Sutton loving on me all night long. I'd had countless orgasms, the first time coming while draped over his lap, my backside littered with handprints I was quite proud of. Squeezing my ass cheeks while showering gave me another zinging sting from the lingering marks, but I didn't stroke my dick to the memory of how he'd taken me slow and sweet then hard and desperate.

Sutton knew how to use his cock to satisfy every craving he woke inside me on a daily basis.

"Delicious man," I murmured to myself, breathing in the scent of bacon and coffee he was making for me downstairs since it was Saturday and he had off work. "I'm one lucky boy."

Grinning and still flying high, I climbed out of the shower after having paid special attention to all my bits—insides too—since we had a stay-in day planned. I expected to be snuggled, pampered, and fucked at least twice before the sun sank behind the mountains.

My hard dick took issue with being tucked into lace

panties, but sneaking down the stairs and putting myself on display in the kitchen entryway and catching my lover off guard would land me sprawled over the island for sure.

Breakfast could wait.

The doorbell rang, and I moved aside the bedroom blind to see who would dare intrude on us without an invite. Probably Jamie, but maybe Dex—

An old, beat-up car in worse shape than my old Chevy sat along the street, one I hadn't seen around town before. I pressed my nose to the cool glass to check who stood on the stoop directly beneath me.

A blonde woman huddled in on herself, arms around her stomach, bruises marring her cheek and temple—

"Fuck," I whispered as the blood drained from my face. I swallowed against the sudden dryness in my throat.

Fucking Darla Forrester—or whatever name she went by these days—had shown up on Sutton's doorstep.

What was she doing back in town, and even more importantly, what the fuck did she want?

Another question whispered through my head, causing me to still, every muscle in my body tensing, dick deflating.

Had Sutton been aware she would be stopping by and hadn't told me? He knew I would flip out. I'd made it clear I was jealous of him and his time.

From what he'd claimed, he hadn't seen her since she'd fled Pippen Creek over a decade ago. I'd believed him about that...no way he would have hidden an upcoming visit from me.

Right?

My insides knotted, I spun to take in the king-sized bed that needed its sheets changed. The two pillows tossed on the floor, the comforter hanging half-off the foot. Evidence of our love fest and the promise of more gluttonous acts to come.

Those plans had flatlined.

What the actual fuck was she doing here?

With the bedroom door open, I could hear Sutton let Darla intrude into our peace. I strained to listen but could barely make out their murmured voices. Shouldn't Sutton have been shouting or at least raising his tone? He'd claimed to not ever having loved his ex-wife, but he'd been hurt and angered over what she'd done.

Had he forgiven her?

Considering his nature, I wouldn't have been surprised. Even worse was the fact she looked beat to hell. Sutton would never turn her away.

I rushed to tug some clothes on over my damp skin, my heart thundering in my ears and making it hard to listen. Panting through parted lips and adrenaline crashing through my system, I crept down the stairs, straining to hear whatever the fuck was being said.

A rustle of clothing—a quiet sob of my lover's name.

"Come here." Sutton's voice held tenderness, stating words he'd said to me countless times when wanting to offer comfort. And now he'd said that same thing to her?

Oh no he didn't!

Heat slammed into me, causing my face to flame and insides to tremble. Thank fuck for the firm hardwood flooring beneath me that kept my feet from creating noise. I peeked into the entryway, and a stab of pain knifed me in the chest at my worst fear coming true.

Sutton pulled Darla to his chest, one hand around her waist, the other cradling her head. No annoyed furrow lined his brow as he clutched her tight. His eyes were closed as though he basked in having her back in his arms, soaked up the feel of her soft flesh when he'd had nothing but my trim, taut body in the previous too-short weeks.

"It's going to be okay—I promise," he murmured, because of course he did. Sutton saw someone in need and couldn't help but run to the rescue.

My limbs went weak to see evidence that he still cared for the woman who had scorned his faithfulness and had attempted to ruin his name.

And he hugged her.

She clung to him like he was the rock she was desperate for—and he fucking *let* her.

Sweat broke out over my forehead, and I gritted my teeth to stop myself from screaming. Sobbing.

Spinning on trembling legs, I hurried toward the stairs. Up to the bedroom. Numb fingers tugged on socks while I attempted to swallow the pain from the back of my throat.

My shoes were in the entryway along with my coat, and no fucking way would I make an appearance, vulnerabilities on display for that bitch to gloat over.

Sutton would be full of excuses for his actions, shit I did *not* want to hear.

"Goddammit!" I grumbled to myself, my voice as unsteady as my eyes were watery.

Chewing on a fingernail, I examined the bedroom window. Could I climb out and drop to the ground a floor below without killing myself? Probably not the smartest choice. I could end up with two broken legs and be unable to escape this nightmare. Sutton would see me at my worst, attempting to crawl away from the pain like a worthless worm—

"Fuck." I choked on the word, blinking my eyes rapidly to keep the tears contained. Nothing could be done about the agony ripping through me, and I clutched at my chest as my heart slowly rent from top to bottom.

Could I possibly sneak into the kitchen and get out the slider before either of them caught sight of me? A quick sprint across the lawn to my car wouldn't be too cold—

The BMW's keys hung beside the front door.

More curses spilled from my trembling lips as I fisted my hands at my sides so they wouldn't shake.

Inaction would only heighten my already thrumming pulse, my inability to draw a full breath.

I *wouldn't* freeze this time and prove what a coward I was. I had to move. Protect *myself* for a fucking change.

One hesitant foot in front of the other, I made it to the landing.

I almost slipped down the stairs in my socks, which sent another burst of adrenaline through my already shaking body. The entryway sat empty, and I could hear the low murmur of voices in the living room. A peek around the corner showed them on the couch—sitting too goddamned fucking close.

Heat flushed through me again, and I clenched my jaw, ready to crawl on hands and knees by the opening to reach the entryway and everything I needed to get away from the sight of them together.

Worm.

Eyes closing, I swallowed hard. I wouldn't crawl—for any*one*, for any *reason*. No matter how badly I wanted to crumple in on myself and disappear beneath the earth's crust, where hiding would be ten times easier than living.

I stepped forward without a whisper of noise, eyes straight ahead as I stumbled past the living room entrance, praying like fuck they would be too wrapped up in each other to notice my presence.

Sutton didn't see me, and if he did, he chose to ignore me because he didn't call out to stop me from leaving.

My lower lip felt raw and chewed to bits before I got my shoes and coat on. The keys made a quiet clinking noise as I lifted them off the hook where they hung beside Sutton's all cozy, like they'd found a new home. A fresh wave of pain slammed into my chest, and I bit on my tongue to keep my sobs contained. A silent turn of the knob, a gentle tug inward, and the door opened without sound.

I stepped onto the stoop, my ragged breaths a puff of white, my lungs instantly chilled by the early morning temperature.

Jamie's SUV flew around the corner, and I only made it halfway down the walkway before he pulled into the driveway beside my car. He hopped out, jeans and flannel unbuttoned, hurrying around the front of his vehicle.

Sutton must have known Darla was in town. He'd invited his son over for fuck's sake—and Jamie rushed forward as though desperate to see his mom again. I'd thought he hated her—he'd spoken of what she'd done with anger and hurt.

But like father, like son.

Again.

My throat went tight as hell, and I swallowed hard, a whine building in my chest.

Jamie stumbled in his haste when his gaze landed on me. "Jimmy?"

I pushed past him, hitting the unlock and yanking open the driver door of my car.

"Jimmy!"

Tears slid down my cheeks as I backed out of the driveway like my ass was on fire. I took off up the road without a destination in mind. I could drive to Canada and never return. Head west and never look back. Hop a plane in Boston, jet across the pond, and never think about Sutton again.

As if.

I swiped the wetness from my cheeks, but the tears continued to roll, making it difficult for me to see the road. Sobs started to tear from my lungs, and I struggled to keep a tight grip on the wheel as my insides shredded, leaving my soul in tatters.

I needed to get off the road before I killed someone.

A parking lot on the left beckoned through my watery eyesight, so I pulled in and cut the engine, forehead dropping to the steering wheel. I'd never cried so hard in my life. Not even when Dad had beaten the shit out of me and left me bleeding on my old bedroom floor the day I'd turned eighteen. He'd called me countless names, blamed me for my mom's death, and that agony didn't compare to how my heart ached like a thousand pound weight sat atop it, slowly crushing its ability to beat.

Stuttered breaths barely allowed me to stay conscious as I sank in on myself and wallowed in my misery.

I'd let my guard down. Welcomed Sutton inside where he could root around and find a place to take up residence.

And the arms that should have been holding me had cradled *her* as though she still meant the world to him.

"Bitch!" I shrieked and slammed my fist on the steering wheel, grimacing as pain shot up to my elbow.

A knock on my window jerked my head to the left, and I scrubbed the tears from my face.

Sarah Kaufman stood on the other side of the glass, bent slightly to see me better. Concern lined her forehead and what I could make out of her eyes through the wetness coating mine.

Sniffing and breath hitching, I put my window down.

"Jimmy? You okay?" She sounded like a loving mom—and I started crying again because of course I couldn't regulate myself and put on my facade today. "We just opened, so why don't you come inside with me and I'll make some tea, okay?"

She coaxed me from the car, and I realized I'd parked in front of her and Stefen's Outdoor Shop.

Hunched in on myself, I managed to get a hold on the tears while following her through the glass door.

"Sarah?" Stefen called.

"Yeah?" She hollered to wherever he was. Sounded like he was down one of the aisles closer to the back of the store.

"Can you help me out for a second?"

"Be right there!" Sarah turned toward me while pulling off her coat. "Why don't you go to the office," she said, pointing at the door behind the counter.

I swallowed the last of my hiccupped attempts to catch my breath.

She squeezed my forearm. "I'll only be a minute."

Sarah hurried away, and I hung my head, feet unmoving, the deep earth calling.

I didn't want to think about, let alone discuss, the mess in my head, what had caused it, or give anyone ammunition to start up the gossip factory. Couldn't begin to imagine the shit that would be flying around town in the coming days.

Forgiveness at its finest from Pippen Creek's most upstanding citizen.

The prodigal kicked out for the person who needed their chief the most.

Sutton had claimed he'd never truly loved Darla, but he and I hadn't exchanged those words either.

Another whine rose from my chest, and my shoulders drooped lower, arms tight around my spilling guts.

Shouldn't have let Sarah talk me into getting out of my car. Hell, I didn't even *like* tea. And—

The door kicked in behind me, and a large body lurched inside, damn near taking me out in the process.

"Stefen! You fucking prick!"

Kurt Wallace.

Drunk off his goddamned ass and waving...

A handgun.

I stumbled back a step and fell onto my backside, what was left of my heart speeding up from a rush of adrenaline. Dizziness swept through my head. My bladder went lax, and I barely managed to keep from pissing myself.

Blazing hazed-over eyes landed on me, but the sound of approaching footsteps lured his scowl off me before I sussed out his true feelings toward me.

Fag. Fairy.

The apology that had seemed so sincere—

My brain shut off. Limbs rooted in place as Stefen appeared at the end of the aisle.

Kurt lifted his arm, shaking, and attempted to train his gun on the man's chest. "I warned you, asshole," he slurred while weaving on his feet. "Told you not to *fucking* touch her again!"

Sarah shrieked, and my lungs to seized along with the rest of my body.

I sat frozen.

A coward.

About to be the victim of drunken rage—again.

Chapter 33

Sutton

I'd gotten caught up in memories of holding Jimmy all night long, how he'd come apart for me countless times before I'd given him the dicking down he'd been begging for since I'd reddened his ass.

I burned the bacon while lost in my head.

Forgot to put the pot under the coffee machine and made a mess before I realized the mistake.

It wasn't until the scrambled eggs began to cook in the pan that I remembered I hadn't added any seasoning to the fluffy yellow bits Jimmy preferred for breakfast..

Chuckling to myself, I salted the eggs a little too late, poured two mugs of coffee, and hoped he didn't mind the bacon crunchier than I'd learned he preferred.

I expected he would still be too blissed out from last night to notice, and if so, I could always make him sit on my dick while eating. That would preoccupy his brain from my first kitchen fail.

The doorbell rang, and grinning, I opened the door.

My lungs deflated, my lips flatlining at the sight before me that I never in a million years would have expected.

"Darla?" I blinked, sure my eyes played tricks on me. I hadn't lain eyes on her in over a decade.

"Sutton." She whispered my name like a prayer, like I was her only hope. Her blue eyes were hazy with tears, despondent. A bruise shadowed her hollow cheek, clear into her hair. The sweatshirt she wore draped over her thinned frame—the woman was no more than skin and bones.

My brow furrowed on instinct. "What the fuck happened to you?" As if I hadn't already known. She'd been leaving me messages at work for weeks.

"C-Can I come in?" She attempted a smile that wavered and didn't reach her eyes.

I stepped back without thought, allowing her into the home we used to share. Where we'd raised our only son. Where she'd lied and manipulated me out of every cent I'd had.

"What are you doing here?" I asked, keeping my tone low. The shower had shut off upstairs, and while Jimmy usually took an hour-plus to get ready for the day, we'd planned to stay holed up inside. I couldn't decide if I wanted him to flounce down the stairs in nothing but lace panties or stay locked up in the bathroom while primping for me.

How the fuck would I explain letting this woman into our private bubble of happiness?

"I'm in a bad place," Darla said, and I shut the door behind her, unable to deny my instincts, the need to keep her safe, now that she stood before me.

Ignoring calls had been easy, but seeing her broken urged me to be the caretaker I couldn't help but be down to my bones.

Even after all she'd done to me, I held no bitterness like

our son did. If I could offer her some sort of protection, I had to give it.

Tears streamed over Darla's cheeks as she hugged herself, and empathy trickled in as it always did for someone hurting.

"Come here," I murmured, and she fell into me, hands grasping at my shirt.

Thank fuck I'd put the damned thing on because of splattering bacon grease, otherwise she'd be pressing against and touching my skin. A shiver rippled through me—not the pleasant kind—while holding her close. I closed my eyes, fighting the desire to shove her back outside into the cold, and took shallow breaths so the stench of her unwashed body didn't flood my nose.

A silent sob caused her to shudder her against me, and I clasped her tenderly, not sure where else she might be bruised and hurting.

What the fuck had happened?

Even worse, why the fuck did my brain care when my body was repulsed by her presence?

Needing space, I pushed her at arm's length, trying to smile. "Let's sit in the living room. You can tell me what's going on, and we'll see if we can get you some help, okay?"

She nodded, sniffling and shuffling where I'd motioned.

I kept a foot between us while sitting and ignored the hand she reached out in hopes I would take.

Darla might need an anchor right now, but I couldn't give her any further piece of me, no matter my natural inclinations pushed me to lay down my life as I would for any person inside my town's limits.

"I'm sorry for showing up like this, but you never returned my calls," she whispered.

And she knew me well enough to trust I wouldn't turn her away if she showed up looking like she did.

Manipulation at its finest.

Heat curled in my guts, but I couldn't be anyone other than the caretaker of everyone who walked inside my town's limits.

"Tell me what happened," I muttered, ready to move this shit along so I could get on with my day with the only person I wanted in my personal space.

A shiver raised the hairs on the back of my neck, and I rubbed at them, giving Darla my full focus until I no longer could. We might have five minutes—forty. Who knew with Jimmy. But what a shit show awaited if his emotions got the best of him before I could explain her presence in the house.

"I've gotten in too deep with an abusive man," she whispered, swiping a forearm across her wet cheeks.

No news there. Her voicemail woes had been confirmed the second I'd laid eyes on her face.

The front door slammed inward, smashing against the wall.

"Dad!" Jamie hollered, and I cursed, my eyes shutting for a brief second as his footsteps stomped toward us. "Dad—" He pulled up alongside the couch, dark blue eyes blazing as they landed on his mom. "What the *fuck* are you doing here?" He spun on me. "And why the fuck would you let her inside this house and send Jimmy packing? That boy is head over heels in love with you, and you'd give him up for...*her?*" The questions spewed in a low, hissed voice, his shoulders tensed, hands fisted at his sides.

"Jimmy..." I glanced over my shoulder toward the hallway and stairs beyond.

"I just saw him outside. He took off like his ass was on

fire, Dad—what the actual fuck!" Jamie trembled in his anger, and I did the same but for a whole different reason.

I shot to my feet to go after my sweet boy, a swell of emotion threatening to choke the air from my lungs. My heartbeat raced, causing pain to lance through my chest. Had to find him. Hold him. Assure him I would never—

Jamie grabbed my shoulder, keeping me in place. "Don't bother. He's already gone."

My entire body stalled out, muscles sagging. "W-What?"

"Gone. Sped off in his car."

I swayed on my feet. What the *fuck* had I done? Outside my son, Jimmy was the only one that mattered. My old instincts had betrayed me, allowed a viper over the threshold of my safe place, the house that I hoped Jimmy would call home.

Jamie glared at Darla, and she hunkered in on herself further, eyes downcast. "Dad finally has shit going his way, and you come crawling back with your filthy tail between your legs?" He huffed, and had we been outside, I didn't doubt he'd have spat on the ground. "Babs called me because she saw you driving downtown and knew she'd go to the most gracious man in this town. Babs tried your cell too, Dad, but I'm guessing you didn't get the warning."

Jimmy and I had both shut our phones off for the day since neither of us wanted our privacy to be intruded upon. And I'd opened the goddamned door without looking out the window. Had my sweet boy seen us hugging? Sitting on the couch together?

Jamie continued to hold me up, and I didn't pull away.

A whine built low in my gut, and I swallowed hard as my eyes began to sting. I couldn't break down and lose my shit. Right now, I needed to be the oak everyone saw me as

—for myself. Then Jimmy. One fucking step at a time to set this shit straight.

"Darla, go upstairs and shower in the guest bathroom," I ordered, trying but failing to use my chief's voice. "I'll find something for you to wear." I grimaced at the truth that only Jimmy's clothes would come close to fitting her small form.

"Sutton—"

"Darla!" Jamie hissed. "For once in your goddamned life, do what he tells you without arguing. And you'd better pray like fuck he's planning to be more gracious than I am, because if shit went my way, you'd be out the door on your ass right this second, just as awful looking as you showed up —un-fucking-invited!"

She swallowed hard, glanced at me, and nodded. Pushing to her feet, she muttered an apology, but neither Jamie or I acknowledged her words.

"What. The. Fuck?" Jamie muttered the second she disappeared up the stairs, his hand finally dropping from my forearm to grip his hips.

"Jimmy was in our bedroom getting dressed—I-I didn't check before opening the door."

Jamie glared at me. "You'd have let her in even if you knew it *was* her knocking."

I rubbed a hand over my face, hating yet appreciating he called me out. "Yeah."

"Fuck, Dad." Jamie shook his head, lips pursed. "You didn't fail her in any way. She needs to own her stupid choices—not you." He poked my chest. "You can't be responsible for every fucking person who enters this town!"

"I know—"

"You *don't*! Jesus." Jamie stalked toward the door and spun again, clearly not having given me enough of his mind. He pointed at me again. "That boy is everything you told me you wanted. He all but *dropped* into your lap, needy as could be, put a smile on your face I don't remember *ever* seeing, and now he's gone."

"I didn't—"

"You gotta to make this shit right before it's too late, Dad. He was running like he didn't plan on stopping anytime soon. You've got your work cut out for you, I can promise you that. He looked hell-bent on escaping this town without a backward glance. Better pack a bag and head to Boston because that's the only other place he has to go."

My mind grasped for ways to stop Jimmy from leaving town, but he was probably already long gone.

"As for that...woman," Jamie nearly spat again, "she manipulates you so goddamned easily. It's time for me to have *your* back—and I won't bend for that bitch. Don't give a flying *fuck* what she's going through or how she's hurting. She gave up the rights to our empathy and love years ago when she walked away without an ounce of concern for the mess she'd made of our lives."

I closed my eyes, head hanging. He was right and hadn't pulled any punches. Running my hands through my hair, I muttered a few curses beneath my breath over my ability to be truthful with everyone but myself. "Who's on patrol?"

"Davidson."

I nodded and straightened, filling my lungs to help steady my nerves. "Call him—tell him to keep an eye out for Jimmy in case he hasn't left town yet. I gotta go get my cell."

Jamie's phone rang before he pulled it from his back pocket. "Babs?" he answered, and I couldn't make out her words even though her shrill tone reached my ears.

I paused from heading upstairs, body tensed as Jamie's gaze slammed into mine. His face went pale, eyes widening.

"Shit," he whispered and hung up. "Kurt is holding

Stefen at gunpoint—and Sarah and Jimmy are in the shop with them."

Time stilled. Everything went to fuzz in my ears like I'd dived underwater.

My heart thumped and went silent for what felt like an hour.

Lungs denied oxygen lay flat inside my chest.

I'd never seen a live crime scene that involved death, but my mind envisioned the shattering of my heart, the loss of someone I had loved for years and wanted more than anything.

"Dad!" Jamie's holler merely buzzed between my ears as I held Jimmy's limp body in my arms. Sobs tore from my mouth, agony ripping me from the inside out.

I wouldn't survive—

Jamie slapped me across the face, and a rush of air and sound slammed reality into my brain.

Couldn't lose him.

Wouldn't.

"Call Davidson," I rasped, focusing on the sting in my cheek rather than the panicked ache in my chest. "Jones too. Hurry." I sprinted up the stairs on shaking legs and threw open the bathroom door.

Darla stood in the shower, thinner than I'd thought and bruised from head to toes.

"Finish and get the fuck out," I hissed, adrenaline crashing through my system, my voice unsteady. "If I find one thing missing from inside these walls you no longer belong in, I'll hunt you down and make you pay for every goddamned cent you took from me a decade ago. We clear?"

"Sutton—"

"Don't! Fucking *don't*, Darla." I shook my head, disgusted with myself and my choices over the last fifteen minutes. "I'll leave some gas money on the table for you, but I want you gone. And don't ever come back. There's nothing left here for you. Call me again, and I'll get a restraining order."

She'd already stolen and ruined more than enough in my life, and I was *done*.

I spun and rushed to my room to grab my cell and Glock, praying like fuck I wouldn't be too late to save the man I loved.

Chapter 34

Jimmy

"Calm down, Kurt." Stefen's voice trembled as he cowered before the gun trained on his chest.

"Calm down?" Kurt shrieked, his eyes bloodshot as all hell and full of fire. "You fucking hurt her *again*! She sent me pictures of the bruises on the back of her neck from when you forced her to heel. Torn fingernails from her trying to rip your hands off her! Don't tell me to fucking *calm down*!"

Stefen rubbed at his wrists that were covered by long sleeves. "Jimmy," he murmured without looking at me, "call 911."

I didn't so much as twitch.

Couldn't.

My eyes stayed glued to the scene playing out before me as I tried to collapse in on myself and disappear like I'd always done with Dad when he was rip-roaring drunk and screaming at me.

Globs of spit landing on my cheek.

A fist to my temple.

My fingers bleeding from trying to untangle Dad's grip

in my hair to keep me upright so he could hit me again. The stinging pain of strands tore from my scalp as he hurled me across the threshold into the living room.

A whimper escaped me as my fingernails dug at my coat, desperate to scratch down my forearm.

"She's a goddamned angel, you psychotic cunt!" Kurt continued his ranting, curses spilling from his lips along with spittle. "She deserves to be worshiped! How dare you call her a *whore!*"

I flew across the room, elbow and chin throbbing from hitting the hardwood flooring. The impact tore the air from my lungs, and I realized I'd bitten my tongue when I choked on blood.

"No son of mine is going to suck another man's dick!" Dad hollered, looming over me, leg drawing back.

I curled in on myself, eyes clenched shut and muscles tensed while coughing over the taste of metal.

"You goddamned piece of shit!"

A boot landed against my spine.

Another on my thigh.

My shoulder.

I cried out, begging him to stop, pleading...sobbing for someone to rescue me because I was powerless to stop the drunkard. "Please," I pleaded for mercy, wishing I could believe a god existed—

Sutton's face appeared in my mind, and I felt his arms cradling me to his warm, strong chest. He held me while I got the shit beaten out of me, whispered words of edification and kindness, soothing what my dad attempted to tear apart.

"I have you. I won't let anything happen to you," my hero whispered against my ear.

. . .

I crumpled, sliding sideways onto the shop's floor, reliving the afternoon I'd gotten suspended for sucking some kid's dick under the bleachers at school. I could feel phantom pain, the emotional turmoil, saw every drawn out second in vivid color as the memory continued to assault me. While taking solace in thoughts of the chief had soothed me, the inescapable trauma had been ingrained in my head.

Dad had nearly broken me that day.

I'd peed blood for a week but had been too scared to tell the school nurse, Gram, or even Sutton, who probably would have tossed my dad in jail. Didn't want the chief believing I was a coward, and ending up in the state's hands would probably have landed me outside Pippen Creek and far from his protection.

Worm.

"No," I whispered, refusing to stay in the past where Dad's voice dug claws into me, attempting to imprison me in the horror of my memories.

Kurt continued his screaming a few feet away from me, helping to keep me in the present, but I was fucked. I'd seen enough law enforcement and reality shows to know how this conflict between two men supposedly in love with one woman would end.

Cops would surround the building, attempting to negotiate with the unhinged drunkard hell-bent on protecting his lover.

Stefen would trigger Kurt somehow, and shots would fire, gun smoke filling the air. Sarah would be prompted by shame to try to protect her abuser from the police and accidentally get hit by a bullet. Even though I wouldn't be able to scramble to safety, I would be a witness to Kurt's crimes. I alone would be the only person left living to doom him to his death with my testimony.

He would end me before I got a chance. I would become a victim when I had taken no part in any of their sins.

Gram and DJ would mourn me, seeing as they were the only family I had left.

Sutton...

A sob ripped from my chest, a whining wail that pulled Kurt's gun my way. "Oh, God. Please," I begged with a teary whimper, praying like fuck Sarah remained hidden back in the aisle, that Stefen would keep his goddamned mouth shut until my hero showed up. The oak of Pippen Creek would protect us—

No.

Not this time.

He was at home—with *her*, his concern focused on the person who had never loved him like I did.

Same as that day Dad tried to kill his faggot son, no one was coming to save the day.

Tears soaked my cheeks as the past dragged me back into its clutches again.

Chapter 35

———

Sutton

My Bronco's tires squealed as I jerked the wheel to tear down Main Street, swerving around cars since I didn't have lights or a siren to warn them out of my way.

Heart racing as fast as the engine, I sent out prayers to whichever gods might be listening to keep my baby boy safe. I'd only just allowed myself to love again—for real this time —the type of devotion that consumed a soul and owned a man's heart.

I hadn't yet found the guts to tell him my truth.

"Please," I whispered, hands in a white-knuckled grip on the steering wheel.

Two cruisers already angled in front of Stefen's shop, and I swerved in behind them, slamming on the brake and hopping out of my truck without turning the engine off.

Pulling my gun from my waistband, I hunched over and rushed toward the entrance.

Screams sounded from inside, curses and warnings to stay back.

Dozens of people littered the area, some hidden in case

bullets flew, others standing upright and pointing, gossiping with those beside them.

"Take cover!" I hollered at the morons, so goddamned disappointed in my townsfolk who couldn't smell danger even if it rotted like roadkill beneath their noses. We'd never had such an event. Peace was our norm.

Had been.

A sense of immense change hung on the horizon of our futures, the kind that clenched my guts and worried at my mind. I was in charge yet felt powerless over the hurricane force winds pushing us forward toward an unseen future.

Officer Davidson crouched on the far side of the door, gun drawn, face pale.

I hurried up the stairs and huddled beside him, heart slamming.

"Sent Jones around to the rear," he said, tone tight and quiet. "No shots fired—yet. Wallace has Stefen held at gunpoint, and it's only a matter of time, Chief. The guy is out of his mind. Fucking batshit crazy. You should hear some of the shit he's spewing."

Jaw clenched, I leaned around Davidson, quickly looking through the glass door. The situation was exactly as Davidson had said.

"You treat her like shit!" Kurt screamed, gun trained on Stefen, who faced our way, eyes wide, body trembling. "And she *still* chose you last week when I asked her to leave with me!"

Stefen's mouth moved, but I couldn't hear him through the glass separating us.

"You're right," Kurt continued to holler, "but this misery ends today for both of us!"

"Fuck," I whispered as puzzle pieces fell into place.

A quick scan of the rest of the interior in my line of sight didn't allow a glimpse of Jimmy.

He could already be broken and bleeding out. Gasping his final breaths. Would he be whispering my name? Begging for me to save him?

My throat tightened as I read the cards before me. I feared what Kurt planned and expected. Possibly even hoped for.

I had heard about this possible scenario at the academy but never expected to be faced with such a situation. This would be my first time putting a bullet into someone in order to protect my town, but I had to try peace first. Attempt to make sure we all crawled into our beds tonight.

Calm leaked in, who the fuck knew from where, but I clung to the roots settling deep, holding me steady. Upright. Strong in the face of storm.

I would do whatever it took to eliminate the threat. I'd sworn to do so even at the expense of my own mental health.

"I'm going in," I murmured, praying like hell I read this wrong.

"Chief—" Davidson's voice cut off as I eased the door open. He kept it from closing with his heel, freeing up both of my hands.

I itched to have my gun held out in front of me, aimed at the man who would dare to bring this kind of drama to our small community. Instead, I made myself as unintimidating as possible, a lesser threat so I might stand a chance of talking him down rather than have things turn violent.

"Kurt?" I called quietly, my voice as friendly as always.

"Chief!" A woman shrieked from inside near the back of the store as I stepped over the threshold, Glock hanging at my side, my free hand up, palm facing Kurt to show him I meant no harm.

Kurt glanced over his shoulder at me, face red, eyes hazed over yet blazing. He swayed on his feet. "It's about fucking time, Chief! You need to know the truth!"

Stefen tensed as though readying to charge, and Kurt swung around toward him, almost stumbling sideways. "One more step, and I'll blow your *fucking* brains out all over the floor, Kaufman!"

A quick glance assured me no one bled—

Jimmy.

The breath left my lungs in a rush at seeing him unharmed. He huddled to my left, pale face wet with tears, his body trembling as he stared into space as though unaware of my presence even though I stood mere feet away.

My heart ached to see him broken and thrust into the past, reliving the abuse of his father.

If we escaped this situation unscathed, I would see my sweet boy through his healing no matter how that might look. Fuck knew how the outcome of this setup would mess with my head too. We could go to therapy together as I had some shit to learn, or perhaps *un*learn, as well.

I wasn't responsible for everyone. Not even those who came crawling back and begging for forgiveness. Like Jamie had said, people made their own choices, and it was simply my job to clean up the resulting messes.

Not grant restitution.

"Kurt—"

A gun exploded, tearing the words from Stefen's lips. He spun, red blooming on his shoulder as he flew backward.

Time crawled, shutting down my brain.

My exhale sounded loud above the ringing in my ears.

Jimmy flinched in my periphery, crying out for mercy.

Kurt began to turn toward him, smoking pistol outstretched—

My arm raised, free hand lifting to offer steadiness.

Feet once more rooted.

My choice made for me by a man bent on ending his misery.

I pulled the trigger, the boom deafening through the fog surrounding me.

Kurt slumped to the floor.

Shrieking flooded my ears, snapping reality into focus.

Footsteps pounded into the shop behind me.

I kept my gun trained on the unmoving man my bullet had torn into.

Damn you, Kurt.

Blood pooled beneath him, spreading outward. His glassy eyes stared unseeing at the ceiling.

Davidson rushed past me toward Stefen, who groaned a few curses while clutching his bleeding shoulder.

Sarah ran up the aisle, bypassed her husband, and fell to her knees beside Kurt, hands scrambling over his face. "Kurt! No! Please, *no*! I *didn't* choose him! I *didn't*!" She sobbed, gathering his limp form against her heaving chest. "Don't leave me!"

I lowered my gun.

Turned.

Jimmy curled in a fetal position, eyes hazed over.

For this man—I'd taken another's life.

Gram and DJ would hate me, even though I expected a suicide note would be found somewhere on Kurt's person or in his home.

It didn't matter Kurt had chosen his fate. Sarah would want my blood.

Stefen would live, a piece-of-shit, abusive husband who was the cause of this drama, even if an affair had taken place behind his back.

And my sweet love…

I went to one knee beside Jimmy, smoothing hair off his forehead with a shaking hand. "Baby boy," I whispered, trailing my knuckles over his pale cheek. "You're safe, sweetheart. Everything is going to be okay."

He blinked up at me, attempting to focus on my face.

"I'm here, Jimmy."

Recognition finally lit his haunted eyes, and a sob tore from deep in his chest.

Someone called for an ambulance behind us as creeping numbness from shock settled into my bones.

More heavy footfalls entered the door.

"Dad!"

"I'm fine," I told Jamie even though I was anything but, setting my gun aside and gathering Jimmy up in my arms.

He clung to me as he used to as a young boy, burrowing his face into my neck. "Y-You're here," he choked out.

"Always." I rubbed his back. Kissed his hair. Held him tight, giving him the solid foundation he—and I—needed at that moment.

A poor decision had almost cost me the future I'd been hoping to share with him, a rewarding existence with the perfect man by my side, one who fulfilled my needs by allowing me to care for his.

I loved Jimmy more than life. More than all of Pippen Creek. Even more than my title and what I'd seen as my purpose when I'd been appointed to watch over this town.

Jimmy was my everything, and I'd almost lost him.

A shudder ripped through me, and I sucked oxygen into my lungs, attempting to keep my stinging eyes from overflowing. "I was so afraid, baby boy..." I swallowed hard, hugging him tighter. "Couldn't let him hurt you—need you so much."

Jimmy sobbed, attempting to burrow deeper against me.

He and I had a serious conversation ahead, but considering the circumstances we huddled in, admissions of what we wanted for the future would have to wait.

Duty called regardless of how shock lingered in my body and mind.

Glancing around while soothing him with gentle touches, I took in the consequences of adultery, abuse, and drunkenness.

Sarah continued to sob even as Officer Jones pulled her from Kurt's body. I didn't need to see the lack of chest movement to know his heart no longer beat. Years of target practice in my backyard ensured I didn't miss.

I'd given Kurt exactly what I had feared he hoped for today.

And now, I, along with the rest of those left behind, would have to suffer the consequences.

EMTs arrived.

Led Sarah from the building, far from the grisly sight of her lover.

Carried Stefen out on a stretcher.

Jamie crouched beside us to block off the sight of disaster, studying my face, hand on my shoulder, helping to ground me in reality. "Tell me what to do, Chief." His tone held assurance—his trust in me even after taking the life of one of our own.

My first priority was the man still clinging to me. Once he was squared away for the time being, I could focus on work and the hours of tedious bullshit ahead for my department.

"Call the Sheriff's department then get ahold of Dex," I said. "He'll take Jimmy home for me while we deal with the fallout."

Jamie nodded and moved off, pulling his cell from his pocket.

Releasing a slow exhale, I closed my eyes and allowed myself one last selfish moment of holding my love before attempting to clean up the mess. While the danger had been ended, the aftermath would linger far into the days ahead of us.

The Chief of Pippen Creek had killed one of the residents beneath his protection—and I would do it all over again.

Would the forgiving spirit of this town remain after what I'd done?

Honestly, I didn't care if the townsfolk scorned me for answering the call of duty.

Jimmy and I would go wherever the wind carried us—together.

Chapter 36

Jimmy

He'd come for me.

Killed a man to keep me safe.

Sutton had chosen *me*.

"I—I can't do this life on my own," I whispered, clinging to Sutton. He would pass me off onto his best friend, and even though I could tell by how he held me that he didn't want me out of his sight any more than I did him, we had no choice.

"I'll always have your back, baby." He assured me, gently pulling me from his neck where I'd finally found the only place that offered me escape and peace.

I'd been a fool to run. Sutton had proven his trustworthiness time and again, and my goddamned trauma, another deranged drunk, had almost taken me from him for good.

Already too well aware of what Kurt looked like sprawled face down and bleeding, I trained my gaze on my hero.

Exhaustion filled his eyes along with pain and concern.

A million questions about his ex-wife filled my head,

but I bit my tongue. He had enough to deal with, and my selfishness in needing answers could wait.

He smoothed my hair off my forehead. "I wish I could drive you home and hold you in our bed, baby, but I can't."

Our bed.

Not his and Darla's.

My throat went tight again. I nodded, hating that I understood his sense of duty.

"Dad—Dex is here."

Sutton brushed a tear off my cheek with his thumb, gaze slipping to my lips and back up. A slow inhale filled his lungs, stretching his T-shirt across his hard pecs. "I want to carry you away from here, but I think you should try to walk, okay? Prove to yourself how strong you really are, Jimmy."

I nodded even though resilience wasn't in my vocabulary.

He clasped my hand and helped me stand. My legs were weak, muscles twitchy, but I could do this with him by my side. "Don't look, baby," he murmured, and I nodded, focus trained on the glass door propped open and letting in the fall's chilly air.

What seemed like a dozen people milled inside the shop, but I didn't glance their way. Refused to make eye contact and allow the townsfolk to see what a weak coward I'd been.

Dex stood at the bottom of the stairs, and I stumbled down the small flight before my feet settled on the ground.

"Jamie called the sheriff's department, but I'm going to need you to give Officer Davidson your statement before you can leave," Sutton said, squeezing my fingers.

I nodded even though I didn't want to.

"Dex will watch over you until I get home," Sutton promised.

I believed every word he spoke because Dex loved Sutton almost as much as I did, and while he might tease the shit out of me, I knew he would lay down his life for both of us.

"I want you to try to eat something when you get home," he continued, his tone not allowing an argument. "Take a hot shower even though you already had one this morning then crawl into bed."

"Okay—wait. Is she..." I swallowed hard, huddling in my coat from the inner chill that seemed settled into my bones. "Is she still there?"

"Fuck." Sutton scrubbed a hand over his beard. "Darla showed up this morning," he informed Dex, his voice low.

"What the actual *fuck*?" Dex muttered, his tone murderous.

"Yeah. I told her to clean up and get the hell out. Left her some gas money on the table, but that was it. Make sure the old Ford she was driving is gone before you let my boy into the house."

His claim thawed some of the coldness inside me, and I shuddered as the physical strength keeping me upright waned.

"Will do," Dex assured him.

Sutton passed me over to his best friend, who tugged me into his side, his heavy arm a comforting blanket across my shoulders, but I missed the connection with...whatever Sutton was to me.

Hero, but more than a friend. Lover, but not yet boyfriend.

I lifted my gaze to his, hoping for the answer I desperately needed.

The sun sat low on the horizon, but its rays reached us, causing his eyes to glint more green than brown.

He loved me, his heart spoke without words—without doubt.

Warmth flooded my chest, and a watery smile curved my lips.

Sutton bent down, calloused palms cradling my face, gaze filled with other emotions I couldn't begin to pick apart. "I would do anything to keep you safe, sweet boy of mine. I'll see you soon."

Mine—his.

Unable to speak past the lump in my throat, I nodded, trusting him to keep his word.

Officer Davidson approached at Sutton's beckoning, and I sat in the back of his cruiser while woodenly explaining the facts of what had happened from the time Kurt had come barreling into the shop until Sutton had cradled me in his arms. What I'd seen, anyway. Half of the torturous minutes had been spent in a flashback from hell. As much as I hated to admit to my childhood trauma and how I sometimes lost touch with reality, I told Officer Davidson so he would understand the missing seconds from whatever timeline the investigation put together.

He was full of empathy and didn't push for more before saying the sheriff's department would be in touch.

Twenty minutes later, Dex managed to get us through the crowd, into his Jeep, and to Sutton's.

The beat-up car Darla had driven was gone.

A heavy exhale sank me into Dex's passenger seat, and he muttered a "Thank fuck," which I heartily agreed with.

We hadn't spoken a word on the short ride, and the quietness remained until we got inside, the door closed firmly and locked behind us.

The scent of coffee and bacon lingered, even though it seemed hours had passed since I'd felt betrayed and had escaped Sutton's house without a backward glance.

Dex and I removed our coats and shoes, and I headed into the kitchen, determined to be a good boy for Sutton. I put the somewhat dried-out breakfast left cold on the table into the microwave and poured two mugs of coffee from the carafe.

"You should eat Sutton's food," I suggested quietly to Dex, who stood in the kitchen doorway as though unsure of what to do.

We sat at the kitchen table, Dex chowing down, me picking at the scrambled eggs Sutton had made for me.

Dex finished and sat back, hand wrapped around his coffee mug. "Want to talk about it?"

I shuddered. "Fuck no."

"I'm sorry for antagonizing you."

I nodded, finding the perfectly fried bacon that had gotten too crisped in the microwave more interesting than meeting Dex's gaze.

"Sutton really cares about you. And even though I give you both shit, you're good for each other."

"I'm a lot," I whispered, pushing aside my half-emptied plate.

Coward. Whore. Worm.

Dex snorted.

"No—I mean I've got too much damned baggage." I shrugged, even though the words in my mind were more hurtful than I wished they were. "I'm broken."

"Ever see a therapist?"

What was with everyone and their brother asking me that question?

"No. Can't stand the thought of living through it all

over again, but what went down today…" I shook my head, trying like hell not to get lost in the nightmare that had played out before my eyes and memory. "Brought everything back, you know?" My voice wavered, and I hugged myself as my lower lip trembled. "But it's time to face this shit head-on," I told myself more than I did Dex. "Take care of it so I can love Sutton without these insecurities and wounds showing up over and over, attempting to ruin things between us."

"Sutton will hold your hand through it if you'll let him. That man would lay down his life—hell, he'd walk away from Pippen Creek and his responsibilities if you asked him to."

My focus jerked up to find Dex's steady gaze on my face. "I would never do that! This town relies on him—needs him."

He reached over and clasped my shoulder. "Glad to hear it. I kinda like having my best friend around."

"Talk about being around…" I raised an eyebrow, just as gossip-minded as the next resident of our town. "Sutton says you *haven't* been."

A muscle ticked in Dex's jaw as he glanced toward the window over the kitchen sink. "That's a story for another day."

Expecting Dex was as stubborn as I'd always assumed, I let matters lie. I was too exhausted to tease or make further attempts to change the topic again.

We cleaned up the kitchen together in silence, and he ordered me upstairs to do as Sutton had said.

I showered, tears once more coursing down my face, but at least the heaving sobs from earlier that morning no longer ripped from my chest.

Blinds closed and room somewhat darkened, I climbed

back into the bed Sutton and I had left rumpled from our morning shenanigans. It seemed a lifetime ago he'd held me tight against his sweaty chest as our heartbeats had slowed, the euphoric tingles of release slowly leaking from our systems.

I rubbed my face in his pillow, clutching the softness to me. While the feathers and cotton were no match for Sutton's flesh, his scent offered me enough reminder of his presence that I rested, my muscles sinking into the mattress.

Blessed darkness crept in, and I carried the memory of my hero along with me to keep me safe from nightmares.

Chapter 37

Sutton

Constitutional law allowed for my actions in protecting the citizens of Pippen Creek, and I'd been trained to use lethal force in certain scenarios.

But I'd never expected to be faced with such a situation and have my instincts dictate the steps I'd taken. Kurt had shot one man and seemed intent on another—could have been Jimmy or me—but I had stopped him before finding out.

I hated having caused heartache to the handful of people who would mourn the loss of Kurt, but I would make the same decision over and over again—even if Jimmy *hadn't* been huddled on the floor or in close proximity. If Kurt and I had been the only two left in the shop, I would have ended the threat to my own life and the town's safety without second-guessing myself.

The sheriff arrived to avoid a conflict of interest in overseeing the investigation of Kurt's death that was required by law. As feared, a suicide note had been tucked in Kurt's back pocket.

Sarah had been manipulated into staying with her

husband rather than leave town with Kurt to seek out happiness together. His intention had been to kill Stefen, assured that Chief Sutton would do what needed doing.

He didn't apologize.

Simply said he couldn't live without his love.

Either his aim had been shit or he'd chosen at the last second not to end Stefen's life.

We would never know.

Kurt had made his choice of violence, and he had paid the price.

Dexter had informed me Darla was nowhere to be seen and kept me updated on Jimmy via text so I was able to focus on my job and comply with the law in the hours that followed what would be the talk of the town for years to come.

I expected, along with the sheriff, for the event to be a justifiable homicide, that Kurt's death would be certified as suicide due to the note he'd written. That meant I was free to go home for the night, but shit was far from over.

Mary arrived at the station around sundown, and although tears lined her face, she hugged me tight. "I'm so sorry."

"I'm the one who's sorry, Mary," I managed to say through the thickness in my throat.

She stepped back, holding onto my forearm with a stern grip. "Don't you dare, Sutton Forrester." Her voice broke, and another tear slid down her cheek. "Never apologize for doing your duty to protect the people of our town."

I swallowed hard and nodded.

"What you did was warranted—I trust you implicitly, Chief. And I heard rumors about a note?"

Lips pressed tight, I nodded again.

She released a shaky exhale. "I'm so thankful Stefen is

going to be okay. I couldn't bear the thought of having raised a man who would take another's life."

He'd been in love. Obsessed with Sarah.

I understood his feelings, couldn't begin to imagine how I would react if Jimmy left me for someone who'd hurt him time and again—manipulated him into choosing evil over happiness.

I'd yet to fully grasp the fact I'd killed a man. He was gone. I'd seen his body bagged up and wheeled out to the coroner's van.

But my emotions were bottled.

"Does DJ know?" I asked what I'd been thinking on most.

"He does, and while it'll be some time before all of this make sense to him, he wanted me to tell you that you're still his hero. His dream of becoming a cop so he can care for people like you do hasn't changed."

My eyes stung, and I managed a nod.

Mary hugged me again, and tears slid down both of our cheeks when she offered me a trembling smile before turning to leave.

After another grueling few hours, the sheriff sent me home for the next week while he and his men took care of business. I was instructed to see a therapist in Berlin who dealt with all local law enforcement issues.

I expected PTSD would be my newest companion, but weariness clung to me like a dense fog, confusing and numbing, allowing me to make it home in the middle of the night without breaking down.

Dex met me at the door, dark eyes empathetic and concerned. He threw his arms around me and held me tight, and I gave over to the need for someone else to be my strength for a change.

I'd informed him of what I could without breaking the law, and he'd texted that he'd been keeping up on the town gossip via various sources.

"You did the right thing," he stated calmly and with authority while I sagged against him.

"I would do it again," I murmured.

He clapped my back and stepped away, eyeing me. "You good?"

I blew out a slow exhale that did nothing to ease the tiredness I felt clear down to my bones. "Probably not, but I'm too damned exhausted to face this shit tonight. Is Jimmy still sleeping?"

"Yep. Haven't heard a peep out of him all evening. He got up to use the bathroom once, came down for a glass of water, and disappeared again."

"He say anything to you about Darla?"

"Nope."

"You and I need to talk about what you've been up to," I said, "but not now."

Dex nodded, clasping my shoulder once more. "I'm fine —*we're* fine."

"You and Christian?"

He shrugged. "No need to worry about me and my love life."

"Love?"

A grimace marred his face. "Obsession? Possessiveness? Need for ownership? I have no fucking clue what to call whatever this is with Cole, but it's hot as fuck. Twisted and probably a little toxic." He shrugged again and turned away to grab his shoes and coat. "If you need an ear, I'll always be here for you, Sutton. And take care of that boy—he needs you just as much as you need him, Chief. I'm happy for you. Hope this shit gets settled soon."

"Thanks." I saw Dex out, locked up for the night, and trudged upstairs.

The various showerheads in the master bathroom called my name, but I didn't want to disturb Jimmy if he was out cold. Peeking into my bedroom revealed he slept like an angel, lips parted and forehead smoothed as though nothing from the day's events lingered in his brain.

I made do with the guest bedroom's single showerhead, noting the used towel hanging on the rack and wet wash-cloth folded over the tub's edge.

Like Dex had told me, Darla's car had been gone when I'd pulled up, and I'd never known such relief.

Hot water pelted my shoulders, and I hung my head, allowing the floodgates of grief to open. Tears slid down from my face, and I bit my tongue, swallowing against sobs that would wake my love from much-needed rest. While Mary's forgiveness and understanding went a long way toward easing my guilt for taking her son from her—ripping DJ's dad from his life—I feared the future. Having studied about PTSD when it came to cops and the choices they had to make in the line of duty, I knew rough days were ahead of me.

Jimmy would no longer be my sole focus, since I would have trauma of my own.

But we would hold each other's hands and hopefully find the healing we needed to find lasting peace.

Once I drained myself of tears, I got out of the shower and dried off, anxious to join Jimmy in our bed.

The sight of him sleeping like an angel—breathing life into his lungs—tightened my throat again, and I crawled beneath the covers, desperate to have his warm skin against mine.

Snuggling against his backside was like coming home. I

soaked in the heat of his lax body, breathing in his natural sweet scent that clung to his skin.

His panties separated his ass cheeks from my bare groin, but my dick couldn't be bothered to stir—not one single twitch of interest over the plump cheeks it snuggled against.

Jimmy laced his fingers through mine atop his stomach with a shuddered sigh. "You're here."

"Mmm."

"Are you okay?" he whispered, concern lacing his words.

"Were you able to rest?" I asked rather than answer.

"Yeah, but I woke up a couple hours ago and couldn't get back to sleep because I was worried about you." He rolled, rubbing his face against my chest, fingers clutching at me. "It was awful."

"It was," I rasped, having to swallow hard again.

"You're not okay." Jimmy didn't ask a question.

I exhaled heavily. "I will be," I assured him.

"I'm here for you, Sutton—even if you can't or aren't allowed to discuss it, I'm here."

"I know, baby boy." I smoothed my hands down his spine as he slung his leg over my waist as though needing to get closer when we already pressed as tightly against each other as possible.

He shuddered. "Can *I* talk about just one thing before we try to sleep?"

"Anything you need," I whispered.

"I'm broken, Sutton." His voice cracked, and I tilted his head away from my chest so I could see his eyes in the light filtering through the door I'd left propped open.

"Will you let me hold you while you get help gluing the pieces back together?" I asked rather than argue or attempt to lessen his trauma. His past was real, and I would never invalidate his emotions that often took control over critical thinking.

"Will you let me do the same for you?" he asked, blue eyes wet and imploring.

"Yes." My answer confirmed how very *not* okay I was.

Jimmy tried for a smile, hugging me tighter. "You're too good to me."

"You're perfect for me," I insisted, tugging him higher so I could kiss his soft lips. "I thought I'd lost you when Jamie came storming in this morning and told me you'd left. Then I feared you would be ripped away from me by a bullet." I blinked away threatening tears.

"I need you so damned much, Sutton." Jimmy whispered words that fulfilled me, something Darla had never once declared in all our time together.

My sweet boy was nothing like my ex-wife—I didn't have to fear him following in the footsteps of the woman who had manipulated me for years with selfish intent. Jimmy might know what he wanted, might be driven to fulfill his desires with whatever wily tactics he had up his sleeves, but he would never intentionally hurt me.

"Please don't leave me," I croaked.

He stilled. "You want to keep me?"

"For as long as you'll stay," I assured him, my voice wavering.

"Forever," he blurted. "I won't settle for anything else, Sutton. I'm going to move into this house, make myself at home, and focus on healing and being your good boy."

I actually chuckled at his breathless declaration, my smile wobbly as fuck. "What about living your own life?"

"*That's* the life I want," he declared. "It's my idea of a dream come true."

"You won't miss the big city? All the excitement?"

"I'd rather be snuggled up in the arms of the man I trust more than my own thoughts."

Something else Darla never had or ever *would* have said to me.

I tucked Jimmy in closer, nuzzling his hair, elation flooding clear through to my soul and easing some of the heaviness from the day.

"What about Darla?" he asked, as though aware of where my mind had gone.

"She tried to manipulate me again, but I wasn't having it."

"I tried to do the same," Jimmy pointed out while gently tugging on my chest hairs.

I grasped his wrist. "Yeah, but Darla never loved me. She simply used me, drained me of everything."

"Do you have anything left to give?"

I held his face in my hands and met his gaze straight on. "Every piece of my heart," I promised. "It never belonged to anyone like it does to you."

Jimmy shivered, attempting to wiggle closer. "Like Gram tricked me into admitting, you've owned mine since I realized what attraction was. I love you, Sutton—have for years but never thought I was good enough for a man like you."

"You're all I want and more, Jimmy. Don't ever doubt my feelings toward you."

My sweet boy muscled me onto my back and settled atop my hips, hands on my chest. His slight weight felt so damned right hovering over me, and regardless of the emotional upheaval and weariness sagging me into the mattress, my dick perked up. "Say it," he demanded. "Say the words I need to hear, Sutton."

I smiled up at him, gyrating my hips enough he would

be aware my cock thickened against his plump ass. "I love you, Jimmy Riley. Cared more than I probably should have even before you were of age, but it's the man you've grown into, the empathetic, caring, sweet soul that I've fallen head over heels for."

"Goddamn." He huffed and shimmied down my body. "I'm gonna blow your mind—" He paused, mid-shuffle down my torso. "Do you...can I? Or am I being too much right now?"

Goddamn, this boy.

I smiled, my chest welled with affection. "Take what you want, baby boy. I'm yours."

He swallowed down my semi, moaning and tonguing me, manipulating my nerve endings and keeping my mind focused on the present. Within seconds, I'd become fully hard, and he hummed in appreciation before shoving me deep into his throat.

"Jesus, baby." I grabbed hold of his hair in a firm grip but remained still, allowing him to have his way with me. "So good—fuck, your mouth is perfect." Hissing, I fought the need to thrust up into the tightness of his throat. A few more curses spilled from me, and he popped off, shoved down his panties, tossed them to the floor, and attacked me again with his adoring lips and talented tongue with its teasing metal piercing.

He sucked on and wet his fingers.

Reached around his hip to stretch his hole.

"Lube, baby," I insisted, but he shook his head while lathing at my cock, soaking my shaft.

"Don't need it—just you."

My lips pressed tight as I'd learned not to question Jimmy over what he thought he did or didn't require to take my cock. I had to trust him to know his own body and heart, and I yearned to be connected with him too much to argue.

He climbed over me, rose to his knees, and grasped my base to hold my rigid shaft upright.

"Easy," I murmured, clasping his waist to make sure he didn't hurt himself in his haste to fill himself with my dick.

"Mmm," he hummed while pushing down until his hole clutched at my cockhead. "I like the sting."

"Jimmy." I groaned, muscles trembling with the desire to thrust balls deep in his tight heat.

He sank down, taking more of me. Lifted and lowered, slowly stuffing himself with my length.

I hissed, and he repeated the action, settling his ass onto my groin.

"Your dick is perfection," he moaned, leaning back, hands on my knees. "Want it every day—tell me I can have you whenever I need you."

"Anytime, baby," I promised, my voice wrecked from the amount of love in my heart for this dear boy.

He hummed his appreciation and began to move, rocking his hips, dragging my cock in and out of his hot hole, easily keeping me in the moment with him.

"Your ass...fucking perfect for me, boy. You were *made* for me." I ran my hands up his taut stomach to his pecs, flicking the rings in his nipples.

"Yes," he hissed. "You make me feel so fucking good." He cursed again, sitting forward to sink his fingers into my chest hair. "Better than my fantasies, every wet dream I ever had of you."

I chuckled, gently thrusting in time with him riding my dick like he'd been born to do. Toying with his nipple rings caused him to shudder and shake until sweat beaded on his brow and slickened our skin where we rubbed together.

Pupils blown and lips parted, Jimmy stared at me like I was the one who made the sun rise on his face every morning, as if I gave him reason to open his eyes to greet another day.

"Christ, Jimmy," I choked out, emotions swelling in my chest to the point my heart felt like it was going to explode. "You're so goddamned beautiful—my sweet angel. Fucking love you."

"Love you too, daddy," he stated breathless, a sassy smirk on his lips.

I swatted his ass, grabbed his shoulders, and yanked him down, clasping him tight in the cage of my arms. "Told you not to call me that."

"What are you gonna do?" He trembled on the edge of release, panting against my mouth while gyrating his hips to fuck himself on my cock. "Spank me? Please?"

"Later," I promised, easing up on my hold of him so I could snake a hand between us. "Right now, I want you to come all over me. Rub your spunk into my skin so a part of you will always be with me."

"Oh God," he croaked, his hips speeding up as he chased release.

"Then I'm going to love on my needy boy until you're hard again, begging me to let you come."

Jimmy whined and sat upright, hands on my knees while arching, working in time with my upward thrusts. "Oh, fuck—right there." He moaned, pouty lips parted. "Gonna come," he gasped, and I took him in hand.

"Yes—my good boy. Give it to me." Two strokes, and he cried out, dick pulsing in my grip, spurts of wet heat splattering over my chest and abs. "That's it, baby," I crooned, while stabbing against his prostate and milking him dry.

He shuddered and stilled atop me, completely spent.

But his loving had revived my body, given energy to my depleted muscles and mind.

I pulled my aching cock from his warmth and flipped him onto the mattress. Smearing some of his spunk into my skin, I stared at his flushed face and lush mouth. With what was left of his release, I lubed up my dick and sank into his gaping hole.

We both hissed, and I lifted his knees, pushing them toward his head. "Ready for me to wreck you, baby boy?"

"Please," he whispered up at me, tears welling in his eyes. "Need it—need *you*. Fill me up and make me whole, Sutton."

I leaned forward and took his mouth, setting my focus on loving him fully until he passed out from pleasure beneath me.

Chapter 38

Jimmy

I stared at the simple grave marker I'd used my boot to dust free from snow.

An "R" lay etched in cold rock below me. A cold fucking grave—fitting.

"I signed over your house to some stranger last week, and even though I live here in Pippen Creek again, I'm not allowing memories of your bullshit to haunt me," I informed the frigid stillness of the town's graveyard, white puffs of air exiting my lungs. "There's no forgiveness in my heart for you. Never will be. But therapy is helping me to crawl from beneath the trauma you rained over me for years. I'm going to live my own life now, exactly how I want, without any bullshit from you in my head to tell me I'm nothing more than a worm."

I huffed a laugh, hunching tighter into my ugly coat Sutton insisted I wear this morning. Thankfulness for his caring flooded through me as it always did when thoughts of my boyfriend filled my head—which was more often than not.

"I'm madly in love with a man—your son is a flaming

gay who gets off on sucking dick and taking it up the ass. You would be so proud of me." I snorted, lifting my chin, never more pleased with how I owned my truth. "I wish you could feel the munching of bugs and *real* worms eating your ashes, digesting them, then shitting you back out."

There was nothing left to say but the same two words I'd whispered to his passed out form that night he'd left me bleeding on my bedroom floor.

"Later, loser."

I sashayed away, truly hoping my dad wallowed in misery in the fiery depths of Satan's realm even though I didn't believe in hell—or heaven for that matter, unless Sutton was loving on every inch of my body.

Shivers rippled down my spine as I crawled into my BMW and started the engine. Warmth blasted from the heat vents, and I didn't even bother glancing at the past over my shoulder while driving toward my future.

Sutton had been cooking since yesterday, teaching me how to prep sausage and sage stuffing, bake pumpkin and apple pies, and make homemade orange cranberry sauce. Brine a massive turkey enough to feed an army, even though only a handful of people were joining us for Thanksgiving.

Jamie and Chaz had already been at the house when I'd gone out for a quick jaunt across town through the dusting of snow we'd gotten overnight. They'd been setting the tables when I'd left.

On Tuesday afternoon, the woman Sutton and I had been meeting with together outside of our individual therapy since that shitty day back in October suggested saying a final goodbye to my father might help in my path toward healing. We'd been so busy yesterday that I hadn't found time, but this morning, I was ready to move forward. Take that one physical step I could toward creating a base for new thought patterns and processes, which was proving to be quite the task, one Sutton focused on too, considering we now shared another connection with motherfucking PTSD.

Some nights, I woke from nightmares. Others, he did.

But we had each other's backs every single time. A warm body to hold. Words of assurance and edification.

He was my oak, and I was his.

As for Dad? I'd expected to spit a simple, "Fuck you," as my goodbye but had ended up speaking my mind as Sutton told me to do almost daily.

His constant encouragement and adoring love gave me confidence I'd never thought possible. The beginnings of freedom had proved addictive, and even though picking apart my trauma every week sometimes left me in tears and huddled in on myself, I was working it out. Wading through the shit to reach the shores of new beginnings, where nothing would hold me back.

Sutton bravely did the same, and his vulnerability and honesty prompted me to respond in kind. There were no secrets between us, no more manipulative tactics to get what I wanted. I spoke my mind, showed him exactly how needy I was—and he loved me as-is.

A half dozen cars parked along the street in front of Sutton's and my home, and I practically skipped to the front door, my heart light, my pulse thrumming with excitement.

My first Thanksgiving with family—of a sort. The last time I'd sat down for a turkey and the fixings had been when I'd been wicked young, living with Dad's parents because he hadn't wanted me. Once they grew too old to care for me, I'd been sent back to him. Not once did he and I celebrate a single holiday.

Sutton spoiled me at Halloween, and now Turkey Day

awaited us, a meal and afternoon we would share with loved ones.

I couldn't wait for what Christmas would bring, the New Year yet another chance to create new goals. Fulfill hopes and dreams.

Dexter pulled in behind me, and I climbed from my car, waiting for him to join me.

No Christian.

I glanced up the road but didn't see another car.

Dex scowled while climbing from his Jeep.

"Where's lover boy?" I teased, and he cursed, striding past me. Chuckling, I followed on his heels.

His on-again/off-again sidekick/fuck buddy—who the hell knew what they were to each other—had been invited to join us.

I guessed he would be a no-show but left the matter lie so as not to antagonize Dex, who'd become like a big brother to me.

The scent of baking turkey wafted over me as he threw open the front door and strode in like he owned the place. His doing so had given him an eyeful of his best friend's backside while railing me right there in the entryway against the wall the day after Halloween.

He'd knocked ever since.

I hung up my coat and meandered into the kitchen while Dex made a detour for the living room.

Sutton lifted a large casserole dish of stuffing out of the oven and popped in two cookie sheets loaded with rolls before turning toward me and pulling me in against his rock-hard chest.

"You okay, baby?" he murmured against my hair that had been flattened by the beanie he'd insisted I wear while visiting my dad's grave.

"Better than I've ever been."

He eased back a bit, and I lifted my head so he could read the truth on my face.

Gaze soft, he peered down at me, a small smile curving his lips. "I'm proud of you."

Four simple words—they never ceased to bring tears to my eyes.

Sutton pressed his lips against mine in a chaste kiss before swatting my ass.

"Oh, yes, please," I wiggled against him, grinding our groins together.

"Behave," he ordered, his tone low.

"Yes, daddy," I whispered and squealed while trying to escape his arms.

Two firm swats on my backside, and he released me.

Winking, I sauntered away, loving how his stare on my ass heated me through and made my heart race.

Jamie and Chaz sat on the love seat in the living room watching football—tradition, they'd said. I checked in with them along with the scowling twins, Kel and Dex, who shared the other couch, to see if I could get them a beer. Chaz's parents held glasses of water—neither drank. Gram and DJ hadn't arrived yet but ought to show up soon.

The first time seeing DJ after his dad's death had been hard. Sutton and I had gone to Gram's where Carrie had brought her son for a visit. There had been a lot of tears, a lot of sharing what each and every one of our therapists had told us.

DJ had been sober, far from his usual wild self, but he smiled at both of us, hugging Sutton tight.

"You're still my hero," he'd whispered with a teary voice, and Sutton had a brief moment of breaking down, his vulnerability and allowing himself to be fully human without excuse a beautiful yet heart-wrenching thing to witness.

Carrie then went on to thank us both for watching out for and investing in her son's life.

We had bonded in grief and shared trauma, strengthening friendships and gaining another with DJ's mom.

After grabbing a couple of beers for Kel and Dex, I meandered back into the kitchen.

"Put me to work," I told Sutton, but he shook his head.

"We're almost ready. Just need to finish up the gravy while the turkey rests. You helped me prep almost everything yesterday." He wrapped me up in his arms, lifted me off the floor, and planted a kiss on my waiting mouth. "Love you, baby."

"Love you more," I assured him, grinning.

He huffed his disagreement but didn't argue.

"What's up with Dex?" I asked once Sutton returned me to my feet and started stirring the pot of gravy he had over a low flame.

"Who knows. He and Christian are probably fighting again."

"That's all they do. Must be miserable." I poured myself a glass of pinot noir and leaned against the counter, watching my man work. He was so damned sexy in his white button-down and jeans, a cartoon turkey apron covering his entire front. I sipped my wine, an appreciative hum escaping me.

Sutton cast a raised eyebrow at me.

I blinked like an innocent who had no intentions other than letting him in on the fact I thought he was hot as hell.

His gaze narrowed.

I winked.

Chuckling, he pulled the rolls from the oven.

The doorbell rang, and I tore myself from his presence, my absolute favorite place to be.

Gram, Carrie, and DJ stood on the stoop, a box of cookies in his hands.

"Come on in," I said, ushering them through the door into the warmth.

Even though Gram had found someone to rent out her shop, she decided to stick around for this winter, helping to care for her grandson on the days Carrie worked. I'd made myself available as well, so he often had his chauffeur—me—pick him up in my BMW. He was my best friend, the years and different maturity levels between us unimportant. Like with Sutton yet definitely on a different level, DJ and I shared a connection I'd always longed for.

That young boy would be in my life forever, no matter where his destiny might lead him.

"Thanks for coming," I told Gram, bending down to kiss her cheek.

She patted mine and smiled as DJ scampered off to the kitchen to gift Sutton their donation to our meal.

"Carrie." I greeted DJ's mom, hugging her extra long and gentle. "Thank you for sharing this day with us. I know you would probably rather be with your parents—"

"We're celebrating tomorrow," she said with a kind smile.

"Two turkey days." I huffed a laugh while taking both ladies' coats. "You're lucky."

"We're lucky to have you and Sutton in our lives," she tossed back, causing my throat to tighten.

"The guys are watching football," I said, my voice slightly unsteady.

"Sounds good," Gram said, shuffling toward the living room. "I just want a soft seat to rest these weary bones."

Chuckling, Carrie followed after her, making herself comfortable with the other guests.

A short while later, we sat jammed around the dining room table and a folding card table, laughter and kindness surrounding us. My eyes smarted as I scanned over the group of people who had become like family to me. Watching Chaz and his dad chat over turkey warmed my heart. While I would never have the type of healing the two of them had found, I wasn't bothered, nor did I feel I'd missed out.

Kel no longer scowled thanks to Carrie keeping him in conversation, but underlying grumpiness lingered as it often did with that man.

Dex was deep in conversation with Gram, and DJ's cheeks were like a chipmunk's, stuffed full of...stuffing.

Snickering, I glanced at the other end of the table where my man scanned the room, ever the watchful sentinel.

A sigh sank my chest in as our gazes met.

Love you, I could hear him declare.

Love you more, I mouthed.

Smiling, he went back to his turkey, and thankfulness welled inside me.

Peace was slowly returning to our lives—and town.

Both of the Kaufmans had moved after selling The Outdoor Shop, Sarah heading south with their son Austin, and Stefen traveling west. It had been an amicable split, although last I had seen Sarah, she'd been gaunt and pale, burdened by grief.

The gossip, at least, had quieted after Kurt's burial and the Outdoor Shop's grand reopening a few days later. Not a single townsfolk left in town limits blamed Sutton for his actions. Adoration and respect for him had only grown.

And me?

I was a happy boy living his best life.

I'd come back here on a whim one warm August afternoon, needing connection and a sense of purpose. The pipe dream had been fulfilled far beyond what I'd ever thought possible.

Eyes smarting like they often did whenever gratitude washed over me, I picked up my glass and held it aloft.

The table quieted around me.

"To family. Forgiveness. Acceptance and love."

Murmurs of agreement flooded my ears, and I swallowed a sip of my wine, gaze fixed clearly on the one man besides myself who had any say in what steps I took or when I ought to rest.

My hero.

The absolute love of my life.

Epilogue

Sutton, 10 months later

I leaned against a log before the fire pit out back of our house, patting the empty space between my spread thighs. Just enough coolness slid through the September night that Jimmy had grabbed a throw blanket off the couch before joining me outside.

Neither of us held our usual after-dinner drinks, so he sank to the hard ground in his thick sweatpants, bundling up in the blanket and leaning against my chest right where I'd wanted him. I wrapped my arms around him, and he rested his head on my shoulder.

The crackling of the fire in front of us caused embers to rise into the night sky that was riddled with brilliant stars. Peace crept in, the kind of quietness that didn't need to be filled with meaningless words or trite conversation.

As we often did, Jimmy and I simply rested, enjoying the now, who we *were* in that moment.

I had considered quitting the force in the aftermath of Kurt's death, but all of Pippen Creek had been verbal in their desire for me to keep my position as their chief. To this day, they continued to remind me of their trust, their support meaning more than I had words for. They also approved of Jimmy's and my relationship—not that I'd have cared either way—but I did appreciate the settled feeling deep in my bones in knowing my town had my back for what I had planned for tonight.

Jamie and Chaz had tied the knot earlier in the summer. Family and friends packed out their backyard on Pippen Creek Pond, and a friend of Kel's had come in from out of town to cater since Jamie had insisted I enjoy the day rather than slave away at the grill.

They had said their I do's in front of his father, who had become a civil officiant simply for the opportunity to make his son's dream come true in marrying the man he loved. There hadn't been a dry eye at the small ceremony, Babs included.

Mary was moving in with her sister next month, since DJ's mom had remarried and transferred him out of our small town's school system for this year. We didn't get to see the kid as often as Jimmy would have liked, but Carrie allowed DJ to spend every other weekend with us and would continue to do so after Mary left for Florida.

On the nights I stayed late at the office, Jimmy often drove to Berlin to hang with him in his new backyard that had a basketball hoop set up by his stepdad, who seemed like a decent enough guy. At least he didn't drink. He also appreciated DJ's hyperactivity because he was the same. Two peas in a pod.

At first, Jimmy had feared losing his young buddy, but DJ had assured him his new dad wouldn't ever take Jimmy's place in his life.

DJ was seeing a therapist through his school in Berlin and was thriving in the new family dynamic. His mom found out in April that she was pregnant, and DJ couldn't wait to meet his baby sister.

As for us...

I filled my lungs with the crisp evening air, thankfulness rising up to thicken my throat as it often did whenever I considered the past year. The return of Jimmy, how desperately he needed my love, fulfilled me in ways I'd never imagined possible.

A lot of healing had taken place in Jimmy, new thought patterns allowing some of his insecurities to fade rather than hold precedence in the forefront of his mind. Rarely did words from the past whisper in his ears, and I made sure to give him all the love and attention he wanted.

I continued to see a therapist on a bi-monthly basis, and although nightmares or PTSD sometimes caused me to lose my shit, I was learning how to manage triggering events or situations.

I'd also found some of the confidence Darla had stolen from me and no longer feared Jimmy leaving me heartbroken.

He'd admitted to loving me for years longer than I had him, and there was one last thing I wished to do, the only way I knew how to tie him to me forever, even though he claimed he was here to stay.

I twisted enough to reach into my pocket, pulling the ring from where I'd hidden it before coming outside to start the fire.

Jimmy grumbled over my disturbing his comfortable seat, but I snuggled him back into place, platinum band held in front of his face between my pointer finger and thumb, the fire glinting through the ring.

He froze but not out of panic. "Oh. My. God."

I nuzzled his temple, my lips lingering in a soft kiss. "Need your love every day, baby boy," I murmured against his skin. "Want you wrapped around me, your sweet scent in my nose, your taste on my tongue. It's my dream to have you sit with me every morning at breakfast, eat the meals I cook for dinner every night, climb into our bed even if it's only to snuggle."

"Are you proposing?" he whisper-hollered, tension stringing him tight.

I clutched him closer since I had plans which didn't include him escaping me just yet. "Say you'll be mine forever—"

"Yes!" He wiggled, and I shushed against his ear, my dick perking up at the friction he caused with his lush ash.

"Hold still."

He obeyed like a good boy for all of two seconds before tossing away the blanket to hold up his hand. "Put it on me, Sutton—right the fuck now. Need it."

I slid the metal band over his ring finger, and he clenched his fist shut, clutching it to his heart.

A low whine rose in his throat, and I rocked us side to side, shushing him.

"Love you," he choked out, and I snaked my hand down over his torso, straight beneath the band of his sweats.

His warm cock lay soft against his thigh—he'd been going without the panties lately. I'd torn too many pairs in my haste to sink into his ass upon arriving home from work the previous couple of months.

Easy access, he'd claimed.

So I took advantage now in order to stop his tears, even though they were happy ones that made my heart ache with a sweet sting.

"Sutton." He groaned and lifted his hips as blood swelled his shaft in my hold.

"Luscious boy," I murmured against his ear, stroking him to full hardness. Pre-cum oozed in abundance as it always did, sliding over my knuckles and easing my strokes over his flesh. "Mmm, so wet for me."

Jimmy whined and thrust upward.

I wrapped my legs around his lower body, keeping him in place.

He submitted beautifully to my hold, allowing me to have my way with him.

Usually, I edged him until he sweated and pleaded for release, but I had no patience tonight. The sooner I could sink balls deep into his tight heat, the better.

"You're going to soak your sweats for me," I said, sliding my hand beneath his shirt to flick the ring through his nipple while fucking his shaft with my fist. "After you're sated, I'm going to carry you inside, where I'll clean you up with my tongue. Suckle your soft flesh while you cry about being too sensitive. Then I'm going to stuff you full of my cock that you can't get enough of."

"Yes—*fuck* yes." He moaned, letting me work him over without argument.

"Gonna stroke over your prostate until you come again hands-free. Fill you with my cum and leave you passed out in my arms."

"Perfect—" He gasped—and hot, sticky shot spunk all over my hand, making a mess of his sweats like I told him to.

"Such a good boy for me," I murmured, and he shuddered in my arms. I kissed his neck, nibbling the slightest bit while gently squeezing his softening shaft. My hard dick bucked against his ass.

He entwined his fingers through mine atop his chest, the coolness of metal against my skin causing my throat to swell shut.

"Love you, baby," I rasped. "More than you could ever imagine."

"Show me," he whispered.

I gathered him up in my arms and gave my sweet boy what he needed.

THE END

About the Author

Spicy romance author Lynn Burke believes everyone deserves healing and a happily ever after. She loves writing hot, inclusive stories of various pairings or triplings and creates characters who will steal your heart.

She is a USA Today Bestselling author, a wrangler of her three spawn, and a farmer's daughter who grows organic food. To escape reality, she hides in a quiet corner with her nose in a book.

You can find more about Lynn at her website: www.authorlynnburke.com

Also By Lynn Burke

Abel's Obsession

Divulging Secrets

Healing Storms

In Between

Reluctant Lumberjack

Resisting his Mate

Billion Dollar Love Anthology

Blood Born Series

Bonds of Worship Series

Dark Leopards MC

Darkest Desires Series

Devil's Outlaws MC

Elite Escort Series

Elite Escorts MM Series

Fallen Gliders MC

Forbidden Obsession Duet

Found by Fate Series

Midnight Sun Series

Missing Link Series

Pippen Creek Series

Risso Family Series

Sandy Ridge Series

Sinful Nature Series

Vicious Vipers MC